ACCIDENTAL INTENT

Also by Marilyn Dungan

Snakebird

The Tape

Field of Stones

ACCIDENTAL INTENT

Marilyn Dungan

Best Wishes –

Marilyn Dungan

Arcane Books
Paris, Kentucky

Published by Arcane Books
P.O. Box 5102
Paris, Kentucky 40362

ISBN 0-9666478-8-2

Library of Congress Catalog Card Number: 2001130565

First Edition 2002

Printed in the United States of America

In memory of

Emmett Conner Williams
Harriet Werle Williams

Acknowledgments

My gratitude goes to these people who helped me in the research for this book: Ralph Rogers, Manager of Madison Municipal Airport; Susan Calloway Nimersheim, Director of Switzerland County Public Library; Mark Wilkerson, Owner of "Aerocolor"; and his father, Fred Wilkerson.

A very special thanks goes to Frank Robinson, a pioneer airman who shared with me his experiences flying a Jenny.

To Linda Hertz, who seems to be able to do just about anything that I ask of her, my heartfelt thanks and love.

Patty Adams, you're the best!

Thanks to the gals of the Paris-Bourbon County Library. Everyone should know how important you are.

My appreciation to the employees of the Mortgage Connection in Paris for receiving packages for this country-bound writer.

Pathway to the Stars

On the cool blue of the sky . . .
in and out among the clouds like a
shadow on the wind . . .
my craft will drift.
Alive am I.
Joyous, jubilant . . .
with the knowledge . . .
with the wonder . . .
that I can fly.
And the steel wings that carry me are
like two outstretched arms
that flex beneath the sun.
With the metal skins of those arms
reflecting light beams so that . . .
they seem to dance in a golden swirl
of unfiltered beauty.
But my craft must land, it must
bury itself beneath the desert of the
clouds and bring me back to earth.
Yet in returning me to the common
path and trials of life,
I shall then know . . . that to fly . . .
is but to taste a sample of the
beauty above the clouds . . .
And that man was only meant in
life to step a few short moments on
the pathway to the stars.

- Frank Guneman

Prologue

A cold gray dawn crept through the twin windows in the small bedroom. Ray rolled over and burrowed into Keely's warm body. She flinched as his cool face nuzzled her neck.

"Ah, Keely," he groaned as the sweet smell of breast milk laced with her scent teased him. He could still taste her on his tongue. Sighing, he took a final long breath of her and whipped off the quilt. Might as well get it over with, he thought. The quicker done, the faster he could return to pleasuring. He tucked the coverlet around her.

In her secondhand crib, Scotty whimpered. Ray stepped to the foot of the bed and peered at his daughter. A tiny foot peeked from the blanket and curled, while above, her lips sucked hungrily on a dimpled fist. Before he ever got to the barn, Keely would have Scotty snuggled next to her in the big bed and that little rosebud mouth would be pulling at a breast he'd left only minutes before.

He dressed quickly in the drafty room, pulling on his jeans and shoving his arms into the year-old Christmas flannel shirt that had lost its fluffiness. Slipping on his quilted vest, pungent with muck, he bent and kissed Keely and her lips tugged a smile. He grabbed his work boots and tiptoed out of the room.

Apprehension cut through him like the biting Scottish wind as he hiked toward the horse barn. He hated winter foaling. Last night's unusual frigid temperature had threatened to freeze the ears off Talia's new foal so he'd quickly rubbed her dry. Talia had nickered softly, nudged his shoulder and for a moment he had thought perhaps this year would be different. Wishful thinking, he thought wryly, as he yanked at the barn door. It creaked open on frozen hinges.

Although the mare was gentle during foaling, within hours after birthing, she would turn ugly—a wild, hateful she-devil. But in a day or so, Talia would reconcile the possessiveness for her new foal with Ray's horse whispering and reassuring touch. Three years, three foals, three frightening mornings after, he thought grimly.

He filled a bucket with two scoops of sweet feed and startled when a snort and a thump against the adjacent foaling stall told him that Talia sensed his presence. Smoky, the barn cat, scooted past him in the doorway heading for the food scraps Keely had saved for him.

Ray peered between the vertical pipes placed four inches apart that served as a barrier in the stall windows that lined the alleyway. Against the far wall of the stall, Talia's sable-colored body shielded her foal. She glared at him with frenzied bug-eyes and her nostrils snorted frost into the morning. She stomped the straw with savage hooves.

"Shit, here we go . . .Talia . . . easy girl," he spoke softly, pulling out the six-inch threaded eyebolt protruding from a shallow hole next to the barred window. The sturdy three-eighth inch diameter pins locked the sliding stall doors in place so that the horses couldn't accidentally slide them open on the tracks. It had happened one morning when he'd forgotten to insert the bolt and he found a mare and her foal grazing in his front yard when he left the cottage to feed. Ray dropped the bolt and it clanked and swung from its anchor chain attached to the frame of the diamond mesh steel door.

Holding the bucket in his left hand, he inched the door open about a foot. With a long breath, he shrunk himself narrow and squeezed through the opening, leaving a space small enough to keep Talia inside the stall, but room enough to provide a quick escape should he need one. He moved quickly to the left corner where a round shallow feed bucket hung from three hooks. Ray's eyes were glued to Talia as he dumped her feed. Her ears lay flat against her head and there was an ominous quivering in her neck. Ray took but a single step to see if the waterer on the left wall was frozen up.

Suddenly, with a long piercing scream, Talia lunged at him with her mouth open, yellow teeth bared. Ray swung the feed bucket at the mare and made his move toward the door opening—only it wasn't there. His fingers grasped the mesh and jerked as the teeth found the fleshy area of his upper shoulder. Pain stabbed through him as the mare's jaws clamped tight. He pulled at the mesh but the door remained tightly in place.

"My God!" he screamed frantically, "I know I left it open! It's though the latch-pin's in!" Jerking his hand from the door, he swung a hard fist at the mare and the glancing blow allowed him to break free from Talia's jaws long enough to reach for the alleyway window bars. Raw terror quickly replaced pain as the mare reared and her form loomed darkly over him. Thrashing black hooves connected, laying open his cheek and crashing solidly against his skull. Dazed and bleeding, Ray dragged his body upward, shoved his arm between two pipes and downward to the hole where the eyebolt shouldn't be—but was.

"What the hell!" he choked.

Just as his blood-slippery finger hooked the eye, Talia spun and her hind legs shot at him like a machine gun volley, her hooves crashing into his side and kidneys. His body recoiled in agony and terror.

"Keely!" he sputtered through bubbling blood. His arms were leaden and his finger slipped from the eyebolt. Slowly, his body slid down the unforgiving oak boards into straw wet with blood and his excrement, while the unrelenting hooves pounded his skull, gut and chest. He smelled the mare's sweat and fear—or was it his own? His consciousness ebbed.

Cowering in her corner, the foal whinnied and abruptly, the fierce strikes pummeling Ray's body lessened and the mare began to calm. Talia tossed her giant head and approached her foal, leaving Ray crumpled in the straw. Through the blur of swollen eye slits and pain, Ray saw Talia nuzzle her colt and begin to eat from the alfalfa hay net that hung from a corner post. Below, the baby nosed a teat, then sucked noisily.

"Sc . . . Scotty," Ray whispered as blackness closed over him like a shroud.

Gloved fingers wiped and yanked the eyebolt from its hole and slid the door open a few inches. Talia moved to her oats and chewed loudly while the bolt swung slowly on its chain.

1

"Your choice of bed sheets beats all," Laney said. "Spitfires and Messerschmitts for a little girl?"

Shar swooshed the sheet over the mattress and pulled the fitted corners in place. "They were the only sheets in the store with planes on them," she said.

"Why planes?"

"Malcolm said Scotty's nuts for them but he didn't say what kind." Shar stuffed a feather pillow roughly into the pillowcase, then plopped onto the poster bed and buried her face in her hands. "Woman, what in the hell am I going to do with the 'Scottish peril' for two whole weeks?" she whined.

Laney McVey smoothed the airplane border of the flat sheet down over the hand-stitched quilt. "Come on, Shar," she said. "Scotty's only five years old, hardly old enough to do much damage." She looked over at her lanky friend and frowned. It wasn't like Shar to allow something as minor as a houseguest to get her down.

Shar slowly raised her head and when she spoke, her voice had an edge. "I personally have never met any of Malcolm's kith and kin, but I have heard him drop scary little comments about Scotty to his sister over the phone."

Laney gave her a questioning look. "Such as?"

"'You shall be forever in my debt,' and the more ominous, 'I hope my wedding will still be on after you collect her.'"

Laney attempted a smile but had a change of heart when she caught Shar's scowl. Instead, she asked, "When did Malcolm last see his niece?"

"Other than a brief visit overnight a couple weeks ago, the last time he had any time with her was last year when she and Keely moved to the states—before Malcolm moved his cattle operation to Kentucky. He even threw a welcoming party for them."

"How did Scotty appear to him then?" Laney asked, sitting opposite Shar on the other twin bed made up with matching sheets.

"Malcolm is rather closed mouth about his family but I discovered, quite by accident, that on the day of the party, the little minx disappeared just before he was about to toast his sister in front of all his guests."

"Disappeared?"

Shar raised her head but not before Laney saw that her roots were cutting a dark path through her strawberry blond, pixie haircut that was growing fast into a shag. Shar picked a purple chip from a ragged fingernail. "Well, disappeared may be the wrong word. Seems Scotty locked herself in the bathroom and Malcolm had to call the locksmith to get her out."

"Malcolm told you this?"

"Hell, no. I wormed it out of his farm manager, Smitty."

"Surely it was an accident. Scotty would have been barely four years old at the time."

"Humph! They never did find the key. Bet she flushed it down the commode."

"Shar Hamilton, it's hard to believe a child that age could have thought that up." Laney stood and crossed to the skirted vanity between two windows. She sat and grimaced at her reflection in the mirror. As she redid the wide barrette holding her dark red hair at the nape of her neck, a thought struck her. "How does Malcolm get along with Scotty?"

"I've never seen them together, of course, but I get the feeling he doesn't quite know how to relate to a little kid. To be fair, he just hasn't been around her very much, although he visited his sister near Edinburgh whenever he could." Shar winced as though remembering something painful. "A few months after Scotty was born, Keely's husband died in a horse-related accident, so one of those visits to Scotland was for the funeral of Scotty's father, Ray Moore."

"I remember you telling me that."

"Keely fell apart," Shar went on. " 'Never quite got over it,' is how Smitty gently put it. He said Malcolm tried to get his sister to move here, but at first she wouldn't leave Scotland. But finally Malcolm convinced her to come and live at the ranch until she found her own place. I guess Malcolm got to spend some quality time with Keely and Scotty until he bought Taylor Ridge Farm last April."

"What did Keely do after Malcolm sold the Florida ranch and moved here?"

"Keely got an apartment in Ocala and worked for a veterinarian for a time. Malcolm said she is quite an accomplished vet tech when she's stable. Anyway, she met another tech down there and they hit it off and moved in together. Frank Rice is his name. The guy took a job with a farm in Northern Kentucky and got Keely a job working with horses too. I hope she can handle it."

"Maybe Keely's unstableness has affected Scotty's behavior."

"Perhaps, but now *I'm* the one who has to deal with the wreckage that is flying into Blue Grass Field today. Like I don't have anything else to do between now and the wedding."

Laney chuckled. Shar and Malcolm Lamont were thick into their wedding plans, the event to be held at Malcolm's home two weeks before Christmas. They were planning Scottish nuptials with all the bells and whistles—in this case, bagpipers and Highland dancers. Last April, Shar Hamilton, her best friend from Pittsburgh, and Malcolm Lamont, who had flown to Kentucky to purchase a Bluegrass cattle farm, had met at Laney's bed and breakfast near Hickory. As was her nature, Shar zealously pursued poor Malcolm with an all-out Scottish attack that included a bagpipe serenade. But she needn't have bothered as Malcolm's devotion was instant and consummate in every way but the sexual act itself, as Shar had worriedly confided to Laney from time to time. Laney, in turn, had assured her friend that Malcolm's chaste behavior only indicated he was saving himself for marriage.

Kudzu, Shar's half-grown tabby cat, tore into the room and streaked under the bed followed by Nessie, a West Highland white terrier. The two of them clattered playfully until bursting forth and jumping onto the twin bed where Shar was sitting. They settled side-by-side in the center of the quilt. The cat stared at Laney and began to purr. Laney was reminded of another gray tabby named Puccini who had the same intimidating M marking between his copper eyes. Puccini was Kudzu's father, however, he didn't have the sweet personality of his offspring.

When veterinarian, Gray Prescott, had moved into Laney's bed and breakfast in August, the haughty Puccini had been part of the package, joining Blackberry, Laney's Border collie. The pets barely tolerated each other and occasionally had to reestablish personal boundaries. Most days, Puccini claimed the dashboard of Gray's restored 1958 pink Buick or two-year-old Jeep Cherokee. Blackberry's preferences included jaunts to the creek crossings for a refreshing dip in good weather and chasing squirrels or Puccini up a tree in the yard.

Just the thought of Gray made Laney long for this day to end so that the two of them could return to the bed and breakfast. She had planned a special dinner. She smiled as she pictured them in the parlor in front of a cozy fire. Unselfishly, Gray would urge her to talk about the final revision of her novel that only that morning she had mailed to her publisher. Perhaps the subject would shift to the plans for their own wedding in the spring and maybe later they would make love. A sudden surge of desire came over her and she sighed imagining the sensuousness that would come from it. Shazam! she thought. It seemed as though all she thought about was snuggling and sex since Gray moved in. There was no complaint from Gray.

Laney blushed and glanced sidewise at her friend, but she needn't have worried that Shar had read her thoughts. She'd fallen back upon the bed next to Kudzu and Nessie, her arms limp at her sides, her gray eyes expressionless and as void as the ceiling that they focused on. All at once, Laney was acutely aware of just how troubled Shar had become over Scotty's anticipated visit. At first glance, she was still the same striking woman Laney loved to death, but lately, Shar seemed to have lost some of her endearing outrageousness. Rare were her cavalier verbal comebacks and when they did fly out of her mouth, they were coated with acerbity. Her saucy fashion statements had been replaced with drab indifference—case in point—her shapeless faded jogging outfit that was missing the characteristic Hamilton tartan accessories and signature thistle earrings. Laney recalled the last few times she had seen Shar, and to be brutally honest, she had found her to be thin-skinned and downright crotchety. She could understand how Shar wanted to be free to plan her special event without the unpredictability of a child under foot, but on the other hand, how disruptive could Scotty be?

"Keely is staying awhile, isn't she? " Laney said, hoping to minimize

Shar's fears.

"How does two days grab you?" Shar said dully. "She'll just get Scotty settled—note I'm using 'settled' loosely here—then poof, she's out of here." She rolled over to her side and began tracing the fan pattern in the quilt with her forefinger. Kudzu reached out a paw to play and Shar snapped her hand back.

"I thought she was staying longer."

"She'd planned on a week here before moving into Frank's house."

"What house?'

"I told you, remember?" Shar retorted. "She's moving in with him. They've lived together in Florida for months."

"No reason to get wolfy," Laney said, her feelings hurt by Shar's petulance. "So how's the plan changed?" she ventured.

"Keely will borrow Smitty's farm truck and drive on ahead to get the house in shape while Mal tries to find a used car for her. When she comes back, she can return the truck and pick up the car."

"*And* Scotty," Laney added.

"Most definitely, Scotty," Shar said intensely, reaching for Nessie. She pulled him into her lap and stroked him roughly until he shot off the bed.

The phone rang on the table between the beds. Shar jumped reflexively but made no move to answer it.

"Shar?" Laney said on the third ring. She moved toward the phone, herself.

"Leave it!" Shar commanded shrilly, her facial muscles twitching nervously.

Laney blinked in surprise. The phone rang one more time and quit.

"Damned telemarketers," Shar said. She forced a smile.

A stab of anxiety ran through Laney. Something isn't right here, she thought. Shar was never one who could let the phone ring unanswered, solicitor or not. Troubled, Laney stepped to a window overlooking the front yard. Her gaze followed a short brick walk through a gate in the straight rail picket fencing around the yard. Unlatched, the gate banged in a gusty cold wind. Beyond, snow flurries swirled and settled between gravel in the drive that led to Squire Road, the road to Hickory.

Taylor Ridge Farm was named for the only other family who had ever occupied the house. Built in the early nineteenth century, the house ranked among the finest examples of Federal style architecture in Kentucky. When Malcolm Lamont purchased it along with two hundred and twenty acres eight months before, he had refused to change the name.

"What's taking Malcolm and Gray so long?" Shar complained. "Arrival time was two-twenty." Shar snatched the phone from the cradle. After the information operator put her through to Blue Grass Field, Shar talked briefly then slammed the phone down. "Plane was on time," she said curtly.

"What's with you?" Laney asked, exasperated with Shar's irritability.

To Laney's surprise, Shar burst into tears and ran out of the room.

2

"There they are," Malcolm announced to his friend, pointing to a group of passengers disembarking the jetway from Delta Airline's Flight 620 from Atlanta.

"I don't see . . . " Gray Prescott began, then noticed a little girl clasping the hand of a young woman. Beneath a ruffled corduroy hat, the child's hair was an explosion of honey-colored corkscrews around a pale, round face.

"Over here," Malcolm motioned to the couple, waving his hands over his head. Abruptly, he frowned. "My goodness, there's Scotty, but where's Keely?" he asked.

It was then that Gray noticed that the woman who held the hand of the child whom he assumed was Scotty, wore a Delta Airline uniform.

Malcolm dashed forward and swept the child up in his arms. She began to scream.

"Sir, are you Malcolm Lamont?" the airline attendant asked as she reached for the child. Scotty continued to wail, arching her back, her face red and contorted with an emotion that was either anger or fear. Several disembarking passengers lingered, concern written on their faces, while two security police appeared from nowhere and asked the attendant if she needed assistance.

"Where is my sister?" Malcolm demanded, while almost allowing the child to slip from his grasp. The attendant took the opportunity to wrestle Scotty from his arms. Scotty struggled until the woman set her down. Scotty immediately buried her face in the woman's skirt.

"Officers, I think I can handle this," the attendant said looking anxiously around at the gathering crowd. To Malcolm, she said, "Sir, if you will follow me, we shall deal with this in private." She pried Scotty's fingers from her skirt and seized a tiny hand. As the agent of the airline led Scotty toward a bank of offices, Scotty, hiccuping loudly, looked back quickly at Gray and Malcolm rushing behind them. The peek was just long enough for Gray to catch sight of a pair of enormous eyes the color of bluebells and a mysterious red and white button secured to the collar of Scotty's navy toggle coat.

Laney was close on Shar's heels as she flew down the hallway toward her bedroom. When the sound of the doorbell echoed up the stairs, Laney paused, not knowing whether she should follow Shar or answer the door. Shar took advantage of Laney's hesitation to slip into her room and slam the door. Laney heard the key turn in the lock.

"Sharlene?" Laney heard Malcolm's muffled call through the front door as the bell rang again. "I forgot my key."

Laney galloped down the staircase to the entrance hall. A cheerless winter glare filtered through the door's twin sidelights and elliptical fanlight, slicing the pine floor into oblique angles. Shivering through her mohair sweater, she turned the lock and pulled the massive door open.

Malcolm and Gray stood on the front stoop with a small child standing between them. Malcolm held Scotty's hand, his expression reflecting exasperation and exhaustion. Laney got only a brief glimpse of a gumdrop nose and a mass of hair before, the child broke from Malcolm's grasp and in a blur, darted by her and disappeared into the house. Gray rolled his eyes at Laney.

"Where's Keely?" Laney asked, noting that Malcolm's green Oldsmobile parked in front of the gate was empty. A lone piece of luggage—a large navy-issue duffel bag—lay on the stoop to Gray's left.

Malcolm threw up his hands and stormed into the center hall. "Scotty, where are you?" he shouted, his words reverberating through the house. Laney had never seen him so agitated. As Malcolm began a search for Scotty, Gray hauled in the canvas bag.

Laney closed the door and spun to face him "What . . . is . . . going . . . on?" Laney demanded.

With his turquoise eyes fixed on hers, Gray said glumly, "Malcolm should be the one to tell it . . . and you'd better get Shar."

Laney opened her mouth to object, then quickly turned on her heel and ran up the stairs.

Laney tapped timidly on Shar's door. "Shar, open up. Malcolm has something to tell us." She could hear quiet sobbing inside. "Ah, Shar, please let me in."

The sobbing stopped. "No!"

"Whatever it is, I can help."

"No!"

"We can't find Scotty."

Silence, a click, and the door creaked open. Two puffy red-rimmed gray eyes peeked out. Laney slipped in and shut the door softly behind her.

"Sounds all too familiar," Shar said in a voice thick with sarcasm.

"Gray said to beat it downstairs."

"I don't want to see Gray."

"Shar, please, something is terribly wrong."

"You have no idea how wrong . . ." Shar's mouth clamped shut like a trap.

The dark blue chenille spread on Shar's sleigh bed was rumpled. Shar snatched a tissue from a box on the nightstand and blew her nose.

This was the first time Laney had been in Shar's bedroom, but she recognized many of the items that she had brought from her apartment in Pittsburgh. Her fixation on things Scottish was in evidence everywhere. Three pillows in her favorite plaid were on the floor where she had tossed them from the bed and two more were on a scarlet chaise lounge in the corner near a door that led to the bath. Stacks of wedding invitations lay on top of a small desk between two windows. She hadn't replaced the white lace curtains with the plaid ones from Pittsburgh, but had tied them back with Hamilton tartan ribbons. Ribbons also adorned the base of a handsome cobalt blue vase on the mantle and tall porcelain candlesticks at either end. Her silver thistle earrings were tarnishing on a small dressing table.

Nessie nosed Laney for a pat and she obliged. "Shar, please, Gray and Malcolm are waiting for us," Laney said. Shar strode angrily across the carpet and abruptly opened the door. The door slammed harshly against the doorstop as she rushed from the room and strode toward the staircase. Laney ran to keep up while Nessie passed both of them and hurtled down the stairs.

As they moved by the guestroom where she and Shar had made up the beds, Laney said sharply, "Wait! I know I left this door open." Laney turned the knob slowly, cracked the door and looked in. "Look, Shar!" she whispered excitedly.

Behind her, with her chin on Laney's shoulder, Shar gasped, "The little monkey! She's climbed under the sheets, shoes and all."

Sure enough, the toe of a tiny red sneaker peeked from beneath the covers of the nearest twin bed and a tell-tell lump in the quilt rose and fell in a rhythmic pattern. Visible under the bed where she had crammed them, were Scotty's coat and hat. Laney surmised that Scotty had found the back staircase and had slipped by Shar's bedroom while she was briefly inside.

Kudzu squeezed between Laney's legs, jumped on the bed and sniffed the form. Finding a gap in the covers along the airplane border, he crawled underneath and formed a smaller lump next to Scotty. She squealed softly but didn't move.

Laney grabbed Shar's arm and closed the door quietly. "Let's leave her be . . . at least until Malcolm tells us his news. Maybe she'll fall asleep."

"In your dreams," Shar said sourly but allowed Laney to lead her away.

They met Malcolm on the stairs on his way up to continue his search for Scotty.

"Shush!" Laney said, a finger to her lips. "She's in the guestroom hiding out. We're hoping she'll nap."

"Thank God," he said, his fingers combing through his hair then pulling at his goatee. Behind tortoise-shell eyeglasses, his eyes darted up the staircase. He frowned as though trying to decide if he should check on the child but then he saw Shar's swollen face. "My dear, whatever has happened, we can reconcile . . ." He couldn't go on.

Laney saw tears in his eyes. "Malcolm, what *has* happened?" she asked, totally confused by the continual emotional outbursts ever since she and Gray had arrived to help welcome Keely and her daughter, Scotty, to Hickory.

Malcolm quickly stepped between the two women and grasping elbows, led them into the parlor off the central hall. "I was unaware that Gray hadn't informed you, Laney." He released their arms and sat down shakily onto one of the twin Queen Anne settees done up in a Lamont green, black and navy tartan. Shar and Laney sat across from him in the second settee covered in the Hamilton red and blue. Laney scooted a plaid pillow toward Shar and slapped another on her lap.

"Keely is missing," Malcolm said with a catch in his throat.

Shar and Laney gasped at the same moment.

"She boarded the plane in Florida but during a layover in Atlanta, she disappeared," Malcolm continued.

Gray appeared with a tray of drinks from the kitchen and passed them around. He kept glancing at Laney.

Laney took an enormous gulp of her Bloody Mary that went down the wrong tract. "She just up and left Scotty in the terminal?" she asked in falsetto, her question culminating with a series of chokes and coughs.

"According to airline officials, it wasn't quite like that," Gray said, then sipped quickly at his own bourbon and water. Above his glass, his eyes blinked nervously.

Shar jetted off the settee and slammed the pillow to the floor. "For God's sake, just how in the hell was it?" she demanded. Her hands formed fists on her hips in a Superman stance.

"Sharlene . . ." Malcolm began, then shook his head as emotion overcame him. Shar crossed to him and laid a hand on his shoulder.

Gray turned to Malcolm and said, "Malcolm, let me," Malcolm nodded and lowered his head into his hands.

Gray swallowed. "During their layover in Atlanta, Keely arranged to have Scotty fly the rest of the way in Delta's Unaccompanied Minor Service."

"I have an idea what that is, but fill us in," Laney said.

"The service allows a child between the ages of five and eleven to fly unattended."

"What?" Shar said, her eyebrows shooting up like twin arrows and her hand tightening on Malcolm's shoulder.

"Actually," Gray said quickly, "an airline agent puts the kid on the plane and another agent meets the child at the destination. "During the flight, a stewardess is assigned to the child who wears one of these to identify them." He showed them a candy-striped button about two inches in diameter that he pulled from the pocket of his tweed jacket.

"I once flew to Florida with two brothers that were flying alone," Laney said. "They were about seven and ten years old. Each wore a button."

"Terrific," Shar said sarcastically. "I bet *that* little tidbit is in chapter one of the pedophile's *How-to-Find-Kids* manual."

With Shar's comment, Malcolm lifted his head. "Sharlene, Scotty wore that button, but believe me, no one could have picked up that child except me," he said. "When I tried to claim her, I had to match the driver's license information that Keely had given the airline officials—my driver's operator's number, height, weight and eye color. Even my signature was compared. They did everything but fingerprint me."

"Wait a minute," Laney exclaimed. "Then Keely must have given the airline this information before the flight."

"How else would Delta have gotten it?" Malcolm wrung his hands. His red-rimmed eyes rivaled Shar's.

"But you didn't give this information to Keely!" Shar said.

"No."

"When you told the airline officials that, why did they release Scotty to you?" Shar asked.

Malcolm glanced at Gray before answering, "I didn't tell them."

His answer was met with stone silence.

Malcolm finally spoke. "If I had told them that Keely had fabricated the documents . . . forged my signature, I wouldn't have gotten them to release Scotty and—"

"And Keely would be in deep doo-doo—as she should be," Shar said caustically. "How could she leave her child like that and where the hell is she?"

"Mither? . . ." a tiny husky voice said with the remnant of Scottish brogue.

All heads turned toward the doorway where Scotty stood desperately trying to hold onto Kudzu with both arms. Although wildly bug-eyed above the hold, below, Kudzu's lower body dangled like overcooked pasta, his hind legs barely grazing the carpet. Laney was amazed at the tabby's calmness and self-control through what must have been a rough staircase descent.

"Scotty," Shar said, rushing to her cat's defense. Her hands reached for Kudzu. "Let me have—"

"Mine!" Scotty screamed at Shar while readjusting the unwieldy load with an exaggerated hip hike. Kudzu's torso swung limply.

Surprised and indignant, Shar stepped backwards.

"Mither?" Scotty repeated, as though she had more to say but couldn't form the words. Her eyes explored the room.

Malcolm leaped to his feet and covered the short distance to the child with unusual speed and knelt on one knee in front of her. "Ah, lass," he said, his voice slipping into a Scottish dialect that Laney had only heard from him one other time. The other emotional event was just after he had witnessed Shar playing the bagpipes in full tartan dress on the foggy banks of Stoney Creek. "I dinna know whair your Mither's gane," he said, his face twisted in anguish for Scotty. Obviously not wanting to deal with the child's distress, Shar walked back to the settee.

Laney, who had left her seat when Scotty appeared, positioned herself behind Malcolm, "Scotty, honey, did your mother tell you where she was going before she put you on the plane?" Laney asked.

With the question, Scotty peered about wild-eyed, her face etched in a desperation that made Laney catch her breath. A chalky circle formed around Scotty's lips. My God, Laney thought, the child's terrified! Scotty tightened her grip about Kudzu. This time, the cat protested and meowed as Scotty's raspy voice exploded out of her tiny mouth, "Mither died like ma faither."

As Scotty's words ripped through all of them, the room went dead quiet. Then, trying to quell Scotty's fears, everyone began talking at once.

"Don't be silly, Scotty, nothing has happened to your mother," Gray said.

"Honey, we'll find your mother," Laney added.

"Lass, she probably only decided to ready your new home and surprise you," Malcolm said.

Shar was the only one who didn't offer any words of reassurance. She sat glumly drumming her fingernails against her glass.

Scotty, her eyes haunted by inner suffering, stood clutching Kudzu as though the cat were her only connection to some kind of permanence in her life.

Finally, Malcolm persuaded Scotty to relinquish the cat to Shar with the promise that Kudzu would be returned to her when they reached her room. He whisked the child upstairs and Shar trailed behind with Kudzu. When Gray swung the duffel over his shoulder and followed, Laney rushed to the kitchen to prepare a tray of food for Scotty.

She made a peanut butter and jelly sandwich and heated a cup of canned chicken noodle soup in the microwave. She added a glass of milk and a couple of store-bought chocolate chip cookies to the tray and carried it upstairs.

Scotty was already in bed with one arm around Kudzu and the thumb of her other hand plugged into her mouth. When Laney asked if she was hungry, she shook her head once and sucked. Laney stepped over an assortment of garments trailing from the duffel and laid the tray on a small desk by the door. While Gray and Malcolm stood by the bed wondering what else could be done, Shar, who had been absent when Laney had arrived with the tray, shuffled into the room. Prepared for bed, she crossed the room to the second twin bed. Scotty watched her every move with wary eyes. Shar kicked off her oversized slippers with the exaggerated likeness of Ronald Reagan on the insteps and shrugged off her purple flannel robe. When she turned out the bedside lamp, her iridescent orange nightshirt glowed until she disappeared between the airplane sheets.

In the soft illumination of a nightlight, Scotty's eyes gleamed like new marbles, then gradually waned behind heavy lids.

The drive home took longer than expected because snow showers made visibility difficult. As the Buick moved through the swirling whiteness and Jussi Björling sang "Salut! Demeure chaste et pure" over the speakers, Laney kept glancing at Gray, who with a grim mouth, seemed only to be concentrating on his driving. Over and over, the snow accumulated on the windshield wipers only to finally slide away in a single wet swipe.

Turning off Hickory Pike, they followed in the single set of vehicle tracks that Laney knew belonged to her farm manager, Aaron Sloan. The scarlet maples that lined the lane were black, wet shapes that hovered over the alley, but no matter how the seasons changed the trees, they always announced to Laney that she was home. Tonight, she especially craved the comfort and warmth of her Victorian stone house, so when they pulled into the circle drive and the beams of Gray's 1958 pink Buick hit the façade, she gave a sigh of relief. She only wanted to lose herself in Gray's arms and forget about the problems that seemed to perpetually follow her.

The evening certainly wasn't going as planned, Laney thought as she and Gray sipped their creamy tomato soup and picked at their salads in silence. The antique cut-glass lamp over the kitchen table cast an amber glow that wasn't unpleasant, but Laney missed the candlelight shining through crystal globes in the red dining room.

"Soup and salad were supposed to be only the initial courses in a spectacular meal," Laney said, breaking the quiet.

"Sorry, but my appetite took off as soon as that flight from Atlanta landed," Gray said as he made a futile stab at a cherry tomato. "That poor child."

Laney dropped her fork. "I promised myself that I was going to get to the root of this," she said as she rose to her feet and threw her napkin onto the table.

"Laney, what can you do?" Gray said as he followed her through the kitchen and down the hall into the library. "Malcolm already checked with the police about filing a missing person's report and they told him he would have to wait twenty-four hours."

"Dammit, *I* don't have to wait twenty-four hours," she said, lifting the phone receiver on the kneehole desk.

Gray covered her hand with his, forcing it back onto the cradle. Laney's eyes darted to his. "Gray, what—" His eyes darted away. With the evading gesture, Laney's throat constricted and she swallowed dryly. "Gray, you're frightening me!"

He moved to the tan leather sofa. "Move over, pooch," he said to Blackberry, Laney's pregnant Border collie who was taking her half out of the middle.

The collie climbed down heavily and found her other favorite spot under the kneehole desk. Gray picked up the *Hickory Times* and pretended to read. Puccini meandered in and by using Gray as a springboard, found his preferred perch—the soft sofa headrest. He sprawled comfortably.

"Oh no you don't!" Laney said, her voice rising hysterically as she slapped the newspaper aside and straddled Gray's legs with her knees, forcing him to look at her. Puccini stood up, made a circle and reclined again.

"Okay," he said reluctantly, "while Malcolm collected Scotty, I checked with the rental agencies at the Atlanta Airport," he said with a mouth that trembled a little. "Keely didn't rent a car."

"What are you saying? That she just walked away from the airport?"

"No, a woman fitting Keely's description took the Jackson Hotel shuttle into the city."

"Description? You've seen her?"

Gray slipped his hand under the crewneck of his Shetland sweater and removed a photo from his shirt pocket. "Malcolm had this picture in his wallet." They studied the snapshot of Keely together.

"She looks like Malcolm," Laney said. Indeed, Keely had his small, compact body and brown curly hair. She stood by a large pine tree, her palm against the rough bark, the other hand closed into a tight fist at her side. She wore soiled tan overalls that were tucked into a pair of Wellington boots. She might have just returned from working in a barn. Behind her and traveling off the photo was a small white cottage. Laney thought the photo might have been taken in Scotland before she and Scotty moved to the states.

"Gray, look at her eyes," Laney said. "They sure aren't Malcolm's good-humored peepers." Although the snapshot was small, Laney could see that Keely's eyes looked incurably sad, almost despairing.

Gray commented, "I wonder if this was taken just after her husband died."

"My thoughts exactly," Laney said as she focused on the beseeching slant to Keely's brows. Abruptly, she recalled that Gray had kept all this information from her. She pushed away from him and rose, glowering. "Surely, you called the Jackson Hotel?"

He also stood, and his face was pinched when he answered, "Laney, she took the shuttle in . . ." While she waited, Gray jangled change in a pocket of his slacks. "But she didn't check into the Jackson Hotel."

Her breath expelled noisily. "Did you check other hotels in the area? She could have taken a cab from the Jackson."

"Laney, I did. Called all over while Malcolm amused Scotty as best he could."

"Why did you keep this from me until now?" Laney asked as a second wave of anger washed over her.

"Malcolm asked me to. He knows you only too well. Look at you. You're like a goddamn nose-to-the-ground bloodhound sniffing around a rock."

"But Gray, this is serious stuff. I get the distinct feeling that Keely doesn't want to be found," Laney mumbled under her breath.

"Laney, your ears are dragging the ground." He tweaked her ear-lobe.

"Maybe I can help."

"Spare yourself, Laney. The police will do what's necessary once the missing person's search begins."

She wrapped her arms around his waist and hugged him to her. She could hear his heart rhythm through his sweater.

"Why don't we finish our salads and reheat the soup," he said.

Laney let him lead her back to the kitchen, but as he pulled her along she told herself that she would keep sniffing around that rock if it would help find Scotty's mother. At the same instant, she recalled a second matter that Gray didn't know about—Shar's baffling cranky behavior only weeks before her wedding.

3

"Here I am, whether you like it or not," Laney said, speaking to the two unfriendly eyes staring at her through the four-inch door opening. "Well, are you going to let me in or watch me freeze on the front steps of Taylor Ridge?" She hugged herself with red-gloved hands and stomped her boots. The eyes disappeared from the gap and Laney pushed the door open to see Shar slogging up the long staircase. She still wore her nightclothes.

Laney unzipped her stadium boots and leaving them on the rug by the door, peeled off her gloves, coat and beret and ran up the stairs. As she followed Shar down the hall, she passed the guestroom and looked in. The beds were unmade and some of the garments from Scotty's duffel were still scattered over the floor. Scotty was gone and there was no sign of Kudzu. The dinner tray on the desk that she had fixed the night before, was untouched.

"Where's everyone?" Laney asked as she moved into Shar's bedroom behind her.

"Malcolm took Scotty into Hickory for breakfast," Shar said, sitting on the edge of her bed. Her face was unwashed and her hair spiked around her face like a medieval mace.

Downstairs, Laney heard voices. They're back, she thought. "Have you heard anything from Keely?"

"No."

She looks like hell, Laney thought, now certain that most of Shar's distress wasn't the result of Keely's disappearance. She stood in front of her and lifted Shar's chin. "Shar, tell me," she said in a velvety, even voice while her eyes drilled into hers, "or you will be pummeled with punishing blows all over your body."

Shar swiped Laney's hand away. Hmm, so much for humor. Blackmail? Laney thought evilly.

"You leave me no choice, my friend," she said. "I'm going to tell Malcolm that you're having second thoughts about getting married." She turned on her heel and charged out of the room.

The yank on her arm hurt. Shar pulled her back into the room, shut and locked the door.

Bingo! Laney smiled.

Shar paced the room. When she finally swung to face Laney, her color was high, her eyes too bright.

"I can't marry Mal. I'm still married," Shar blurted.

A whoop exploded from Laney's mouth. Surely she hadn't heard her correctly. Laney searched Shar's eyes and saw that she was dead serious.

Laney's mind sped dizzily back three years when Shar was married to her third husband, Paulie. "But Shar," Laney sputtered, "You divorced Paulie. I went to the divorce hearing with you in Pittsburgh. You celebrated that night by burning your marriage license in the fireplace." Laney didn't add that Shar also toasted the event over and over until Laney had to put her to bed.

Shar began to sniffle. "I don't mean Paulie," she cried.

"You married someone else after Paulie?" Laney shrieked, "and didn't tell me? . . . your best friend?"

Shar swung to face Laney. "Of course not."

"Then what in the hell are you talking about?"

"Simon."

Laney looked at Shar quizzically.

"Simon Anderson, my second husband."

Laney scratched her head while searching her memory. "Simon? I'm afraid that's before I knew you, Shar, My god, surely you divorced Simon before marrying Paulie."

Shar's silence said it all.

"My God, Shar, why!" Laney screeched, but before Shar could answer, she added, "If you didn't divorce Simon, then you weren't legally married to Paulie."

Nothing from Shar.

Laney tried to put together what Shar was trying to tell her. She quickly came to the only solution for her friend "Then," she said, jabbing Shar's shoulder with her forefinger, "you must get a quickie divorce from Simon *now*. When did you last hear from him?"

Shar crossed to a Sheraton-style mahogany dressing table and opened a narrow drawer under the mirror and removed a small white envelope. She slipped out a photo and held it out to Laney. "This came about a month ago."

Laney took it from her trembling fingers. It was a photograph of a man.

"Simon," Shar said.

Laney stared at the picture. The man was bending over an engine of some sort and his face was in profile, his straight blond hair hanging over his cheek and eye. He wore coveralls that were smudged with grease and held a tool in his hand as he reached down to work on the motor. He seemed to be inside a garage. "Okay," she said, "so this is Simon." She handed the photo back to Shar.

Shar's mouth twisted. She waved the photo at Laney. "If this is Simon," she said with a flourish while her other hand swept to the fireplace, "then who in the hell is that on my mantle?"

Laney's gaze shot to where Shar pointed, to the cobalt blue vase on the mantle, its base tied with the Hamilton plaid ribbon. Realization slowly hit her. She rushed to the vase, lifted it down and removed the lid. Inside, gray ash and withered slivers of bone filled the vase to the brim. "Oh, my God! You mean these are Simon's remains?" The urn almost slipped from her fingers and she quickly returned it to the mantle.

"Woman, Simon died in a plane crash five years ago."

"Then . . . then that man in the photo isn't Simon Anderson," Laney said. She grabbed the photo and envelope from Shar and looked again. "The man's face isn't clear."

"It's Simon," Shar said strongly.

"How can you be so sure?"

"The blond hair. His cute little butt. The shape of his hand resting on the metal."

Laney could see one hand supporting himself while the man reached into the motor with the other. "You can't identify someone by the shape of his derriere, Shar." Laney said. "And even if this *were* a picture of Simon, it could have been taken years ago before—"

"The phone calls . . . " Shar interrupted.

"What calls?" Laney said and instantaneously remembered the phone call that Shar had refused to answer the day before.

"I would get phone calls about the same time almost every week. I could tell someone was on the line. Then they would hang up."

"I get those . . ."

"Then, about a month ago a woman whispered Simon's name. Two days later, I got the photo."

"So, you haven't actually spoken to Simon." Laney said with her arms spread in an I-told-you-so gesture.

"It was a woman, but—"

"Jeez, Shar, I was beginning to worry that you had gone off the deep end . . . that you thought you were communicating with the dead, somehow."

"Woman, this is not hocus pocus."

"You know what I think? I think someone is playing some kind of cruel hoax on you," Laney said, slipping the photo into her pocket. "If you get anymore calls, change your phone number. And mail those invitations. You and Malcolm are going to have the most beautiful wedding in the world. Poor Simon would have wanted it that way," Laney said.

"If only I could believe . . ."

"You *must* believe it. You have Simon's remains," she said and straightened the bow on the urn.

With those words, there was a knock on the door and Malcolm softly called Shar's name. When she unlocked the door, he stood in the hallway holding Scotty and Kudzu in a fumbling grip. Scotty's red corduroy overalls were hiked up under his grasp, exposing her worn unlaced sneakers over unmatched socks. Her hair snarled around her round face like a lion's mane. "We have company, Sharlene," Malcolm said, his face ashen, his eyes downcast. "Laney, could I prevail upon you to take Scotty for a few minutes while Shar and I see to this?"

"Of course," Laney said, reaching out her arms to the child. Scotty stiffened and turned her face into Malcolm's shoulder.

"Lass, it will be all right," he said, setting her down. "I shall be back directly."

With a single glance at Malcolm, Shar had rushed into the bathroom and Laney heard the water running as she hurried Scotty down the hallway to her room. Her hand, in Laney's, felt tiny and cold.

Kudzu scampered down the steps.

"Kitty," Scotty called after him.

"He's probably getting a bit of breakfast," Laney explained. "He likes you and will be back. Anyway, Nessie's here to keep you company." The Westie waggled about Scottie's feet but when he didn't get her attention, he followed Kudzu down the stairs.

Once in Scotty's room, Laney made up the two beds and picked up several garments from the floor. She emptied the rest of the contents of the duffel on the second twin bed and began folding the little blouses, overalls, panties and pajamas. Scotty picked through the few toys her mother had packed: several books, a Kay Bojesen wooden elephant, a well-worn Velveteen rabbit. But she reached for a plush airplane in bright colors. Once in her arms, she climbed onto her bed. She inserted a thumb in her mouth, the four remaining fingers wrapping tightly around the stuffed plane's propeller and her eyes promptly closed.

Laney covered Scotty with a blue and white afghan from a quilt stand and stared at her for a long time before continuing her task. She was sure that Scotty slept to help forget the pain of her mother abandoning her. Laney wondered what could have made Keely do such a thing. She tucked Scotty's little garments into a deep drawer of a large powder-blue painted chest adjacent to a window. Laney couldn't help herself. Curious to know who was visiting Malcolm and Shar, she parted the chintz draperies. She squinted as the white glare from the sun reflecting off the snow struck her eyes. Through a watery blur, she saw two vehicles parked behind the Whooptie, the 1989 Nissan her sister, Cara, had left to her when she had died almost two years before. Although Malcolm had called Sheriff Gordon Powell inquiring about filing a missing person's report, Laney hadn't expected to see the St. Clair County Sheriff's car parked there. Behind it, a gray Mazda looked vaguely familiar, but the name of the owner escaped her.

Suddenly, a man appeared from under the covered front stoop and walked toward the car. When he opened the passenger door and lifted a bag from the front seat, Laney briefly saw his face.

"Mark Lyons!" Laney cried out, recognizing her family doctor. She spun from the window and with a quick glance to make sure Scotty still napped, Laney rushed from the room. She started down the staircase.

"Mark," she called to the doctor who had just closed the front door.

He turned. "Laney," he said, forcing a smile and waiting for her.

"Why . . ." she swallowed, "why are you here?" she asked with trepidation.

"Gordon called me. He knew it would be a great shock . . . and Malcolm and I are friends, as you know."

"Shock? Dear God, no!" Laney whispered as her body turned cold as marble. "Keely?"

"Yes. A car ran a red light in Atlanta . . . struck and killed her," he said, rushing by her with his well-worn bag.

From the den, Malcolm's cries of anguish wrenched the old house until gratefully, someone closed the door.

4

As Laney put together her mother's Swedish meatball and rice recipe, she reflected about the events of the previous three days. She and Gray had driven back and forth from their bed and breakfast to Taylor Ridge, doing their best to help Malcolm and Shar arrange for Keely's funeral and help Scotty cope with the loss of her mother. When Malcolm and Shar, supported by Laney and Gray, had told Scotty the dreadful news, Scotty's eyes brimmed with tears and the tiniest of whimpers, like a keening wind, escaped her lips before she buried her white face in Kudzu's soft fur. Laney had wept into Gray's own trembling shoulder when she saw how Scotty struggled to suppress her grief. Laney suddenly remembered Scotty's cryptic comment the night she'd arrived, "Mither died like ma faither." It was as though Scotty had been prepared for the loss.

When Malcolm had received the news about his sister from Gordon, Dr. Lyons had given Malcolm a sedative and Shar had accompanied him to his room. Downstairs, Gordon explained the scant details about Keely's death to Laney. Keely had been struck by a hit and run driver about six a.m. as she crossed the street in downtown Atlanta. An eyewitness to the hit and run saw a dark blue car with tinted windows run a red light just as Keely stepped off the curb. The woman, a homeless person, said the vehicle seemed to slow after hitting Keely, then raced on down the block. The same woman had added one final detail. She had seen Keely in Ivy Park the evening before.

Laney wondered if Keely had spent the night in the park instead of a hotel where she might have been found. If that was true, the big question was why had she gone to all that trouble to disappear.

"Can I help?" Gray asked, hugging Laney from behind. His lips whispered shivers on her neck behind her right ear.

Laney shoved the mixing bowl with ground beef, minced onion and egg across the butcher block table. "Mix this," she ordered, slipping away from him but wanting to stay. She gathered the rest of the ingredients while Gray tossed with a wooden fork.

"I think Scotty is getting closer to Shar," Gray said while Laney dumped a cup of Italian breadcrumbs, a teaspoon of baking powder, and half a cup of milk into the mixture. As she sprinkled seasoned salt and pepper, Gray blended the ingredients briskly.

"Closer?" Laney said skeptically. "Maybe . . . if you believe Kudzu is Shar's third arm." She carried the bowl to the counter next to the stove. She dipped fingers into the concoction, formed a small meatball and dropped it into a hot frying pan.

"No doubt about it. Scotty has put up a barrier, all right. But I see signs she's weakening her resolve a bit," Gray commented.

"How?" Laney asked, doubting that Gray had seen anything she hadn't.

"It's not much, mind you, but Malcolm told me this morning she shoved Kudzu at Shar to hold while she took her bath last night. Evidently, the evening before, the cat had scratched Scotty when she had attempted to carry him into the tub with her."

"You're right, it's not much," Laney remarked.

The phone rang on the kitchen desk. "Get that," Laney struck a savage pose with hamburger-covered fingers and went back to making meatballs while Gray talked on the phone. Blackberry scarfed up a spill from the brick floor and sat expectantly near Laney's feet, hoping for more.

"Laney, a Bonnie Day would like to reserve one of the rooms," Gray said, placing his hand over the phone. "She says she was related to Keely by marriage. She'll be here for the visitation tonight and funeral tomorrow."

"Bonnie Day? . . . oh, Ray Moore's sister," she said washing her hands at the sink and speaking over her shoulder. "Remember me telling you Ray was Keely's husband that died in that dreadful horse accident five years ago? Malcolm must have referred Scotty's aunt to our bed and breakfast. Get all the information and give her directions how to get here."

While Gray completed the call, Laney finished browning the meatballs and mixed together catsup thinned with water, teaspoon of pepper, Worcestershire sauce, and a hefty shake of Louisiana hot pepper sauce. She poured it over the meat, covered the skillet and turned the temperature to a low simmer. After measuring a good portion of rice and water into a huge covered casserole she slipped it into the microwave.

"Dinner, huh?" Gray said, back to chilling her neck with his lips.

"Don't you dare touch it. I'm taking it to Malcolm's tomorrow."

"Speaking of Malcolm, do you think it's wise that he's not taking Scotty to the funeral?" Gray asked.

"She's going to the funeral home with me this evening. I certainly think visitation is enough," Laney said. "What time is Bonnie Day checking in?" she said, turning the heat on under the teakettle.

"She's going straight to the funeral home, then will check in here afterwards. If you'd like, I'll let her follow me home so you can spend the time with Scotty until Shar and Malcolm get back."

"That'll be good."

"Shar looked a bit more presentable this morning. Lately, I swear she's looked like something the cat dragged in," Gray said as Puccini rubbed against his pant leg.

"Goodness! With all that's been going on, I forgot to tell you . . . but you must promise this will not get to Malcolm," Laney said.

"I can't promise," he said with a grin as he took two delicate blue and white teacups and saucers down from one of the dark oak cabinets.

Laney swiped at his buttocks. "Then I won't tell you Shar's bigamy story," she said with a wicked smirk.

"Shar was married to two guys at once!" He plopped into one of the oak chairs. "My lips are sealed," he said, giving her his undivided attention.

Laney quickly related the story while hopping up and down from her chair, checking on the meatballs. On one of her trips, she dug the photo from her purse where she had transferred it from her pocket and dropped it in front of Gray.

"How did you get this?" Gray asked.

"Snitched it from Shar."

"Is there a reason you felt compelled to do that, sticky fingers? I hope you're not—"

"Let's just say I thought it odd that some practical joker was trying to get Shar to believe Simon had returned from the dead, but I didn't want Shar to know I was concerned. She's been consumed over the phone calls and this photo for a month."

"But as you said, Simon's remains are on Shar's mantel," Gray said, making a face, "and, by the way, that's disgusting. Hope you can convince her to give Simon a decent burial."

"I'll try," Laney said as she poured water over the teabags in her blue and white teapot.

"Laney, in case you are getting any ideas about taking your magnifying glass out of storage, let me remind you that you can't even see the man's face in the photo."

"That's what I told Shar." Laney hung over Gray's shoulder studying the photo with him. "Hmm," she said, and suddenly hurried to the telephone on the desk and lifted the receiver.

"Don't like the sound of that 'hmm,'" Gray said.

Laney raised a palm and punched in Shar's number. She turned her back to Gray and spoke softly and held the phone away from her ear when Shar went on a tirade when she heard her question. A minute later, she hung up.

"Well, Agatha?" Gray asked.

The microwave dinged. Laney took the hot fluffy rice from the microwave and placed it on the range and poured the meatballs and sauce over. The spicy tomato and meat aroma filled the kitchen.

"Laney!" Gray said impatiently.

Laney poured the tea and nervously stirred artificial sweetener into her cup.

"What?" she answered innocently. She snatched the photo away from Gray and he promptly snatched it back. "It's probably nothing, anyway," she said, but knew she was postponing the inevitable.

"Come clean, you wench," he said. His mouth lines deepened with his smile but his brilliant blue-green eyes cautioned her.

"Look again at the photo," she said and Gray did. "The hand resting on the metal . . . which hand is it?"

"His right."

"And the hand with the tool?"

"His left . . . oh, I getcha. The guy's left-handed."

"Yes, and so was Simon."

5

All thoughts of the photo vanished with Laney's concerns about the evening ahead. As she buttoned her navy suit jacket over her white silk blouse, she could just imagine how trying the visitation would be for Malcolm. Keely had been his only sibling and Scotty was now his only surviving relative.

While Gray showered, Laney sat down at her vanity to attempt to control her hair that had worked into a rambunctious frizzle not unlike Scotty's untamable curls. Scotty, she thought and sighed. What would become of her? She suddenly wondered if Malcolm and Shar had discussed the possibility of raising the child themselves. To Laney, that option came with the dubiety of Shar's relationship with the child. Could Shar overcome her negative impressions about Scotty and could Scotty learn to trust Shar, or for that matter, *anyone* again?

For Scotty not only had lost her father and mother in her short lifetime, but also her only grandparent, Mabel Moore. Curiously, with the death of Keely, Malcolm had suddenly become generous with information about his family and had explained to Laney, Gray and Shar, that Mabel was the determining factor for Keely's decision to come to the U.S.

Through the years, Mabel had traveled to Scotland numerous times to visit Scotty and Keely until she had become too frail to travel. Unfortunately, Mabel died before they could see her one last time. Gran, as Scotty called her, had adored her only grandchild and had heaped upon her an endless supply of attention via airmail and transatlantic phone calls.

Laney finally settled on two strategically placed combs to restrain her hair and moved to the war of the freckles.

"Leave them be," Gray said, snatching her makeup puff away. "I like em."

Laney looked in the mirror at his body behind her. Rosy from his shower, his skin contrasted with his white T-shirt and boxers. "You must. There are two manure freckles on your neck that you missed in the shower."

He snuggled her and grabbed a tissue from her vanity and with a touch of spit, wiped the spots off, then turned on a frown. "Laney, I know I should butt out of this, but I'm going to put in my two bits anyway."

"You always do," she said into the mirror.

"Then heed my words. Stay out of this one. That the man in the photo resembles Simon Anderson and that they're both southpaws is just a coincidence." He gave her shoulders a tiny shake for emphasis. "Simon is in a jar. Let's concentrate on our wedding plans and your book coming out in the spring."

Laney got to her feet and smoothed the furrows between his eyes "I'll be good, I promise," she said, giving him a hug. Over his shoulder, her eyes blinked owlishly at their reflections in the mirror and at her crossed fingers on Gray's back.

6

Laney didn't recognize Scotty's outfit as one from her duffel bag. She wore a dark green velour jumper and a white ribbed knit top over green plaid leggings. Shar must have found time to run to the mall, Laney thought, and she could bet Scotty hadn't agreed to accompany her.

Shar and Malcolm had rushed out the door as soon as she'd arrived at Taylor Ridge. Shar's face was pinched and white and she glared at Laney as she passed. Laney knew the look was the result of her earlier phone call when she had asked Shar if Simon was left or right-handed. Laney suspected that with her question, she had rekindled Shar's suspicions about Simon Anderson.

"I dinna want to see ma mither," Scotty said, her raspy voice breaking through Laney's thoughts. Stooped to fasten the silver buckles on Scotty's new black Mary Jane's, Laney gazed up at Scotty sitting on her bed. Kudzu was draped across her lap sloughing gray cat hairs on her dark jumper. Laney's reply to Scotty's dread of going to the funeral home was, "Your mother has gone to be with your father, Scotty."

Scotty looked at her with such suspicious bewilderment in her eyes, that Laney blushed. God, she thought, what a deficient explanation that is for a small child. She searched for how she had reconciled her own father's sudden death when she was very young. In a burst of memory, she recalled the soothing words her mother had spoken to calm her at his funeral.

She sat back on her heels. "Scotty, when my father died when I was twelve years old, my mother told me to think of him doing what he loved the most. Poppy loved to fish so I like to picture him in his boat catching fish after fish on a crystal blue lake."

Scotty's face brightened fleetingly. "Gran said Granfaither dives his airplane ower an' ower through clouds, wigglin' them into faces an' puffy people."

"Why Scotty, I always wondered why clouds did that."

Scotty reached behind her and grabbed her stuffed airplane. "Gran gave me this," she said, trying to hold both Kudzu and the plane on her lap at the same time.

"What about your mother, Scotty? What did she like to do best of all?"

A groove formed between Scotty's eyes as she thought. "Mither's garden was bestest in the whole warld," she said, her funny voice breaking with the memory.

"Then why don't you think of her as a butterfly in a garden, roaming from flower to flower, kissing all the pretty buds?" Laney said with a catch in her throat that Scotty should have to imagine her mother anywhere but right here with her.

But the analogy seemed to work as Scotty abruptly grinned. It was the first smile that Laney had seen since she had arrived three days before. Scotty momentarily forgot Kudzu and the plane and raised her arms into the air and fluttered her tiny fingers about her head."

"Two butterflies, Scotty?" Laney asked.

"Mither an' ma faither," she said with moist eyes.

7

When Laney and Scotty arrived at Chase's Funeral Home, Laney hung their coats on the coat rack by the door. Neither Shar nor Malcolm was a native of Hickory nor did they have any relatives in the area, so Laney was surprised by how many friends had turned out to pay their respects. Laney spotted Jesse Mills, a dear friend who was assistant manager of the Finish Line Restaurant, speaking to Rose Cohen, an ample-sized woman who owned Second Hand Rose, an antique and collectible store across from the courthouse. At one end of the spacious room, Malcolm and Shar stood by the closed casket talking with Sheriff Gordon Powell and Deputy Freddie Rudd.

A magnificent spray of creamy yellow rosebuds covered the center of the walnut casket and a silver, framed picture of Keely sat to one side. As Laney and Scotty approached the foursome, she could see that the photo was an enlargement of the one that Malcolm had given to Gray the day of Keely's disappearance. Keely's haunted eyes seemed to reach out in a silent appeal for help. Laney shivered.

Upon spotting her mother's photo, Scotty broke her handhold and darted toward the casket and stopped. Standing on tiptoes, she craned her neck to better see her mother's image.

Observing Scotty's effort, Shar retrieved a sturdy armchair and dragged it to the front of the casket. She lifted Scotty and positioned her so she was standing on the chair in level with the photo and the roses. She placed one of Scotty's hands firmly on the chair's backrest for support and left her there, standing quietly. The corners of Scotty's mouth curved upward in a contented smile and her gaze briefly followed Shar as she walked back to Malcolm, Laney, Freddie and Gordon.

"Malcolm, we just wanted to stop by for a couple minutes," Gordon was saying as Laney joined them, "and to drop off the carry-on that was found near your sister."

"I put it in your trunk like you asked," Freddie added, handing Malcolm his car keys. "She sure traveled light." Freddy's jaws chewed as he spoke and a crack of gum punctuated his sentences.

"Most of her things were being shipped to Northern Kentucky," Malcolm said with a pained look on his face. "I had to stop the move and instead, her clothes and a small amount of furniture were transported to Taylor Ridge. They arrived earlier today and are being stored temporarily in one of my barns. Tell me, Gordon, have they found the driver who struck my sister?"

Gordon, who looked out-of-his-element dressed in a tan suit, heavily starched shirt and red tie, tugged at his collar. He rubbed his fingers, like a brush, twice through his crewcut and shook his head. "I'm afraid not, my friend, but the search goes on for a dark blue car with tinted windows. Most likely, it was a drunk driver. Seems like there has been an epidemic of hit-and-runs in Atlanta this year. Many of the drivers have been located so I wouldn't despair." His gray-green eyes, the color of the ocean on a cloudy day, were hopeful but held an underlying sadness for his friend.

Laney scanned the room for Gray while Gordon and Freddie chatted a while longer with Shar and Malcolm and then left. Laney finally spotted Gray in the second row of chairs talking with a woman she didn't recognize. As the woman talked, she was gesturing so animatedly with her hands, she could have been blazing a trail through a jungle. First glancing over at Scotty who was still standing on the chair, Laney slid into an empty seat in front of Gray.

Gray, who saw Laney approach but wasn't able to interrupt the one-sided conversation, gave Laney's hand a grateful squeeze across the backrest as the woman rattled on.

". . . so you see, I've come to collect Scotty," the woman was saying and abruptly turned her head to Laney.

A panicky expression passed over Gray's features and his eyes settled on Laney for help. "Uh . . . Mrs. Day, my fiancée, Laney McVey," he stammered. "Laney, this is Bonnie Day, the woman who reserved a room at the B & B. She is Scotty's aunt."

Did I hear correctly? Laney thought. She wants to take Scotty? She swallowed a sudden lump in her throat and shakily offered her hand, her fingers suddenly as stiff and cold as though she had just dipped them in ice water. Bonnie Day pumped her arm like she was drawing water from a well.

"Nice meeting you," Bonnie said, her rouged cheeks popping into round apples that squeezed her bottle-green eyes into slits. Below her beige, felt fedora, listless auburn bangs hung over her brows like a limp awning. The beginnings of a fleshy wattle under her chin hinted that she was pushing fifty. Momentarily, Laney's attention strayed from Bonnie's revelation about Scotty to the shriveled fox heads biting foxtails in an unbroken circle of fur around Bonnie's shoulders.

"My pleasure," Laney murmured, and abruptly returned to the possible dilemma facing Malcolm and Shar. She wondered if they had met the sister of Keely's late husband, Ray, and if they had been informed of the woman's intentions. "Mrs. Day, is your husband here?" Laney asked, glancing about innocently but actually trying to find out as much information as she could about the intriguing Bonnie Day.

"I'm afraid he isn't," Bonnie said loudly. "But I hope Dwayne can make the funeral. Today he is meeting with lawyers in Vevay about the temporary guardianship of Scotty."

"Vevay, Switzerland?" Gray asked, his voice choking.

"No, no," Bonnie said with hands, palms out, waving rapidly from side to side. "Vevay, Indiana, across the Ohio River from Kentucky."

Bonnie looked in the direction of the casket. "Isn't it all absolutely dreadful . . . the little angel losing her mother in that accident? Believe me, I know what it is like to lose those close to you." Tears spurted from her eyes. "My poor brother, Raymond, five years ago . . . and my mother just last fall." She wiped her eyes with a handkerchief trimmed with a pattern of red and yellow flowers.

"Scotty was just a infant when her father died," Laney said, "but she seemed very fond of her Gran, as she calls her."

"Yes, and the feelings were mutual. She was the only grandchild." Bonnie blotted again at her eyes.

"May I ask how your mother died?" Laney asked cautiously, worrying that her question might appear insensitive, and at the same time, wondering why she needed to know.

Bonnie blinked with surprise at her question. "Uh . . . complications of pneumonia." She fidgeted in her seat and chewed on her lip. "Mother was ninety," she said quickly.

"I'm sorry," Laney said, puzzled why Bonnie was suddenly so ill at ease.

"Laney?" Gray said with a nod toward something behind her.

Laney turned to see Scotty climbing off the chair. "I have to go," she said to Bonnie, rising. "Gray will show you the way to the house." Bonnie nodded.

Gray stood and gave her a quick peck on the cheek. "See you at home, later."

When Laney reached Scotty, Shar was pulling a couple of rosebuds off the coffin spray. She wrapped the stems in a wad of tissue from her pocket and folded Scotty's fingers around them.

"There you are, sweetheart," Bonnie gushed behind Laney. Squeezing between Laney and Malcolm, Bonnie stooped and hugged Scotty, a fox head from her scarf pressing into the child's face. Scotty shoved her back.

"Where are your manners, child?" Bonnie said stiffly.

"You broke it," Scotty said with a stricken look at the broken stem in her bouquet.

"It's okay, Scotty," Shar said, hurrying to pluck another from the spray.

"You remember me, don't you?" Bonnie said to Scotty. "Your Uncle Dwayne and I were at your party last year when you arrived from Scotland."

"Hello, Bonnie," Malcolm said with his hand outstretched. "How kind of you to come."

The sister of Scotty's father and the brother of Scotty's mother shook hands. Scotty's last living relatives, Laney thought.

"Please meet my fiancée, Sharlene Hamilton," Malcolm said.

"How do you do," Bonnie said with a starchy glance at Shar who was stooped in front of Scotty replacing the rose in her nosegay.

Shar nodded and forced a cool smile.

"Scotty, you certainly have grown since I last saw you," Bonnie said. "Uh . . . why don't we sit over there and get reacquainted, child." Bonnie smiled affectedly at Scotty and reached for her hand but Laney beat her to it.

Quickly, Laney explained it was past Scotty's bedtime and whisked her off. As Laney guided Scotty between mourners toward the coat rack, she smiled inwardly at how cleverly she had snatched Scotty away from a second wave of Bonnie Day. But her self-satisfaction was overshadowed by a serious concern. She doubted Malcolm was aware that Bonnie had already begun the temporary guardianship process. What if they both wanted Scotty? Could this be the beginning of a painful custody battle?

Later, on the way home in the Whooptie, Scotty was so quiet, Laney first thought she was asleep until her scratchy voice pierced the darkness with a question so simple and guileless, Laney didn't know quite how to answer:

"Why does Aunt Bonnie wear dead dogs?"

Laney read from *The Wee Scotch Piper*, one of the books Scotty had brought with her from Florida. On the bedside table, the two roses nodded in a bud vase. Kudzu purred with his striped head on the plush toy plane and Scotty sucked on her thumb. By the end of the first chapter, Scotty was asleep. Laney heard the front door slam and the strident sounds of Shar's voice carrying up the stairs. Laney turned off the bedside lamp, and tiptoed out of the room, closing the door behind her.

Laney stepped over a black carryon at the foot of the stairs. Keely's, Laney guessed, remembering that Freddie had put it in the trunk of Malcolm's car. Laney went directly to the kitchen where she mixed two Bloody Marys and a scotch and water for Malcolm before carrying the tray into the parlor.

Shar was sitting quietly next to Malcolm on the Lamont settee. Her head was resting on his shoulder and her long fingers entwined with his.

"I only got through one chapter of a book before Scotty conked out," Laney said, passing the drinks and collapsing onto the Hamilton loveseat.

"You sure rushed her out of the funeral home in a hurry," Shar said, then drank most of her bloody in four gulps.

"I was trying to spare her from Bonny Day's 'dead dogs' as Scotty called them," Laney said.

Malcolm chuckled, the first that Laney had heard from him in days.

"Malcolm, did you get a chance to speak to Bonnie at any length?" Laney asked.

"Other than to thank her for coming—no."

"As Scotty's aunt, she's concerned about her future," Laney said and quaffed down her bloody.

Shar addressed Laney. "That's what we were discussing when we came in."

Laney had thought it sounded more like a quarrel and raised an eyebrow at Shar.

Shar sent back a withering stare. "Mal feels we must make some kind of decision about Scotty immediately. I thought it wouldn't hurt to wait until after the funeral tomorrow. Poor Keely isn't even buried yet."

"Bonnie has an ulterior motive for her visit," Laney said. "She's come to get Scotty."

A roar exploded from Malcolm and he jumped to his feet. Shar's jaw dropped.

"Get Scotty? How do you mean?" Malcolm shouted. He laid his drink down hard on the coffee table and it sloshed over the brim.

"Get—like in custody, Malcolm," Laney said and winced.

"Well, she can't have her."

"I'm afraid the decision may already have been made," Laney said. "Bonnie and her husband have initiated legal action to gain temporary guardianship of Scotty."

"Legal action!" Malcolm cried, beginning to pace behind the settee where Shar was seated.

"Malcolm, are you suggesting that you might want to adopt Scotty?" Laney asked, her eyes on Shar as she spoke. Shar quickly lowered her chin and pealed off a broken fingernail.

"The lass has no one," he said with eyes glistening, his voice softening. He halted his pacing and turned his back to Laney as though embarrassed by his tears. Just as abruptly, he swung around to face her. "But what do I know about raising a wee one?" He shook his head and a sob caught in his throat.

"You know, Malcolm," Laney said, "Since her mother died, Scotty has taken to you more than to anyone, except Kudzu, of course." She smiled at Shar. "No offense, Shar."

Shar ignored the remark. Sensing her detachment, Malcolm ran his hand over Shar's shoulder gingerly and sighed.

"Bonnie's husband . . . Dwayne, isn't it? What's he like?" Laney asked.

"He seems like a good enough chap, I suppose. He was at the party I gave for Keely last year when she and Scotty arrived in the U.S." Malcolm resumed his pacing. "Maybe Bonnie and her husband *could* do an adequate job of it."

All at once, Shar lunged to her feet. "Mal, we can't let her go!" she said in a sudden outburst. She caught up to Malcolm behind the sofa. With a quick jerk on his arm, she pivoted him as effortlessly as though he were a world globe on an axis. He gasped.

Shar's gray eyes drilled down on the little guy. "Please, Mal, Scotty may hate my guts right now, but I . . . I think I'm beginning to care for the little catnapper." Her face folded.

"Sharlene, dear." Malcolm wiped her tears with a Lamont tartan handkerchief that he produced from his jacket pocket.

"Shar, Scotty doesn't hate you," Laney said. "She's afraid . . . afraid she'll lose anyone she gets close to."

"But look how she is with Kudzu," Shar said, sniffling.

"Scotty knows Kudzu doesn't expect anything back from her," Malcolm said. He led Shar to the sofa where they sat. He took her hands in his. "What do you think, Sharlene? Do you think we could handle a ready-made family?"

Before she could answer, Laney interjected, "Bonnie will fight this."

Evidently incited to action by the word, "fight," Shar catapulted off the sofa, and immediately called Attorney Marshall I. Knight.

8

"Finally," Shar said with a sigh in her voice, "we can talk. I thought Mal would never hit the sack." She disappeared for an instant into the center hall.

Laney knew exactly what was coming up.

"The phone call, woman," her voice echoing from the hall. "Why did you want to know whether Simon was right or left-handed?" Shar asked as she reappeared carrying Keely's carryon.

Laney sighed. She hated to get back into the subject that might pull Shar down again. After Shar and Malcolm had made the decision to keep Scotty, in minutes, Shar seemed to have returned to her old lively self. The two of them were to meet with Attorney Marshall Knight after the funeral to also file for the guardianship of Scotty.

"Shar. I can barely keep my eyes open. Tomorrow, I have to get up early to prepare Bonnie Day's breakfast, then beat it back over here to stay with Scotty while you're at the funeral." She began to rise.

"I'll fix you a cup of coffee," Shar said. She tossed the small bag over to Laney and called over her shoulder. "I promised Mal I'd go through Keely's things for him. Stack the stuff on the coffee table. I'll be right back."

As Laney unzipped the tapestry bag, she tried to think of something fast to explain Shar's question, but instead, she got interested in what Keely had packed.

Just inside, she found a cosmetic bag and several cards jutting from an unsnapped wallet. Since no purse was found with Keely, it made sense that she was using the carryon for a duel purpose. The contents of the wallet must have been disturbed by the police searching for identification after the accident. The usual toiletries were stuffed here and there between a couple of underwear changes. A green, cotton turtleneck and cardigan sweater were rolled up to conserve space. Keely definitely had only planned for a night or two, Laney thought. There was nothing in the bag that seemed to belong to Scotty. She checked the only inside pocket but found it empty as was the large outside zippered pouch.

Shar entered the parlor with a tray holding coffee mugs, a tiny pitcher of cream, sugar bowl and two packets of artificial sweetener for Laney. "Your phone call to me—*now!*" Shar demanded.

She slid the tray onto the coffee table that held Keely's few possessions and in doing so, knocked the cotton turtleneck off the stack. As it hit the floor, it rolled open at Shar's feet. As she snatched it up and flung it onto the pile, what looked like a photo fluttered to the floor in front of Laney. She picked it up and turned it over.

"Laney!" Shar squealed. "It's the same photo! Simon!"

Laney was dumbfounded. "Shar . . . remember . . . he's on your mantle." But her voice lacked conviction. Oh God, she thought. What was Keely doing with the same photo that had been sent to Shar? She remembered the phone calls Shar had received from a woman who'd whispered Simon's name.

"Laney!" Shar's voice whined, imploring her to come up with some explanation.

"Let me think."

"Woman, think fast before I go into cardiac arrest."

Shar's wide gray eyes reflected fear and what Laney was conjuring up, wasn't going to relieve her panic one iota. "Shar, maybe Keely was the woman who was calling you and later sent you a copy of this photo."

"Keely? But how would she know Simon?"

"Shar . . . remember the urn," she reminded her weakly.

"Woman," Shar said, "Either Keely knows this guy or the person who sent me my photo, also sent one to Keely. And I don't care what you say . . . this *is* a picture of Simon. Now, what about your phone call to me, woman."

Laney knew when she was defeated. She pointed to the man in the photo. "Look at the hand the man is holding the tool with."

Shar was way ahead of her. "He's left-handed! I told you he was Simon!"

"Coincidence."

"Bullshit!"

The two of them had reached an impasse. "Shar, we need more information before we can draw any conclusions from this. As they talked, Laney was going through the rest of Keely's clothes to see if there was anything else that could explain the photograph. Nothing. She removed everything from the wallet—sixty-three dollars in cash, a state of Florida driver's license, two credit cards and another photo of a handsome man holding an infant. She shared the photo with Shar.

"I bet this is Scotty's father, Ray Moore," Shar said.

"Probably." Laney could see a vague resemblance to Bonnie—the round cheeks and his smile.

The only place Laney hadn't checked, was the cosmetic case. She unzipped it slowly, certain she had reached the last source for any information. She was about to toss the case on the table with the rest of the luggage contents when a flash of white from an inside pocket caught her eye. Her heart thumped with expectation as she unfolded a sheet of copy paper.

"Shazam! This is a scan of Malcolm's driver's license—the information Keely needed to get Scotty on the plane unattended. How would she get this? She would have had to snitch his license," Laney said.

"Maybe she just borrowed it for a few hours."

"When, for God's sake?"

"I don't know. Wait! Two weeks ago, Mal flew down to Ocala on cattle business. He stayed at Keely's apartment overnight. Maybe she would have had time to do it then."

"You're saying that Keely may have had Scotty's unattended flight planned for at least two weeks."

"Oh, I just thought of something," Shar moaned. "Do you think that somehow Keely found out about Simon still being alive and didn't want me to marry her brother?"

"Why wouldn't she just tell Malcolm her suspicions?"

Shar shrugged.

Personally, Laney believed Keely's trip to Atlanta had nothing to do with Simon. Something very serious forced her to send her daughter on to Lexington without her. A sudden chill shook Laney's body. And thank God Scotty *hadn't* been with her. She might have been lying in a casket next to her mother. Laney's heart did a sudden flip-flop as another theory began to form in her mind. Had Keely wanted to keep Scotty from harm by sending her on? Come on Laney, she answered herself. Don't let your evil mind grope for something sinister behind Keely's death. It was a hit and run—a drunk driver. An accident.

Her eyes slid back to the paper. The handwritten words "Peachtree Courtyard—Atlanta" were scrawled at the bottom, along with a phone number.

"A hotel," Shar mused. "Maybe Keely stayed there the night before she was killed."

"It might be somewhere to start to find out why Keely stopped over in Atlanta," Laney said and rushed to the desk. "Surely the hotel would have a record of her reservation." She dialed the number.

A woman answered. "Peachtree Courtyard, an assisted-care facility."

"Huh?" Laney said. "This isn't a hotel?"

"Honey, this isn't the first time we've been mistaken for a hotel," the woman said with a chuckle.

"Well, I'm sorry to have bothered you. I . . . I was trying to track down a friend who's visiting Atlanta," Laney lied. "The name was on her list of places to visit."

Shar's eyes grew large with Laney's whopper.

"We're normally not one of the top attractions in Atlanta," the woman quipped. "But maybe she planned to visit a friend or relative here while she was in the city."

"I can't imagine who that might be, but just in case I need to call you back, what's your name?"

"Betsy. I work four to midnight this week. Have a good one. Bye-bye."

Laney rang off. "Now why did Keely write down the name of an Atlanta nursing home and hide it in her cosmetic case?"

"Got me."

"I wonder . . ." Laney quickly redialed. "Betsy?"

"Why hello again. What can I do you for?" the woman asked cutely.

"I still don't know where my friend is staying in Atlanta. Perhaps she did visit someone at your facility and they'd know where she's staying," Laney said, lifting her eyes skyward in a silent prayer for God not to strike her dead.

"What's your friend's name?" Betsy asked. "We keep a log of all visitors."

"Keely Moore."

"What in the hell are you up to?" Shar whispered. Laney hushed her with a wave.

"Oh, Ms. Moore was here all right," Betsy said dryly and paused as though considering whether she should say more.

"Wonderful. Could you tell me who she was visiting so that I could talk to the person?" Laney waggled her hands at Shar in an emphatic gesture. Her mouth winced in anticipation.

"What is your name, please?" Betsy asked. The lilt had vanished from her voice.

Uh-oh, Laney thought. "Laney McVey," she said.

"I can tell you whom Ms. Moore came to inquire after, but I'm afraid you can't speak to the party," Betsy said.

"For heaven's sake, why?" Laney asked.

"Mabel Moore died last year."

"M . . . Mabel Moore? Keely Moore's mother-in law? But Keely knew—"

"Yes, she knew Mabel Moore had passed away . . . but . . . " Betsy paused. "Perhaps I shouldn't say anything more."

Laney was losing her. "Betsy, please. Why did Keely Moore come to Peachtree Courtyard if she knew Mabel Moore had died?"

"I'm really not supposed to—"

"Betsy, please."

"Ms. Moore was very upset. She wanted to know all the details of Mabel's fall and subsequent illness. She especially wanted to know if Mabel had had someone with her when she fell."

Laney's face flushed with alarm. "Had she?"

"No one had signed in to see Mabel," Betsy said, her voice warming the longer she spoke with Laney.

"How *did* she fall?"

"Mabel toppled over the balcony railing while watering her fushias. She had no business on that step stool. She lived on the second floor and the distance wasn't great, but she was ninety and very frail. It was all very mysterious."

"Mysterious?" Laney echoed.

"First, the fall, then while she was in the hospital, someone broke into her apartment."

"Goodness, was anything taken?"

"Her purse, but Mabel's daughter had already taken the wallet out of it for the medical insurance cards. The apartment was turned upside down. Pictures were torn from their frames, her mattress and sofa sliced open. It was though they were looking for drugs or some hidden treasure."

Laney listened with growing amazement.

Betsy continued. "When pneumonia set in, Mabel was gone in a few days. She never gained full consciousness or was aware of the robbery. Her daughter saw to that."

Bonnie Day, Laney thought. "How did the burglar get into Mabel's apartment?"

"Police thought he came in through her balcony door—shimmied up the balcony support like some slippery Romeo."

"Did Keely Moore know about the robbery?"

"She did when she left here. I told her myself. You would have thought that Mabel's daughter would have filled her in. But Mabel was dead and buried before Keely Moore was even told about her death. She had a right to know, didn't she?"

"You'd think so."

"Who knows, maybe the sisters-in-law weren't on the best of terms. Happens more often than you'd think."

"Gee, Betsy, thanks for talking to me."

"Sorry I can't help you find your friend. If you had called three days ago when Ms. Moore was here, maybe you two could have hooked up."

I'm afraid Ms. Keely Moore will never hook up with anyone again, Laney thought sadly as she hung up the phone.

Shar pounced the moment the phone hit the cradle. "You'd better have a good explanation for all those fibs, and it better not concern a certain dead husband of mine who has suddenly been yanked back into a state of limbo."

"Shar, I still don't believe Simon is alive," Laney began, "but I *do* believe that the reason Keely stayed in Atlanta was to get more information about her mother-in-law's fall that led to her death."

"I heard enough of your end of the conversation to realize Mabel was robbed."

"Yes, the robber slashed the place up looking for something and stole Mabel's empty purse."

Both of them were pensive.

"Humph, I bet the purse was taken as an afterthought," Shar said.

Laney looked at Shar with surprise. "To make it look like a robbery, huh? Damn, you're beginning to think like me."

"Woman, what does all this tell us?"

"Nothing, nothing at all," Laney hedged.

"Hogwash! Keely was suspicious of Mabel's accident—enough so that she made a special effort to check it out. She was killed right after snooping around Peachtree Courtyard. And don't forget the burglar wanted something more than an empty purse if he tore her apartment up. Don't you wonder if he found what he was looking for?"

Laney nodded in agreement. To be honest, Shar had reeled off her own list of concerns.

Shar's eyes suddenly welled. "I'm thinking . . . Keely's death may be my fault," she moaned.

"How in hell?"

"The phone call."

"Which phone call?"

"The one I didn't answer the day Keely and Scotty were supposed to arrive. Remember, you wanted to answer it, but I wouldn't let you." Tears sprang from her eyes.

Laney could only wonder in silence.

"What if that call had been from Keely," Shar blubbered. "What if it was a call for help? Maybe if I'd answered the phone, I could have—"

"Shar, don't go there."

9

Gray left for an early morning emergency call, but promised he'd get back in time to dress and take Malcolm and Shar to the funeral while Laney stayed with Scotty.

Much to Laney's relief, Bonnie Day had chosen the breakfast-in-her-room option. Laney placed the large wicker tray on the little table in the upstairs hall and tapped lightly on Bonnie's door. She rushed down the hall, hoping she'd make it downstairs before having to face Bonnie Day. Although already dressed in black slacks and ribbed turtleneck, she hadn't yet put on her face or reined in her hair.

"Ms. McVey," she heard Bonnie call to her as Laney reached the stairs.

Damn, Laney cursed to herself. She turned with an artificial smile.

"Could I have a word with you, please?" Bonnie asked, her hand waving in a summoning gesture.

"Surely," Laney said, retracing her steps. Bonnie, in a maroon flannel robe, stepped aside to allow Laney, lifting the tray, to enter the room. Laney ceased worrying about her own appearance when through the open window shutters, the white dazzle from another overnight snow played unkindly with Bonnie's unwashed morning face and dull auburn hair. Laney placed the tray on a skirted table by the window and poured a mug of coffee for Bonnie from the white carafe. Bonnie lifted the cover from over her plate and licked her lips as the aroma of thyme wafted from the cheese and mushroom omelet.

Bonnie sat and began to eat after offering the other chair to Laney.

"Mmm," Bonnie breathed while rolling her startling green eyes upward in pure pleasure with the first bite of the omelet. "Delicious. I hate that I won't be staying at your bed and breakfast after today."

"Is something unsatisfactory?" Laney asked as she watched her devour the breakfast.

"No, no," she said with one hand waving away Laney's concern and the other reaching for the covered breadbasket. "Your place is just wonderful, though a bit pricey," Bonnie said, her mouth closing down on a pecan muffin. She took a quick swallow of black coffee. "I only agreed to stay here last night because Malcolm suggested it and I know you two are friends."

"I understand," Laney said, somewhat relieved because of Malcolm and Shar's quick decision to also pursue guardianship of Scotty.

Bonnie stabbed at a bite-size slice of honeydew melon with her fork. "As it has turned out, Dwayne won't be able to make it to the funeral this morning. He can't get off from his job." After nibbling at her speared fruit, Bonnie sighed and slouched back in her chair.

"Really?" Laney couldn't imagine any job that wouldn't allow an employee go to a funeral. "Where does Dwayne work?"

"Madison Municipal Airport in Indiana."

"What does he do there?"

"He's an aircraft mechanic. The flu bug hit the other mechanic so Dwayne's been working a lot of overtime this week and he already had to miss a half a day yesterday to go to the lawyer's office."

"Has any decision been made about Scotty?" Laney probed casually.

"Not as yet . . . but," her forefinger shot upward, "Dave Wells, our lawyer in Vevay, told Dwayne yesterday that I shouldn't have any problem getting guardianship because I'm Scotty's only aunt. So, I'll just go home after the funeral and sit tight until I can come back and take her home with me." She slapped the arms of her wicker chair for emphasis. "Scotty's a dear child, but sorely in need of discipline, don't you think?" She turned a cold eye on Laney followed by a disdainful lift of her right eyebrow.

Laney bit her tongue but felt an overwhelming urge to punch Bonnie in the nose. She didn't know why she suddenly remembered Bonnie's uncomfortable reaction the night before when Laney had asked her how her mother had died. Not once had Bonnie hinted that the pneumonia that had killed Mabel was the result of a fall. Nor had she mentioned the apartment robbery.

Laney rose and with her face flaming, turned and said impulsively, "Bonnie, are you aware that Keely visited Peachtree Courtyard just hours before she was killed?"

A tiny strangled cry burst from Bonnie.

"She evidently had some questions about your mother's accident, the subsequent break-in and if someone was present when she fell," With a sense of pleasure, Laney watched Bonnie's mouth drop open.

Bonnie's face paled, then splotches of color flooded in and out like a scrolling screensaver. "No one was with her," she said uneasily and a shaky hand flapped in a dismissive gesture.

Laney, not sure if she could control her temper much longer, excused herself, spun on her heel and stamped out of Bonnie's room. She closed the door behind her a bit too forcefully.

"I'll be damned," Laney snarled as she went down the hall. "I wonder why Bonnie Day tried to conceal the facts behind Mabel's accident and robbery." Blackberry sat at the foot of the stairs, her tail thumping for a pet or two, but Laney walked right by her and into the library. There on the desk, lay the two photos side by side—the blond man intent on his engine and Keely, her sad eyes seemingly begging for help.

"How can I help you?" Laney addressed the woman in the picture. Quickly, the answer came to her: She had to continue the search that Keely had begun, the search to discover what really happened to Scotty's Gran in Atlanta and why her apartment was vandalized.

And somehow—and this might be the most difficult undertaking of all—she had to help Keely's daughter find some happiness in her life. And as sure as the sun came up every morning, Laney knew Scotty wouldn't find it with her Aunt Bonnie.

10

Eleven o'clock. The services for Keely were just beginning, Laney thought as she added the milk to the cocoa and sugar and set the mixture on the burner to heat. Scotty sat on an oval braided rug on Malcolm's kitchen floor teasing Kudzu with a gray toy mouse on a red string. She looked adorable in a red jumper, white sweater and red and white polka dot leggings, but Shar hadn't been able to persuade her to put on any other shoes but her faded red sneakers. She had coaxed her hair into two wild bundles tied with blue and red plaid ribbons.

While Malcolm took Scotty downstairs to help feed Nessie and Kudzu, Laney had watched Shar get dressed for the funeral. Her black dress dropped over splayed hips and gapped at the sweetheart neckline. It made her look as long and narrow as a licorice stick. At least sometime during the past three days she had taken the time to restore her strawberry-blond hair color and get a pixie cut. While Shar carelessly brushed blush over her pale cheeks and dimpled chin that jutted with thinness, Laney related the conversation she had had earlier with Bonnie Day. Shar also wondered why Bonnie had kept the details of Mabel's last days under wraps. Her reply to Bonnie's criticism of Scotty was typical of the old Shar, "The woman is so self-righteous, I bet she doesn't have sex in broad daylight."

Shar, Malcolm and Gray left at ten o'clock and Scotty hadn't said boo for almost an hour. Laney wondered what was going on in her troubled mind as the cat leaped and pawed at the mouse in a practice hunt. Nessie was taking a late morning nap on his favorite spot, the needlepoint hearthrug in the parlor.

"Scotty, if you sit in the breakfast nook, I'll bring you some hot chocolate."

Laney poured the cocoa into two mugs on a tray and dropped miniature marshmallows into each. To the tray, she added a package of graham crackers, a tub of butter and a knife.

"If you'd like, we can play a game after," Laney said carrying it all to the cozy alcove.

"I dinna want . . ."

"Well then . . . how about more of *The Wee Scotch Piper?*"

Laney took her silence as a yes and ran upstairs, leaving Scotty spooning the cocoa into her mouth. When she returned, Scotty was bobbing the marshmallows with a graham cracker.

Laney began where she'd left off the night before. She wondered if Scotty's interest in the book was because she identified with the motherless lamb that Ion, the young son of a Scottish shepherd in the story, was struggling to rear so he could win a coveted set of bagpipes.

Laney paused to sip her cocoa. "Shar Hamilton plays the pipes," she said, and noticed that Scotty's eyes widened noticeably with the information.

"I learned to—"

Whatever Scotty was going to tell her was interrupted by the ringing of the phone. Laney scooted out of the booth and lifted the receiver hanging on the wall in the kitchen.

A man's voice, animated and pleasant, though muffled as though he was on a cell phone, asked. "May I speak to Keely Moore?"

Laney drew in her breath and her heart thudded with the thought that she might have to break the news of Keely's death to the caller. "M . . . may I ask who is calling?"

"Frank Rice from Goshen. Is Keely there?"

"No . . ." She puzzled over the name, "Frank Rice?"

"Yes. I was expecting Keely and the moving van at Riverview Farm yesterday. When neither arrived by last evening, I thought perhaps there had been a change of plans. I'd been out of town for several days and may have missed her call."

Oh God, she thought, Malcolm had been trying to reach the man for three days. "Excuse me, Mr. Rice, would you hold on for a moment?"

"Yes . . ."

Laney covered the receiver with her hand and called to Scotty, "Scotty, honey, would you see if I left my purse in the parlor?"

Scotty scooted off the bench and with Kudzu following, scampered out of the kitchen.

As soon as Laney was sure that she was out of hearing distance, she took a deep breath and said into the phone. "Mr. Rice . . . we tried to reach you . . . I have terrible news." She heard his intake of breath. "Keely was struck by a car and killed in Atlanta. Her funeral began just minutes ago."

He began to sob "No . . . no," he breathed into the phone. She waited a long time for him to speak and when he managed, his voice was thick with anguish.

"Scotty! Was Scotty—"

"Scotty is here with her Uncle Malcolm."

"Thank God." His voice broke to a whisper. "Keely . . . oh God, my Keely!"

"Perhaps there is someone you could call . . . a friend or relative?"

"Oh Lord, her funeral. I . . . I've missed it?" He cleared his throat.

"I'm sorry," she said as Scotty entered the kitchen with the purse slapping against her calf. Laney turned her back to the child and spoke quietly into the phone. "Mr. Rice, I must hang up now. I'll call you at another time." She jotted down the number he gave her.

"I . . . I'll let the farm know . . . goodbye," he said, his words fading away before he clicked off.

Laney became aware of Scotty's penetrating stare. "What is it, honey?"

"Frankie come doon?"

Of course, Laney thought, she must have heard me say his name and after all, he was the man Keely had been living with for months. Laney recalled his reaction upon hearing of Keely's death.

"I don't know. I don't think so," Laney told her.

"Frankie dinna like Aunt Bonnie," Scotty said guilelessly, her eyes wide. She shook her head for emphasis.

Laney recalled that Bonnie and Dwayne had been at Keely's welcoming party in Florida. "Was Frank Rice at the party in Florida?" she asked, taking her purse.

Scotty nodded.

"Do you like your aunt?" she asked.

Scotty shrugged and murmured what sounded like "crabbit," as she climbed back into the booth.

Laney sat down across from her. "How about your Uncle Dwayne?" Laney urged.

Scotty's eyes flashed to Laney's and then dropped to her mug. She shrugged in reply.

Laney buttered a graham and offered it to Scotty.

"Nae thank you," she said, her eyes seeming to lose some of their brightness with Laney's questions. She inserted her thumb in her mouth.

"Scotty, can you remember back to the party your Uncle Malcolm had for you and your mother?"

She nodded. "I was wee."

"Your Aunt Shar told me you locked yourself inside the bathroom."

Scotty scowled but nodded.

"Why, Scotty?"

"The bairn. He took ma plane a hunner times. Mither told me I should share it."

"Oh, it was a child?"

She nodded. 'I ran in the bath and locked it."

Laney smiled at her possessiveness of a favorite toy. She couldn't blame the child. "Where did you hide the key?"

"It went doon the hole," she said and Laney laughed.

Not proud about her shameless probe of Scotty's feelings about her aunt and uncle, Laney again picked up the book but Scotty curled up on the bench cushion and shut her eyes.

Laney munched on a graham and mulled over the guardianship situation. With a heavy heart, she recalled the surge of pain that had wrenched Shar's face when she realized that Malcolm might have to surrender Scotty to Bonnie and Dwayne Day. Laney was certain that both Malcolm and Shar would be devastated if the court decided against them. She only hoped that Marshall Knight, the attorney whom Shar and Malcolm planned to see after the funeral, would have some answers.

11

W hile Scotty slept in the nook, Laney laid out the food that friends and neighbors had dropped off as was southern custom when there was a death in the family. Even though no one in Hickory had ever met Keely, both Malcolm and Shar had acquired a phenomenal group of acquaintances since their arrival in Kentucky. One after another, Laney heated the casseroles in the microwave and placed them on electric warming trays in the dining room. When she heard Malcolm, Shar and Gray at the front door, she popped two trays of her mother's yeast rolls in the oven and set the timer.

Malcolm received people in the entrance hall. Most were the same mourners who were at the funeral home the night before. Laney's mother, Maddy, and Sheriff Powell, who had been dating for over a year, were first to arrive. Laney's close friend, Jesse Mills, helped keep the food coming and the coffee and teapots brewing.

Scotty, who had wakened when some of the visitors overflowed into the kitchen, shyly slipped out of the room and into the foyer. With tight fingers, she clung to the hem of her uncle's suit jacket while she sucked on the thumb of her other hand.

Laney stood near Malcolm when Bonnie Day, again wearing her fox scarf over the same pant suit, swept up to Scotty and pulled her thumb from her lips with a pop and said, "Dear, you mustn't do that. Your teeth will buck out like a bunny's."

Malcolm, his eyes swollen from crying, lifted Scotty into his arms and she rubbed her face into his shoulder. Quickly, Laney urged him to take Scotty to get something to eat and was relieved when he headed for the dining room.

Shar, descending the staircase, must have heard Bonnie's reprimand for a frown creased her forehead as she nervously polished the newel post with Scotty's stuffed airplane that she had retrieved from upstairs.

"Mal," Shar called and he stopped and turned. Shar tucked the plush plane under Scotty's fingers, pushed her thumb back into her mouth and winked at her. The subtle gesture didn't escape Laney, nor for that matter, Bonnie Day, who because of her impeccable manners, could only suffer the slight in silence. Scotty's small smile briefly broke the suction on the thumb before Malcolm continued into the dining room.

A steady stream of people murmured their condolences to Malcolm, snacked and quickly left. Laney knew just about every mourner except a blond woman wearing a black cloche who arrived alone, slipping inside the door while Laney was talking with Tina Findley, her husband, Eugene, and two daughters from Washington, Kentucky. Every time Laney would spot the mysterious woman—one time in the dining room and another time as Jesse tottered past her with a tray of sandwiches from the kitchen—someone would waylay her. Finally, while Laney chatted with Jesse who was taking a quick break from kitchen duty, the woman clicked by her in high heels and rushed out the front door, leaving a whiff of perfume in her wake. Curiosity pecking on her, Laney excused herself and peered out the sidelights of the door as the woman's heels slid deep into fresh snow before she climbed into a vehicle with Indiana license plates near the front gate and drove away.

An hour later, even before everyone had left Taylor Ridge, Malcolm, Shar and Attorney Marshall Knight retired in private to discuss Malcolm's potential guardianship of Scotty. Laney and Gray, with Scotty tagging along, talked with guests and helped Jesse whenever they could.

"So you see, Malcolm, the Circuit Court considers many factors before choosing a guardian for a child," Attorney Marshall Knight was saying as smoke from his second cigarette in less than thirty minutes hung over Malcolm's den like blue smog. "It's more than just the potential guardian's age, health and resources that are taken into account. Character, values and even personalities are considered," Marshall said while his long, thin forefingers traced circles on the arms of his chair. He spoke to Malcolm and Shar who sat side by side on a dark red leather sofa facing the lawyer who was sitting on a matching chair.

Shar knew what Marshall was leading to. Damn her marital history.

"But all things equal . . . " Malcolm began. He slipped his arm behind Shar's waist.

"But all things are not equal," Marshall interjected. His rubber galoshes squeaked as he crossed his feet at the ankles.

Here it comes, Shar thought.

"Much will be remedied with our upcoming nuptials," Malcolm said, exasperation wearying his words.

"Even with your marriage in the near future, I'm concerned that Bonnie Day and her husband may still have the advantage," Marshall said. "Mrs. Day is Scotty's only female relative and the fact that she is unable to have any children of her own may be given special attention by the court. She and her husband are already in a stable union—married seven years, so you told me, and they go to church regularly."

Shar shot to her feet. Only briefly did her beautiful Celtic wedding plans flash through her mind before she blurted, "What if Mal and I get married immediately."

"Is that possible?" Marshall choked. He snuffed out his cigarette in a bronze ashtray.

"Give me three days. How about it, Mal?"

"Sharlene, are you sure about this?"

Marshall stirred the ashes with the butt. "The court may find a quickie wedding as contrived and—"

"To hell with the court. We're only moving it up a few weeks," Shar said.

"There are other factors." Marshall briefly made eye contact with Shar. "Please forgive me, Sharlene. I hesitate to mention your previous marriages, but they can only be a detriment," Marshall said.

"Cr-ap," Shar said. Double crap if Marshall gets wind that Simon may still be alive and kicking, she thought.

"It's not fair," Malcolm said, standing and pulling Shar to him in a fierce hug. "I just know that Keely would want me to have Scotty and would be certain that I would choose a suitable mother for her." Behind his thick lenses, his eyes welled. He looked straight into Shar's eyes. "The very traits that drew me to Shar would contribute to Scotty growing into a smashing lass."

What a sweetheart he is, Shar thought, and kissed him thoroughly on the lips while her fingers pinched a buttock.

Marshall went red in the face while Malcolm, mostly used to Shar's brashness, only cleared his throat.

Marshall's suffusion slowly faded to pink. Then suddenly, his gaunt body jackknifed out of the chair. He drew his fingers through his sparse gray hair that lay like threads across his scalp. "I should have thought of this sooner. Did Keely leave a will?"

Malcolm's lips parted, then closed. It was a couple of moments before he spoke. "If she did, we haven't come across it, although I haven't had a chance to go through her personal effects except for those in the carryon that she had with her when she died." A cheek muscle twitched with the memory.

Shar recalled the photo and copy of Malcolm's driver's license that she and Laney had found in the cosmetic bag the night before. She had later hidden them away in her vanity drawer. "How could a will be significant?" she asked Marshall.

"Many parents put in their wills the name of the person who they would want to raise their child in the case they die while the child is still a minor. Of course, the parents should always ask the potential guardian if they would want the responsibility. Did Keely ever speak to you about this?"

Malcolm's face dropped. "Never."

"Do you know if Keely ever contacted a lawyer in Ocala, Florida? A copy of a will would be kept on file. Or perhaps she had a safety deposit box."

"I don't know but I think it's worth checking out," Malcolm said with hope in his eyes.

"Marshall, how much weight would this endorsement have with the court?" Shar asked.

"The court normally gives first consideration to the person that's named, however, you can't pass on a child's custody like chattel. It is only a recommendation that the court appoint the guardian that the parent prefers."

"Mal," Shar said, "in case Marshall doesn't come up with a will, maybe we should go through all Keely's stuff in the barn on the chance it might be there."

But Shar knew it was unlikely that even if Keely had written a will, she would have thought of including the recommendation, unless Keely had been afraid that something might happen to her? She suddenly thought of the hit and run in Atlanta and chills climbed her arms.

12

"Scotty had her airplane before Mal and I met with Marshall in the den," Shar said to Laney and Gray while she dug beneath the cushions of the Lamont settee in the parlor. "I've torn this place apart twice."

"She's certainly fond of that little plane," Gray said. "I'm surprised she went to bed without it."

Laney looked up from the carton that she was cutting open with Gray's penknife. When she and Gray had learned that Marshall encouraged an all-out search for a possible copy of Keely's will, Malcolm had asked his farm manager to haul in several of Keely's boxes from the barn.

"Mabel gave her the toy. Scotty told me that her grandfather was a pilot," Laney said in answer to Gray's comment.

"Where's Malcolm?" Laney asked as she pulled out a couple of ledgers and a black notebook from a carton marked "personal."

"He promised to stay with Scotty until she was asleep," Gray said, "but I have a suspicion that he fell asleep before she did."

"I promised I'd have it for her in the morning," Shar said, her butt jutting as she searched under the secretary. Anxiety coated her voice.

"Maybe Nessie got hold of it," Gray said, turning the pages of an old cardboard covered notebook that Laney had handed him.

"That's a thought," Shar said, "although I thought he'd gotten out of the chewing stage a long time ago." She groaned to her feet and dashed out of the room.

Gray had removed his navy suit jacket. A catsup stain on his light blue oxford-cloth shirt swiped at the edge of his striped tie. Laney suspected it might be from her Swedish meatball casserole because she had seen him go back for a seconds.

"Look at this," he said. He shoved the open notebook toward Laney.

Laney stopped shuffling through papers in the bottom of the carton and began leafing through the notebook that contained page after page of newspaper clippings and a few photos of old airplanes. The clippings were in terrible condition—yellowed and crumbling. Most told of forced landings and hair-raising stunts at air shows. One article included a photo of a handsome mustached man in an unfastened leather aviator's cap, the goggles resting crookedly on the crown of his head. He stood in front of an airplane with two sets of wings held rigid with struts. The caption under the picture read, *Pilot, Victor Moore, escapes injury in forced landing.*

"Scotty's grandfather!" Laney exclaimed.

"Seems he was a barnstormer during the late twenties and early thirties," Gray said, taking back the book to look through the pages.

"Well, I found it," Shar said, entering the room and dumping an armful of stuffing on the coffee table and dangling a blur of colored fabric in front of everyone, "in Nessie's bed."

"Oh my," Laney said.

"Ruined! What do I tell Scotty?" Shar was close to tears.

"Wait, Shar. Maybe it's repairable," Gray said, reaching for the cover that was turned inside out. He turned it to the outside and stretched it out on the table, smoothing out the wings and fuselage. He poked his fingers inside the opening and pushed out the tail, propeller and button wheels. "See, all we have to do is re-stuff it and sew it up." All at once, Gray paled and his eyes darkened.

Alarmed, Laney asked uneasily, "Gray, what is it?"

Gray lifted the fabric and studied the edges of the opening. He looked up at the two women. "Unless Nessie has suddenly grown scalpels for teeth, this toy has been slit open with a razor blade."

"Gray, no!" Laney snatched the fabric and scanned the opening with Shar hovering over her shoulder. Unmistakably, the four-inch gash had been cut with a sharp edged instrument and it was nowhere near the seam that ran along the bottom of the toy.

"Woman, the slasher has struck again!" Shar blurted. "Remember what Betsy at Peachtree Courtyard told you about the burglary at Mabel Moore's apartment?"

"I remember, I remember," Laney said, her mind in a whirl.

"What are you two women babbling about?" Gray asked, his eyes riveted on Laney's face, his stern expression demanding a quick answer.

"I was planning on telling you," Laney said lamely. "I just haven't had a moment all day."

"No time like the present," Gray said evenly, but his turquoise eyes flashed angrily.

So, while Shar scurried to find needle and thread, Laney related her conversation with Betsy at the assisted living center after she and Shar had found the second photo of the blond man and the copy of Malcolm's driver's license hidden in Keely's carryon luggage. She paused briefly, then reluctantly concluded with her suspicion that Keely may have sent Scotty on to Malcolm because she was afraid, perhaps afraid for her life.

Shar returned to the parlor with a tray containing three drinks, straight-pins, and black thread with a needle woven through the paper disk on top of the spool. Her face reflected the strain of the past few days and Gray's ominous revelation that Scotty's toy had been deliberately tampered with.

Gray hadn't commented throughout Laney's long account of the recent happenings. In fact, during her narration, he aimlessly turned the pages of the notebook.

But Laney saw the stress lines forming on his forehead and the twitching jaw muscle as though words were lining up inside his mouth to spew from his lips any second. But he remained silent.

"I know what you're thinking," Laney said to Gray.

Shar, who had been struggling to thread the needle, handed it to Laney and she welcomed the diversion. Once threaded, she handed it back. Silence crackled.

Laney watched Gray turn the pages.

"Stop that!" she cried and pulled the notebook from his hands. "Say something!"

But before he could respond, words in old English type on yellowed newsprint jumped up from her lap. *The Vevay Rev . . .* she read, and beneath the partial name of the newspaper was the subtitle fragment,

Covers Switzerland County like the dew from . . .

Beneath the fragment, a smaller headline began, *Occupants of plane*— But the complete article had crumbled away. There was only one word remaining in the date— *Thursday.*

Gray's controlled voice broke her concentration. "It's obvious that someone who was here after the funeral cut the plane open." His face hadn't regained its color.

Shar was furiously stuffing the airplane with the fiberfill. "But there were only caring friends and relatives here," she said.

"Someone so caring, they wasted a grieving child's toy," Gray said sarcastically and picked up his drink and sipped.

"I agree with Gray," Laney said, amazed that the two of them would be of one opinion on this. "Just like at Peachtree Courtyard, they were looking for something," Laney said.

"Laney, I didn't say that. This may have been no more than a malicious prank," Gray said, "but I'm willing to be proven wrong."

"Prank?" Shar exclaimed. "Who in the hell?—"

"Bonnie Day," Gray said.

Laney knew Gray was referring to the snub in the center hallway when Shar had given the plane to Scotty and winked at her. He had laughed when Laney had told him about the episode but no one was laughing now.

"Not even goody two-shoes would destroy something her own mother gave to Scotty," Shar said as she tried in vain to turn under the edges of the fabric and pin it together.

"Unless she was searching for something inside the toy that was either worth a lot of money or could incriminate them somehow," Laney said. "I think the same thing could be said regarding the motive for the burglary in Atlanta."

"Dammit," Gray moaned.

"Oh, before I forget," Laney said, trying to distract Gray, "who was that blond woman with the black hat that was here today?"

Gray frowned, trying to remember the woman. "I have no idea. I thought she was a friend of yours."

"Some people will do anything for a free meal—even go to a funeral luncheon for someone they don't know," Shar quipped as she pulled out a tuff of fiberfill and began pinning again.

Laney smiled thinly at Shar's attempt at humor. Her friend had bounced back somewhat from her deep depression, she thought. But she was sure that it had nothing to do with Shar's assurance that Simon was still resting peacefully on her mantle. Rather, that Scotty was beginning to warm toward her and the possibility that the youngster might become a permanent resident at Taylor Ridge, were more likely the causes for her renewed buoyancy.

"The woman came alone and left alone, in a car with Indiana plates, I might add," Laney said. She suddenly jumped to her feet and dashed to the phone on the secretary. She dialed Sheriff Powell's home phone number. When she didn't get an answer, she called her mother's number.

As she figured, Gordon was there and fifteen minutes passed before she rejoined Shar and Gray. Shar waggled the repaired airplane at her in greeting. Laney wondered what Scotty would think of the heavy black sutures, like a botched surgery, zigzagging along one side of her favorite toy.

"Listen up," Laney exclaimed. She drank some of her watery bloody as Gray rolled his eyes at her impatiently.

"You won't believe this," she said putting the drink down. "Indiana license plates don't have the name of the county on them like Kentucky plates do. When I told Gordon that I saw only the first two numbers of the plate, he said that was all he needed to search the county code. The first two numbers of the mystery woman's plate were 78, the county code for Switzerland County."

"So-o," Shar said.

Vevay's in Switzerland County."

"Lay ee odl-oo," Shar yodeled.

Laney ignored her. "Vevay's a town I'd never heard of until yesterday when Bonnie said she lived there. Look, you guys." Laney pointed to the notebook clipping. "Victor Moore, who was Mabel's husband, may have crash-landed his plane near Vevay and now we find that the mystery woman had Switzerland County plates."

"Coincidence?" asked Gray weakly.

"Too much of a coincidence," Laney retorted. "Shar, want to go to Vevay?" Laney asked.

"Oh woman, I'd love to . . . but I can't. I've got a wedding in three days . . . and there's Scotty, and I have to help Mal search for the will," Shar said, about to cry with disappointment.

"I'll go with you," Gray said.

Laney blinked with surprise. "You will?"

"Vet business is really slow around the holidays. I'll get Doc Mike to cover my calls. But what about the new novel?"

"I put it on hold three days ago," Laney sighed with regret. "I'll take my laptop, but I doubt I'll have time—"

"You two won't miss my wedding, will you?" Shar cried.

"Fat chance," Laney said patting her hand.

"What'll you do up there?" Shar asked.

"First off, I want to check newspaper microfilm at the public library to get a copy of this clipping. I'll see where that leads me. We'll try to be back day after tomorrow so we can help with the wedding. Ah, Shar, I hate that you won't have the blowout wedding you wanted."

"Who said I won't? This wedding may be smaller but it will still be the blast of the social season."

Laney thought of the blond man in the photo who Shar feared was her second husband. If somehow Simon wasn't dead after all, Shar's wedding could be more than a blowout. It could be a downright explosion.

13

The following morning, Laney and Gray were in the breakfast room devouring slices of Maddy's date-nut bread slathered with cream cheese and mugs of hot coffee, when Jesse Mills arrived to clean the bed and breakfast. Every Thursday, Jesse's day off from the Finish Line Restaurant, she worked for Laney.

"Have some nut-bread and coffee before you begin," Gray said. "We'll be out of your way in a few minutes. We're off to Indiana."

Jesse poured coffee, removed a plate from a glass-fronted cabinet and sat down across from them. She took a bite of the bread and Blackberry, under the table, licked up a couple of crumbs that fell to the floor.

Jesse peeked under the table and scratched the dog's ear. "God almighty, she's a sight. I won't have to play mid-wife, will I?"

Laney looked at Gray anxiously.

"She has a few days to go. I think we're okay to leave her, but just in case, I'll leave Mike's number for you and Maddy."

Jesse had agreed to spend the night. Three guests from Houston, Texas were arriving in the afternoon for a single night's stay while they attended a surprise fiftieth anniversary party for an aunt and uncle who lived in Hickory. To prepare breakfast for the guests, Maddy would spell Jesse early the next morning. Fortunately, Maddy's boat dock was closed over the winter so that she could help out whenever Laney needed her. Laney felt comfortable leaving the bed and breakfast in her mother's hands. She had an easy, friendly manner with guests and her country breakfasts were always accompanied by a homemade yeasty bread, savory muffin or mouth-watering biscuit.

"Gra-ay," Laney whined. "If there is any chance at all Blackberry will deliver while we're gone, we can't go."

"It's okay, Laney. I'm sure of it," he said.

She tossed him a skeptical look, then turned to Jesse. "Jesse, did you see the blond woman with the hat who was at Taylor Ridge yesterday after the funeral?"

"I thought she was a friend of yours from Pittsburgh," Jesse said.

"I'd never laid eyes on her before," Laney said, licking cream cheese off her fingers.

"She sure made herself at home. Spent a lot of time in the bathroom and I saw her coming down the stairs once," Jesse said, then sipped her coffee.

Gray's brows lifted. "What was she doing upstairs?" he asked.

Puccini had displaced Blackberry under the table and Gray was scratching the cat's belly with his foot.

"Maybe she didn't find what she was looking for inside Scotty's plane and she was searching the joint," Laney said sourly.

Gray laughed but Jesse looked puzzled.

"It's a long story, Jesse," Laney said.

"Well, that *other* woman has a story that ought to be told," Jesse said.

"Huh?" Laney queried. "What other woman?"

"The gal with the den of foxes around her neck. Caught her with her ear to the door while Shar, Malcolm and Marshall Knight were meeting with the lawyer."

"You don't mean it! Bonnie Day eavesdropping?" Laney shuddered with the thought that Bonnie may have overheard confidential information between her friends and their lawyer about Scotty's guardianship. Maybe she was wrong about the other woman cutting open the airplane now that she knew Bonnie could stoop to eavesdropping. And Bonnie was in Atlanta the same time Mabel's apartment was ransacked. Maybe she was the one who had made it look like an attempted robbery.

Jesse cleared the table and took the dishes to the sink.

"Gray, we'll go as soon as I call Frank Rice. Laney waved an index card with his phone number on it. Yesterday, I promised to call him back."

Laney took her coffee to the kitchen desk and dialed the number Frank had given her. After four rings, his answering machine picked up and she left a message that she planned to stop by while in the area. She looked at the number again and dialed directory assistance.

"Well, well, well," she said after hanging up the phone and returning to the table. "Guess where this number is located."

"Don't tell me it's in Switzerland County too." Gray said sarcastically. "For sure, I'd have to don my lederhosen."

"No, smart nose, it's in Carroll County, Kentucky, across the river from Switzerland County."

"What in the hell is the attraction up there, anyway?" he said.

"I don't know, but I'm sure as hell going to do my best to find out."

14

Because of the bright morning sun and the salt trucks with their scraper blades working through the night, most of the secondary roads were clear of snow. Gray picked up Route 421 in Frankfort and traveled north through quaint little towns named Defoe, Pleasureville, New Castle and Bedford. He had brought an ample supply of opera tapes and CD's and they mostly listened rather than talked. Only when they crossed the Ohio River at Milton and turned east at Madison, Indiana, did Laney begin to feel the stirring of expectation, that at last, she might discover some answers to some questions about Keely's death. Paramount in her mind, was why Keely had sent Scotty on to Malcolm without her? Was she afraid for her daughter? Had Keely been the person who had called Shar and told her Simon was alive? If so, how had she acquired the photo of the blond man in the first place and why had she inquired into the accidental death of Mabel in Atlanta? Half a dozen other questions nagged at her as they followed scenic Highway 56 along the river toward Vevay.

Vevay. Could the little Swiss town hold some answers? Bonnie and Dwayne Day, the mystery blond woman, and now even Mabel Moore's husband, Victor, had connections to Switzerland County, Indiana. Also, Frank Rice lived just across the river where Keely and Scotty had planned to move. Was there a common link that tied them all together?

It was noon when Gray's pink Buick swung into the parking lot of the Switzerland County Public Library. When they left the car, they were awestruck by an enormous mural painted on a brick wall of a building overlooking the parking lot. The colorful painting portrayed the town of Vevay during the era of the steamboat.

They crunched through a sprinkling of salt that had already done its job in front of the library—a one-story brick building set back on the lot. Once inside, Laney explained to the director, Louise Maynard, that they would like to review newspaper microfilm for the years 1927 through 1930, the years she thought she might find the headline that began with *Occupants of Plane. . . .* She had come to this time span from the dates of other flight clippings in the black notebook and a Western Union telegram dated November 1927 from the Director of Aeronautics in Washington DC. The telegram informed Victor Moore that he had been issued a temporary license number for his JN-4D biplane.

The director led them to the genealogy room in the rear of the library and pulled three boxes containing reels of the *Vevay Reveille=Enterprise* from a drawer. After scooting a second chair over to the microfilm machine, she fed the earliest film into the machine. Laney thanked her and she left them.

"No telling how long this might take," Laney said while she turned the forward dial until she came to the front page of the first newspaper.

"At least the newspaper is a weekly, not a daily," Gray said noting each issue was dated on a Thursday.

"And since the article was on the front page, we only have to scan one page of each issue," Laney added.

"Laney, what exactly do you hope to gain from this search?"

Laney grimaced. "To tell you the truth, I don't know. Something . . . anything . . . a connection between the past and present, I guess." She continued to scan each front page from the 1927 newspapers.

"Well, we know some of the connections already. Victor and Mabel Moore were the parents of Bonnie Moore Day and the late Ray Moore. Ray was Keely's husband and the father of Scotty."

With Gray's brief review, Laney's insides took an unexpected sickening drop. She flipped the dial to the vertical position and the film stopped with a clunk. She looked at him. "What's wrong with that picture, Gray?"

"Huh?"

"Mabel. Ray. Keely. Scotty's grandmother, father and mother. All dead from accidents." Laney said. Her heart lurched with the realization.

"Accidents, Laney. It does happen in families sometimes."

"Like my sister's so-called accidental death." Laney said sarcastically.

"That was different."

"That was murder."

Gray reached for the knob and the film advanced. November's Thursdays came and went in silence, then December's. He rewound the film, removed the reel and put it in the box. He fed 1928 into the machine.

They found it on the front page of the August thirtieth newspaper:

OCCUPANTS OF PLANE UNHURT WHEN THEY ARE FORCED DOWN

A Curtiss JN-4D airplane was forced down on the Fry farm west of Vevay last Thursday by a faulty gas line. The plane is owned by Victor Moore of Madison, Indiana and was piloted by him. He was accompanied by his mechanic, also of Madison.

The young men were returning from Cincinnati and planned to land at Madison. While flying over Vevay, the motor began spitting and losing speed, and the plane gradually began descending.

Moore, realizing he would have to make a landing, began looking for a convenient field. As the plane passed over the west end of Vevay, it seemed to be almost skimming the tree tops. Moore fairly jerked the plane over a string of telephone wires and it came to earth slightly on its nose, the propeller plowing up the dirt. The plane was not heavily damaged and neither of the occupants was injured.

The plane remained on the field for about three hours until necessary repairs were made and then took to the air again headed for Madison.

"Not much there, Miss Marple," Gray said triumphantly while Laney pushed the copy button.

"True," Laney said. She grabbed the sheet from the tray and began to re-read it while Gray rewound the film. She waved the copy in front of his face "We already knew that Victor owned a Curtiss JN-4D airplane by the telegram in the notebook."

"I read somewhere they nicknamed that early plane "Jenny" from the slurring of the two letters, J and N," Gray said.

"Well, now we know that Victor Moore and his Jenny lived in Madison and his mechanic was also from Madison."

"The knowledge is overwhelming," Gray snorted.

"Listen, if Victor and Mabel lived in Madison in 1927, perhaps their children, Bonnie and Ray, were born there. That could explain why Bonnie and Dwayne settled in the area. Switzerland County is only the next county over.

"Your mind moves in strange and mysterious ways." Gray stole a quick kiss on her neck.

"I agree it's not much to go on, but it's a start. Let's go." Laney turned off the microfilm machine and stood.

"Where to, Sherlock?"

"Madison Airport," she said, replacing the three film boxes in the drawer.

Gray followed Laney to the front desk where they paid for the copy and thanked Louise for her help. After a quick duck into the restrooms, they were soon back on Highway 56 in route to Madison.

By Gray's silence, Laney knew he was hoping that any information found in Madison would put an end to her suspicions once and for all. But as they drove along the Ohio River, Laney pictured Scotty's fluttering butterfly fingers symbolizing her dead mother and father and it wrenched to the core of her. Keely's unexpected death just didn't ring true and she wasn't going to let it go until it did.

15

Shar's mouth clamped tightly over the blowpipe and she began to play "Highland Cathedral" one more time, but she just couldn't seem to get it right. She collapsed the airbag under her arm, lowered the chanter, bag and three drones and laid them on Malcolm's desk. Her concern that the month of not practicing the bagpipes would take a toll on her technique had been realized. But it just couldn't be helped, she thought ruefully. The phone calls and that photo had ripped her apart. And now there was dear Scotty who slept between bed sheets of airplanes to worry about.

Shar had spent another restless night in the other twin bed. At dawn, she slipped into her robe and tiptoed to the door. Kudzu left his cozy cuddle next to Scotty and followed her into the hall.

As the cat darted down the stairs, Shar peeked in on Malcolm in the master bedroom. Normally an early riser, Malcolm, instead, was lying on his back snoring tiny puffs, a book and his glasses beside him, the bedside lamp still glaring. The pace and stress of the past days had worn him to exhaustion, so Shar let him sleep. After feeding Kudzu and Nessie, she let them outside and secluded herself in the den to practice.

Still thinking of Scotty, Shar gently fingered the worn velvet of the bag and felt her eyes begin to water. Never in a million years could Shar have thought she could have such a turnabout of feelings for a mere snippet of a girl. Not tough and flippant Shar Hamilton, she thought. But whenever she imagined Scotty being taken away from her and Malcolm, a thumbscrew kind of pain squeezed her heart. Whoever said you must bear a child before you could know how you would feel to have her taken away?

She sighed and lifted her pipes once more. Malcolm had requested that she play at their wedding and she needed to get the tune right. Maybe the lively "Highland Fling" would get her fingers limbered up, so she began the dance of joy traditionally performed at the end of a victorious Scottish battle.

Halfway through the song, the door to the den flew open. Startled, Shar stopped playing in mid-blow and the bag collapsed in a whining succession of off-notes. Scotty stood in the opening with a hand on the doorknob. Barefoot, she wore only a pink flannel nightgown that barely reached to her knees. A section of the ruffled hem had become separated from the gown and hung to her left shin like a rosy peninsula. The morning sun streamed through the window giving her sleep-tossed ringlets the sheen of new pennies.

As Shar watched in amazement, the child placed her fists upon her hips and took two steps into the room and stood ramrod straight in the first position of dance, her heels touching, her knees turned out with her toes pointing in opposite directions.

"Mither took me to learn it," Scotty said, trilling her r's.

For a moment, Shar didn't grasp her meaning. " 'The Fling,' Scotty?"

Scotty gave Shar an endearing exaggerated nod.

"You have learned one of the Highland dances?" Shar asked again in wonder, still not believing Keely had provided instruction for her daughter.

Scotty's vivid eyes sparkled like dew-kissed heather. She looked expectantly at the pipes in Shar's arms.

What the hell, Shar thought, and quickly adjusted the drones on her shoulder and raised the blowpipe to her lips.

With the first tone, Scotty's lips silently counted to the unchanging tempo. On the eighth count, Scotty bowed at the waist for a second count of eight. Quickly, she sprang into the second position with her right foot up, then behind her, in front, then again in back before springing to her left foot. She repeated the steps three times while alternating her arms, one arched over her head, the other in a fist at her waist.

Shar almost choked with the excitement of what she was witnessing. At Scottish festivals, Shar had been present when children under seven competed in the Highland Dance. Once she even played for an afternoon competition when the scheduled piper had become ill. Most of the youngest competitors danced only four steps of the "Highland Fling." But Scotty performed six steps of the fling, including the toe heels and the shakes. All were done with surprising control and skill. Her timing was perfect and her balance remarkable for someone so young. When Scotty went round with arms overhead, her second finger and thumb of each hand touched in a graceful curve and her other fingers spread like antlers of a deer, as the arms and fingers represented in the dance.

Shar trembled with delight, her eyes moist in awe of Scotty's unhurried and supple hops and springs. Her "working foot" was always pointed, her "supporting foot" on the ball with hardly a wobble. When Scotty concluded the dance with a bow—again in the first position—only damp curls at her hairline hinted that Scotty's dance was less than effortless. Shar knew that only an uncompromising instructor and Scotty's obvious love of Highland Dance could have produced such precision in a child so young.

Collapsing her pipes on the desk, Shar couldn't get her hands on the child fast enough. She swooped Scotty up before she had even straightened from her bow and they whirled round and round until they both giggled from dizziness and joy. Scotty's tiny arms went tight around her neck and her bare legs caught Shar about her waist. The instant Shar felt Scotty's soft mouth and silky ringlets press against her neck, she swore to herself that she would fight to the death to keep this child.

16

"Our secret, Scotty? Until the wedding?" Shar asked. "Your Uncle Mal will be blown away by your dancing." What an exciting present for him, she thought.

Scotty's eyes looked troubled "Blown away?" she said with alarm.

"No, no, Scotty. It's just an expression that means he will be pleased."

Scotty pulled on her red sneakers, apprehension still lurking in her eyes.

Shar stooped and began to tie her laces.

"I want to do them," Scotty said, and while sitting on the edge of her bed, she pulled her knee up to her chin and did a fine job of it.

Definitely independent, Shar thought, but Scotty's lingering anxiousness brought to mind one of the first sentences out of the child's mouth the day she arrived, "Mither died like ma faither." Shar risked keeping the painful memory alive, by asking, "Scotty, when your mother was missing, why did you think she had died like your father?"

Scotty gave Shar a sidelong look and reached for her airplane on the quilt behind her. She fingered the new black stitches that Shar had blamed on poor Nessie rather than frightening her with the true story. For a moment, Shar thought she hadn't heard her question.

"Mither told ma cheet."

Cheet? Wasn't that "cat" in Scottish? Shar asked herself. Had Keely told the cat something? "Whatever do you mean?" she asked.

"Mither told Smoky that someone made ma faither die."

Shar gasped. "Scotty, you are mistaken. It was a horse, honey . . . an accident."

"Mither dinna know I hear when she told Smoky. Her eyes were full of fricht."

Shar's knees began to quiver and she sat down hard on the bed next to Scotty. Pulling her into her arms, she began to rock back and forth. "When did you hear this?"

"Before we go to America an' we have to leave Smoky."

Last year, Shar thought. Perhaps Keely was just emotional about leaving the cat. But Scotty said her mother's eyes were full of fright. Unconsciously, Shar squeezed Scotty tighter and tighter until she wiggled free. She crossed to the bedside table where the two rosebuds from her mother's casket were drooping. The airplane under her arm, Scotty fingered the withering petals and several fell to the tabletop. "Mither's roses are gone," she said.

And also gone was the bloom in Scotty's cheeks that had transformed her when she'd danced only a couple of hours before. With Scotty's weariness of spirit, Shar vowed to never ask her about her parents' deaths again.

Struggling to put a lilt in her voice, Shar quickly changed the subject. "I must measure you for a kilt."

Immediately after Scotty's dance, Shar had phoned a local seamstress and for an elevated fee, the woman had agreed to make the kilt from a Lamont tartan throw that Malcolm kept on the sofa in the den. After breakfast, Shar had secreted away the fabric when Malcolm left to check his Angus herd with his farm manager.

Kudzu slithered around Scotty's legs and she scooped him up. "I have a bonny kilt, Saugh," she said casually.

Shar blinked with astonishment, not only that Scotty owned a kilt, but because of the name she had called her. "Saugh" was Scotty's first attempt to say her name and Shar didn't mind the mispronunciation.

"Mither make ma kilt."

"Where is it, Scotty? It wasn't in your duffel."

"I dinna know."

"The cartons in the barn!"

"Mibbie."

Shar rushed to the closet and ripped Scotty's toggle coat off the hanger and grabbed her ruffled hat off the shelf.

"Let's go search!" she cried, while Scotty's frightening words about her father still beat in her ears like Scottish drums.

17

A man about sixty years old stood behind the counter in the small terminal.

"We're here to inquire about a former resident of Madison," Laney said, after introducing herself and Gray to Elliot Cook, the Madison Airport manager.

Terminal would be stretching it, Laney thought. Actually, the building was a one-story clapboard house with two cluttered rooms. The front office was crammed with flight memorabilia, a computer station and a desk whose surface held several inches of files and papers that had no chance of finding a niche in a cabinet that was spilling folders.

Various plastic models of planes hung from the ceiling on fishing line. One, a yellow and white radio controlled Piper Cub, was on a collision course with a blue and white twin-engine Comanchee.

"His name was Victor Moore," Laney shoved the copy of the 1928 Vevay newspaper article on the counter in front of Cook, who with his bulldog build and thick hands, could have been a wrestler in his younger days. His full lips pursed as he read about the forced landing.

"1928," he commented, reading the date.

"Do you recall anyone by that name?" Laney asked. "He had a son named Ray and a daughter, Bonnie. Bonnie lives in Vevay."

"I don't understand," he said. "If you know where Victor Moore's daughter lives, why don't you ask *her* about her father?"

With Laney's growing suspicions about Keely's and Mabel's deaths and the possible guardianship dispute over Scotty, that was the one thing Laney didn't want to do—ask Bonnie Day anything.

"I'd rather not talk with her directly," she said truthfully.

Cook raised a gray eyebrow in a questioning arch. "Uh . . . what about the son?"

"I'm afraid Ray Moore is deceased," Gray said.

"May I ask you what you want to know about . . ." He glanced at the clipping. "Uh, Victor Moore?"

"I am a freelance writer and I am doing an article on the Curtiss JN-4D airplane and the barnstorming years. Not too many people are left that have ever flown a Jenny and when I came upon this article, I thought maybe someone knew about Victor's experiences with the plane and could relate them to me," Laney lied. Well, all weren't fibs, she thought, although Gray's castigating look foreshadowed soap-in-her-mouth when they got back in the car.

Elliot Cook's jowly face broke into a doughy grin. "If that's all you want, I know just the man to talk to. Barnaby Biddle."

Laney pulled a notebook and pen out of her bag. She wrote down the name and looked around for Gray. Peeking around the partition, she found him sipping from the water fountain that was between two restrooms in the waiting room.

"Barnaby's the eighty-nine year old authority on biplanes around these parts. In fact, he's providing the know-how for a guy who is restoring a 1932 Navy Stearman."

"Where can I find him?" Laney asked, thinking that perhaps the fellow just might have heard of Victor Moore.

"He owns a small grass airstrip near Vevay," he said.

"There's that famous town again," Gray whispered in her ear as he joined her back at the counter.

"But you might find him here at the hangar where Dwayne is working on the Stearman," Elliot said.

"Here at the airport!" Laney exclaimed.

Elliot grabbed a set of keys off a hook on the wall near the computer. "If you don't mind a grungy ride, I'll take you by the hangar. Can't guarantee he'll be there though."

Elliot wasn't kidding about his mode of transportation. The eighty-eight Ford 150 was pretty gruesome. Laney could have autographed the dust on the dashboard with her finger and dried muddy pawprints on the blue vinyl front seat looked suspiciously as though Elliot had recently taken "Beethoven," for Sunday drive.

Elliot drove through an opening in the cyclone fencing, turned right and followed alongside one of the runways toward a distant oasis of metal hangars.

"Don't see any parked vehicles," Gray said next to Laney.

"There's Dwayne's car," Elliot said, pointing as he passed the next to the last hangar. Parked between the structures, a vintage Volkswagen Beetle screamed a poor, yellow paint job. He braked in front of the last hangar.

"Dwayne? His last name wouldn't happen to be Day, would it?" Laney asked.

"It most certainly would," Elliot said, surprise in his voice that she might know the man. "He's one of two mechanics who work for the airport."

Laney elbowed Gray in the ribs and whispered "Uh-oh" in his ear. Quickly, she tried to think of an excuse to avoid meeting the man who, along with his wife, were trying to get guardianship of Scotty, but Elliot had already stepped down from the truck and had opened the door of the hangar. She and Gray followed behind like puppies.

Laney was struck by the eerie greenness inside the hangar caused by overhead florescent lighting that bounced off plastic-covered wall insulation. In the center of the space, the steel carcass of the Stearman plane, minus its skin, wings and motor, was painted a bilious green. Below a narrow, yellow-tipped black propeller, a man on one knee was tightening a nut on a wheel assembly.

"Dwayne, have you seen Barnaby?" Elliot asked the man who jumped as though startled.

The man, somewhere in his forties, slowly got to his feet and turned toward them. He tossed his finely textured black hair out of his eyes and smiled crookedly through a Clark Gable mustache. His cobalt eyes darted from Elliot, to Gray, to Laney and back to Elliot. "Hey," he mumbled in a deep voice.

"Seen Barnaby, today?" Elliot inquired again. "This lady wants to talk to him about the Jenny."

"Uh-uh." Dwayne's eyes shot back to Laney.

"Say, do you two know each other?" Elliot asked.

"H . . . haven't had the pleasure," he said. He wiped his hands on his overalls and extended his hand, never taking his eyes off Laney. "Dwayne Day."

"Laney McVey," Laney said while shaking his hand, "and my fiancé, Gray Prescott."

Dwayne's smile collapsed behind his mustache, but nevertheless, he shook Gray's hand stiffly. He certainly knows who we are, Laney thought. From his wife, Bonnie, no doubt. She wondered whether Dwayne had somehow learned about Shar and Malcolm's plan to also fight for Scotty's guardianship, hence the cool reception. But how could he have learned about it so soon?

"I'm afraid I have to get back," Elliot said to Laney. "I'll give you directions to Biddle's Flying Service at the terminal. He held the door open for them while Dwayne walked slowly back to the plane.

Elliot turned the truck around. Suddenly, the yellow Beetle backed out in front of them, squealed a doughnut and ate up the snow-dusted turf next to the runway like it was revving for takeoff.

18

The waitress seated them in a dark wooden booth at Mundt's in Madison. Constructed in 1835, the building was known for the candy store, home and candy factory of the Mundt family between the years 1893 and 1966. Mundt's had recently reopened and now served lunch along with its fine chocolates, ice cream and confections.

Laney scanned the menu. When she spotted the desserts, she decided to skip lunch. She chose "The Hill," three scoops of ice cream layered with caramel sauce and topped with creamy hot fudge. Gray ordered the Al B. Core Salad on wheat berry bread.

"Did you see Dwayne's reaction to our introductions? He froze up like someone had dropped an ice cube down his coveralls," Laney said after the waitress served their coffee. "It's not even public knowledge yet, but he's definitely heard about Malcolm going after Scotty. And there's only one way he could have heard about it, through Bonnie who listened at the door during Shar and Malcolm's meeting with Marshall yesterday."

Gray had been oddly reticent ever since leaving the airport. "Laney, I've chewed on this for half an hour. Dwayne's transformation began before he even heard our names."

"Huh?'

"His eyes shot icicles the instant Elliot said you were after info about the Jenny."

"Really?"

"I'm sure of it."

"Odd . . . I thought the mention of our names was what wiped the smile off his gorgeous face."

"I'm not saying that he hadn't heard about Malcolm and Shar's intention, only that your interest in the Jenny triggered his disquiet," Gray said and gulped his coffee.

"Aren't you the perceptive one? But why in heaven's sake would that shake him up?"

Gray shrugged but Laney had a feeling he was purposely being tightlipped.

The waitress brought their lunches. Laney plunged her spoon into the "The Hill." "Real whipped cream!" she swooned while licking it off her upper lip. Gray remained uncommunicative as he worked his way through his sandwich.

"Okay," Laney said when she finished scoop number three, "Let's go find this Barnaby and see if he can throw some light on the subject of the Jenny. Or more to the point, on Victor Moore."

19

"Marshall, we were just going out the door," Shar said. She put her hand over the mouthpiece. "Scotty, would you go see where Kudzu and Nessie have gone. Please don't leave the yard."

Scotty, a red woolen scarf tied around her neck and wearing matching new mittens, bounced out the kitchen doorway into the sunshine. Her glossy, scarlet boots reached to her knees. With outstretched arms she was an airplane buzzing the curved walkway cleared of snow that morning. She banked into a fast melting pile next to the walk and made a quick angel before marching high through the whiteness to search for the pets.

"Sorry, Marshall," Shar said into the phone.

"I'm afraid I'm the one who is sorry, Sharlene," Marshall said. Shar's heart did a dive.

"I have not located a will," he said softly. "Malcolm told me when Keely arrived in the U.S., he gave her a list of names and phone numbers including those of his lawyer, insurance agent, bank, doctors, et cetera and I've found that she took advantage of some of these professionals. I called Malcolm's former lawyer in Ocala and he said that she had made an appointment last month but later cancelled it."

"Crap," Shar said. "What about a safety deposit box?"

"None where she banked in Ocala. Perhaps she had planned to finish her personal business after moving to Northern Kentucky."

"Too late for that, now."

"Shar, let this be a lesson for you, albeit it's a hard one to swallow at this time. Never put off making legal decisions. Tomorrow can be too late."

Shar answered with pin-drop silence.

"Sharlene, are you still there?"

"Yes."

"The judge has set the date for the hearing for November seventeenth—three days from now."

A day after our wedding, Shar thought with a dull empty ache already gnawing at her heart.

After Marshall rang off, through the window of the storm door, Scotty, holding Kudzu in her arms, came into view. The cat's tail trailed the fluffy snow. Beside her, Nessie's nose furrowed like a snowplow as Scotty giggled with glee. Shar's question about her father obviously forgotten, Scotty's face was aglow with exertion and happiness.

Shar watched them frolic until the scene blurred behind a curtain of hot tears and she had to turn away.

20

"This must be it," Laney cried. She pointed to four orange cones at one end of a closely cropped field that was barely covered with snow. A stand of trees bordered the far end of the airstrip that Elliot had told them measured approximately 1700 feet. They had come upon the runway almost by accident, Elliot's directions having taken them on several wild goose chases.

Beyond the strip, Laney could make out a haphazard arrangement of outbuildings: a wooden barn, several sheds, white metal hangar and behind them all, the Ohio river sparkling diamonds in the bright sunshine.

Gray followed a long asphalt drive that had been cleared of snow the width of a scraper blade. The lane ended near the cluster of structures. To their left, a tiny gothic cottage with gingerbread trim was partially hidden by overgrown hedges.

Gray swung a right and parked beside a maroon Chevy van in the lot next to the large hangar. A northwest breeze ballooned an orange windsock attached to the peak of the structure. They splashed through slushy footprints to a side door and ducked inside under a steady drip of water melting off of the roof.

The cavernous area was unlit, but a dim light shined from behind a figure of a woman standing in the doorway of a tiny office. "Yes?" she growled as though they had interrupted her beauty sleep.

"We're looking for Barnaby Biddle," Gray said, taking a step closer to the woman. He introduced himself and Laney.

Instead of inviting them into the office, she quickly stepped into the gloom of the building and made no move to turn on the lights. "He's not here." In the shadows of the interior, Laney thought she saw the faint outline of a plane.

"Where?"

"The house next to the drive," she muttered and didn't elaborate.

"Well . . . uh . . . thank you," Gray said while Laney opened the door to the outside. The sunshine burst into the hangar but as though the woman had anticipated the brightness, she rushed over the threshold into the office and closed the door softly behind her.

Barnaby Biddle's wife—Elaine, as she introduced herself—answered the door with an inviting smile. Below an upsweep of wispy white hair, her umber eyes flicked golden lights. Laney would have given ten years of her life for Elaine's shiny, high cheekbones and clear skin.

"Elliot called and told us you were on the way. If there's one thing Barnaby likes to talk about, it's the Jenny," she said, leading them through an arched doorway to the right of the entrance. Her trim legs disappeared into black, oxford lace-ups.

Laney and Gray stepped into an oak-paneled den where aviation seemed to have been born. Every available inch of wall space held photographs and prints of aircraft from the early twentieth century. Laney was immediately drawn to a grouping of three framed lithographs: the first heavier than air flight of the "Wright Flyer" at Kittyhawk, Lindbergh's "Spirit of St. Louis," and a "Sopwith Camel," the most successful fighter of the First World War.

A mahogany desk at right angles to a sunny window was lit by matching lamps with bronzed bases depicting World War II fighters. Barnaby looked up from his desk, stood and offered his hand in greeting.

"Well now," he said, grasping Laney's hand and smiling brightly into her eyes. With his snow-white hair, lively blue eyes squeezed into mirthful crescents and lips in an upward curve, Barnaby was a dead ringer for Santa Claus, minus the facial hair. Wow! Laney thought as he released his firm grip and turned to Gray. Laney couldn't believe he was pushing ninety.

He offered two mahogany chairs across from the desk and sat back down.

"Could we have that fresh pot of coffee now?" he addressed his wife. With a thumbs-up and a smile that warmed the whole room, Elaine, a woman about seventy, exited with a bounce in her step that Laney had seen only in much younger persons.

"My life," Barnaby said, his eyes misting as they followed his wife. He blew his nose into a white handkerchief and shoved it back into the pocket of his pants.

"Now, what can I tell you about the Jenny? I cut my teeth on that sweetheart. Fire away."

Normally, Laney would have loved to hear all about the biplane but she didn't want to lose sight of why she was here—to find out about Victor Moore. "First, I'd like you to read this," Laney said, sliding the 1928 newspaper article across the desk.

He picked up his spectacles and placed them on his nose. As Barnaby read, his bow mouth slowly straightened into a thin line. When he finished reading, he looked over his glasses at her. "May I ask how you came across this article?"

"It's a copy from the microfilm files at Switzerland County Public Library."

"But how did you know to look for it?"

Laney explained that the damaged clipping was in a scrapbook that belonged to Keely Moore, Victor Moore's daughter-in-law.

"Ah, Keely," he murmured.

"You knew . . . I mean . . . know her?" Laney asked.

A shadow of alarm spread over his face with her slip of the tongue. "Yes, I know Keely, and knew her husband, Ray, also. His father and I flew together."

"Laney," Gray interjected. "I think you should get to the crux of the matter or we shall be here all day."

"You're right, Gray," she said and took a breath before plunging in. "Barnaby, Keely was killed in a hit and run accident in Atlanta four days ago." She cringed inwardly.

Barnaby jerked to his feet. "No, that can't be. I only spoke with her . . ." His eyes brimmed, then tears overflowed to stream down his face. He pulled out his handkerchief again. As he dabbed at his face, he mumbled, "How can this be? God in heaven, the child! . . . is she all right?"

"Scotty is with her Uncle Malcolm in Hickory, Kentucky."

Barnaby's hands began to shake violently and he collapsed back into his chair. Laney was afraid the shock had been too much for him. At that moment, Elaine entered the room with a tray of mugs and a carafe of coffee. She still wore the pleasant smile. With one glance at her husband, the smile vanished. She dropped the tray heavily onto the desk and ran to his side.

"Darlin, are you ill!" she exclaimed.

"These folks have brought the most disturbing news," he said, patting her hand. "Keely Moore has been killed."

Elaine's face blanched and her hand flew to her heart. She swayed. Jumping to his feet, Gray led her to his chair. Laney poured coffee into two of the mugs and passed them to the couple.

As though she was watching a tennis match, Laney's gaze bounced back and fourth from Barnaby to Elaine. It was difficult to determine who was the palest.

"I . . . I had no idea you actually *knew* Victor and Mabel," Laney said. "Thank God! Please . . . maybe you can help us." Had she inadvertently found the break she needed?

Unexpectedly, Barnaby's hands ceased trembling and his sorrowful eyes turned dark with consternation. "You are here on false pretenses? You don't want to learn about the Jenny?"

Laney shifted in her chair. "I must be honest with you," she said. "I only used my interest in the Jenny to find out more about Victor and his wife Mabel." She suddenly felt compelled to tell them about her suspicions about Keely's death. Who else could she trust to give her information about Victor? Laney sat on the edge of her seat as she told the couple about the hit and run while Keely was in Atlanta checking on how Mabel died. "You see, I believe Keely was afraid she was in danger so she sent Scotty on to Malcolm while she checked out Mabel's death in Atlanta."

As Laney voiced her suspicions, Elaine's knuckles turned white. She turned her face as though reeling from a blow, but recovering quickly, her question masked her shock, "The child flew alone?"

"Under the care of an airline attendant," Gray said. "Malcolm met her when she arrived in Lexington, Kentucky."

"We were visiting Mabel the week she had that dreadful accident,"

Barnaby said almost remotely.

"No!" Gray cried.

"Yes, we stayed in Atlanta through her pneumonia, subsequent death and the funeral."

"So you know about the break-in at Mabel's apartment?"

"Yes. The place was completely wrecked."

"You began to tell us that you had recently spoken with Keely. When was that?" Laney asked Barnaby. Elaine swallowed dryly and she stared at her husband with unblinking eyes.

"Saturday morning," Barney's voice was wooden with grief. "She was getting ready to leave for the airport."

"She died early Sunday morning," Gray said quietly.

Elaine began to cry softly and Barney rose and went to her. "Would you excuse us?" he said. Suddenly, the two of them looked every bit their ages as they shuffled out of the den.

21

"Scotty, I've gone through every box," Shar said with an edge of impatience. She shoved the final carton with "clothing" marked on the side, away from her in exasperation.

"Mibbie Mither forgot to send ma kilt," a rough voice came from above.

Shar looked up at Scotty perched on a stack of hay bales where Shar had lifted her before beginning to search through the cartons. Scotty's denim hat, mittens and the matching scarf lay on the bale beside her. She had gradually peeled off the clothing as the temperature in the barn moderated. Released from their confinement, her curls poppled in a disheveled mass.

One at a time, Shar lugged the four boxes over to the others that she had rummaged through since the moving van had unloaded them two days before. Looking for a will, Laney, Gray and she had explored the three cartons marked "personal" and Malcolm had helped her search eight others containing household trinkets and dishes.

"I just can't afford to spend any more time looking," Shar said grumpily while they watched Kudzu's barred tail disappear behind an elaborately carved headboard made out of dark oak.

"Anither, Saugh," Scotty said, pointing to a stray carton jutting from behind a plastic covered mattress in the area where Keely's furniture was stored.

There's that name again, Shar thought. I must ask Malcolm if it means something or she just can't pronounce my name.

"So it is, Scotty." Shar scooted the mattress further down the barn siding until the whole box was exposed. She carried it to the single bale of hay she had been sitting on and carefully cut the tape seal with her razor. She spread the flaps and under a covering of tissue, there it was!

"Oh Scotty, it's beautiful!" Shar lifted the green, black and navy Lamont tartan fabric. Made of the finest light worsted wool, the tiny kilt seemed hardly big enough to fit a doll, let alone a child of five. But she knew that just by the painstaking attention Scotty's mother had put into arranging for the best instructor to teach her child to dance, the garment she had made for Scotty would most certainly fit her perfectly.

Shar lifted the kilt and showed it to Scotty, still sitting high on the hay bales. Her instant smile suddenly illuminated the dreary barn. Shar returned to the carton and dug between layers of tissue and found a black velvet vest trimmed in silver braid and silver embossed buttons. And below them, she could see a white blouse, hose and the black Highland dancing pumps called guillies.

"We're all set," Shar said swishing the kilt back into the box, wishing she felt as cheerful as she pretended to be. But Scotty's recapitulation of her mother's cryptic remark about her husband's death, and Marshall's fruitless search for a will lay like a boulder on her chest. Only days remained before the judge would make the decision that could affect the rest of their lives.

22

"I think we should check on them," Gray said, "They've been gone for twenty minutes."

Laney, peeking through the mini blinds for the fourth time since the Biddles had left them in the den, suddenly squealed, "There's that snarly troll. The one in the barn."

Gray joined Laney at the window. "Look," Laney continued, "she just got into Dwayne Day's yellow Bug." She separated the blinds so he could see.

As they watched, the car turned around and sped down the driveway.

"Gray, what if Dwayne and that woman are involved."

"Involved? In the way I think you mean?"

A hollow chuckle came from directly behind them. Laney spun and almost smacked into Barnaby who had somehow managed to enter the room without them hearing. The blind clattered into place.

"That's not so," said Barney who obviously saw the woman get into the car. "They're running an errand for me."

Embarrassed that Barnaby had overheard her rather catty remark, Laney left the window and slipped into the chair she had occupied earlier. Gray sat beside her and snatched up her hand and held it in his lap. His thumb massaged her palm.

"To erase any misconception, the woman is our daughter, Patricia," Barnaby said as he again sat across from them at his desk. His eyes had lost their twinkle. "She lives here in a basement apartment and is vice president of my flying service. Quite the aviator, I might add. She's a licensed instructor and manages the office."

Laney mumbled a quiet, "Oh."

"Dwayne Day is married to Ray Moore's sister, Bonnie," Barnaby explained further. "He is an excellent aircraft mechanic. That's how Patricia knows him. He helps me out sometimes."

"We met Dwayne this morning at the Madison Airport," Laney said, "and met Bonnie at Keely's funeral."

Barney's eyes dulled further with his next statement. "We would have come to the funeral had we known. I'll never forgive Bonnie for not informing me of Keely's death . . . but then, I've always known Bonnie was nothing like her parents." He swiveled his chair toward the window and fiddled with the blind. Pulling the cord, the bright sunshine defined the lines around his eyes and mouth. He lifted his face as though he thirsted for warmth.

"Barnaby," Laney said softly, "you were about to tell us about Keely's phone call to you the day she left for Atlanta."

"Yes . . . yes," he said, pulling himself from his thoughts. He faced them. "Keely told me she was flying with Scotty to Lexington to visit her brother, Malcolm, before moving to Northern Kentucky."

"Did Keely call you often?" Gray asked.

"After Ray died, she would call us about once a month. We grew very close. Elaine and I were looking forward to her move north so we could see her more often. Carrollton, Kentucky is just across the river." His eyes reddened with the realization that all that had changed now. He wiped his eyes with his handkerchief.

"So, there was nothing unusual about her call?" Laney asked. "She didn't sound frightened?"

"No."

"Did Elaine also talk with Keely? Maybe she told her something that she wouldn't have told you."

"No, Elaine was in Florida on one of her art club jaunts."

"Barnaby, we know for a fact that Keely arranged ahead of time to send Scotty on to Lexington alone," Laney said. "According to someone at the Peachtree Courtyard care facility, Keely had doubts about what caused Mabel's fall."

"I don't know why. I'm sure it happened just like we were told," Barnaby said. "Remember, we were there that week. On more than one occasion, Elaine and I chastised Mabel for climbing on that stepladder to fool with her flowers. When we got the call at the hotel that she had fallen, I knew instantly that she must have toppled off that ladder." He stared out the window and frowned. "Keely seemed to always have a wary view of life."

So Mabel's fall was an accident after all, Laney thought. "But Barnaby, the break-in. The burglar was looking for something. Why else cut open cushions, tear the backs off pictures?"

"The police thought that the burglar was looking for cash. We old folks have a way of stashing money away in odd places."

Gray got to his feet and with both palms on Barney's desk, leaned forward and stared directly into Barnaby's eyes. "Yesterday, there was a second occasion that someone willfully destroyed property belonging to the Moore family," Gray said. "A stuffed airplane that Mabel had made for Scotty was sliced open during a funeral luncheon."

Barnaby's eyes widened.

Laney also hopped to her feet. "We believe someone was looking for something valuable. Maybe this person thinks Mabel might have given that something valuable to her granddaughter, Scotty."

Barnaby's face grew chalky. He stood, perspiration erupting on his brow and his nostrils dilating. His hand shook as it combed through his silver hair.

Laney felt the small hairs on the nape of her neck stir. "Barnaby!" she cried. "You know something! I can see it in your face!" She grabbed at his arm as he tried to move away from her to collect himself. Her skin grew clammy as though she had entered a sauna.

"Victor," Barnaby whispered.

"What about Victor?" she demanded.

"Perhaps it's nothing." He shook his head with quick frustrated motions. "So long ago . . ."

Gray snatched at Laney's hand, hoping to calm her as she sank into her chair. He sat next to her, never releasing his grip on her fingers.

Barnaby collapsed into his chair and again stared out of the window. It was a time before he spoke again. "We were both so young. Victor was twenty-five and let's see . . . I guess I was about nineteen. We had first gotten acquainted at a flying club that met near Madison." Barnaby swung back around in his chair to face them.

"We hit it off from day one. He had just married Mabel and they were expecting their first child—Ray as it later turned out. They'd recently moved to Madison from D.C. where he'd worked for the government."

Dammit, Laney thought, get to it, Barnaby Biddle. She squirmed impatiently. Gray's mouth was set tightly, his cheek muscles working.

"But flying that rickety Jenny was Vic's first love. When he found out I also flew and was a mechanic of sorts—for sure better than he— he asked me to work on his plane sometimes. I'd been tinkering with aircraft engines ever since I was fourteen."

Barnaby lifted the 1928 article about Victor's plane crash. "The mechanic who was flying with Victor in this article, was me."

"You're kidding." Gray and Laney said in unison.

"One night Victor and I were ground flying—"

"Excuse me . . . ground flying?" Laney interrupted, not wanting to miss a single bit of information.

Barnaby forced a quick smile before continuing. "It's the term used among pilots for telling flying experiences," He waved the article. "It's ironic that this particular forced landing was what we were discussing that night. I guess the close call in the Jenny and too much moonshine triggered a bit of melancholy in Vic."

Laney couldn't stand one more minute of delay. "Barnaby, please . . . what did Victor tell you?"

As I remember, it was about midnight on that hot, August night in a pasture that our flying club used for an airstrip up near Madison. We were sitting on a couple of crates under the stars and the two of us were passing a Mason jar of white lightning back and forth. His voice and his eyes faded into the past.

> *Vic began to slur his words. "Barnaby" he said, "maybe I-I- I need to quit flying."*
>
> *I took a throat sizzling swallow of the hooch. "Quit?" I asked. "What the hell for?"*
>
> *"W-well, maybe not hang it up. But I'm go-going to have to settle down some now that a baby's on the way," he said, "Costs too d-d-damn much money."*
>
> *Then he said, "Wish I could sell them. I-I-I'd never have to worry about money again. I could buy one of those new mono- planes." Under the full moon, his eyes were shiny wet with tears of real regret. Behind him, his Jenny loomed like a ghost plane.*
>
> *I said something like, "Sell what? You got something worth a*

lot of money?"

The alcohol was really getting to him. All teary-eyed, he began to blubber, "I'm not proud of what I did. Too s-s-soon to sell them. Feds would get me for sure. But maybe my grandchildren will get their benefit some day."

"What in the hell did you do, Vic?" I asked him.

"Nothing . . . nothing," he said thickly, looking at me all blurry-eyed. Then, in a move surprisingly quick for someone so boozed, he suddenly grabbed my shirt collar and with a drunken grip that about turned me blue, he threw me to the ground. "Forget I ever told you, Barnaby Biddle!" he roared in my face, his whiskey breath stinking all to hell. With that, he rolled over onto his back.

"Did he tell you what was so valuable?" Laney was beside herself with excitement.

"You don't understand. He'd passed out."

"Shit," Gray said.

"He never brought up the subject again and I never asked."

"What!" Laney said.

"If you had seen the look on Vic's face when he thought he had told me too much. And to be honest, if he *had* done something illegal, I really didn't want to know about it anyway."

Disappointment flooded Gray's features. "Do you have *any* idea what he might have done?" Gray asked.

Barnaby shook his head. "Vic was a son of a gun, but during all the years I knew him, he never did anything worse than drink some hooch during prohibition."

"Do you think he ever changed his mind and sold what was so valuable?" Laney asked.

"If his lifestyle was any indication, definitely not. He even had to sell his Jenny to get Ray through animal husbandry at Indiana University. Post office jobs back then didn't pay much."

"How did his son, Ray, end up in Scotland?"

"That's a story in itself. Elaine and I had met Malcolm's parents on a trip to Edinburgh, Scotland. At the time, Malcolm was a little tyke and Keely hadn't even been born yet. Later, in the fall of eighty-three, long after the Lamonts had moved to America, Keely visited her parents and brother in Florida and she and Malcolm drove up to see us.

"We had a small dinner party. Vic, Mabel, Ray and Bonnie were there. With one look, Keely and Ray were incurably smitten. Neither had ever married, even though Keely was thirty and Ray, forty-five. It was like they had been waiting for each other.

"Malcolm tried his darndest to get Keely to stay in the U.S., but Keely loved Scotland and wanted to return there.

"At the time, Ray was working with horses in Goshen near Louisville. He was good with animals. If he had had any money, he could have gone on to vet school.

"With Keely's Scottish horse farm connections, she got Ray a job as manager of a brood mare stable near Edinburgh and within a year, she and Ray were married."

"What did Ray's sister, Bonnie, do?" Gray asked.

"Back then, she worked in an antique shop in Madison and lived with Victor and Mabel."

Almost afraid to ask, Laney inquired. "How did Victor die?"

"As it turned out, our dinner was the last time we saw Victor alive. He died in his sleep, two days later. He was eighty."

Natural causes, Laney thought with relief.

"Mabel was heart-broken. Bonnie, who'd been caring for both parents for several years, moved Mabel to that nursing home in Atlanta. She visited her once or twice a year—a little more often after she married Dwayne. I never understood why Bonnie placed her mother so far away from the friends she had left and her only daughter. But then, like I said before, she wasn't anything like her parents."

Gray stated the obvious. "It's apparent that Victor didn't pass his illegal treasure to his children. I wonder if Mabel knew about it . . . *whatever* the hell it was."

"Or even possessed *whatever* the hell it was," Laney said. "If Mabel did have it, maybe at some point, she gave it to Keely to keep for Scotty." She recalled the hit and run that she didn't believe was an accident.

"If Mabel did have something valuable in her possession, maybe the burglar found it when he ransacked her apartment," Gray said.

"Doubtful. Remember Scotty's sliced airplane," Laney reminded him.

"Scotty . . . " Tears filled Barnaby's eyes again. He blew his nose. "A little miracle, that one. Keely and Ray were married nine years before she came along. Scotty and I would chat over the phone whenever

Keely would call. His lips formed a shaky smile. "Scotty loves airplanes just like Vic."

"Does she ever!" Laney said. "Although Scotty never met her grandfather, Mabel must have written and talked about Victor's flying with her. The toy plane that Mabel made for her isn't a biplane, but it's hardly ever out of her sight. Unfortunately, one of the times it was, it ended up requiring an additional line of stitches."

Barnaby rose. "Come," he said, "it's time I show you something."

As Barnaby led them toward the hangar that Laney and Gray had visited earlier, Elaine dashed out the door of the cottage jamming her arms into the sleeves of a black parka. "Wait," she called, and they did. "Why didn't you waken me, darlin?" Her eyes were swollen from crying but her steps hadn't lost their briskness. She hugged Barnaby's arm and walked with them toward the hangar, her head lightly resting against his shoulder. His other hand reached across to her face, the back of his fingers brushing softly over her cheek as though he knew instinctively that a tear might be there. His gesture was so intimate and delicate, Gray blushed that he had seen.

As they approached the hangar, Barnaby pointed a remote toward the building and the door slowly folded and lifted. The amber, afternoon sun inched its way into the interior, over a pair of wheels with smooth rubber tires, then upward to a hub tightened over a large wooden propeller. Behind the prop, a boxy fuselage, interrupted twice by open cockpits, tapered to the tail. As the golden glow slowly eased over the cotton-covered, double wings, Laney and Gray involuntarily gasped at the same moment.

Gray drew in his breath. "My God, a Jenny!"

Barnaby smiled at their shock and admiration. Elaine seemed quiet and withdrawn.

"*You . . . you* bought Victor's Jenny!" Laney said.

"I did," Barnaby said.

"Tell them the shape it was in," Elaine said, quietly nudging him.

"Vic cracked up at Madison. The plane broke apart and Vic sustained a concussion and three broken ribs. It was amazing that he survived at all. Mabel was fit to be tied and she put her foot down. She said she would leave him if he so much as tried to put the pieces back together. So they gathered dust in a barn for years until I bought the plane about the time Ray was getting out of high school. I paid dearly for that bunch of bolts and nuts—a hell of a lot more than the hundred dollars he paid for it."

"Hundred dollars?" Gray exclaimed.

"The Curtiss Jenny had been used as a pilot trainer by the U.S. Army Air Service during the First World War and afterwards, they were auctioned as surplus to civil flying clubs and barnstormers. Victor borrowed money from friends to buy it and worked several jobs to pay it off."

Laney and Gray inspected every inch of the plane that Barney had restored so lovingly through the years.

"How did you do that?" Gray asked, referring to the drum tightness of the fabric over the wings.

"You apply a nitrate and acetate lacquer to the cotton. It not only shrinks the fabric to the wooden spars and cross-ribs, but also protects and waterproofs the wings."

Gray was reminded of the balsa wood models he put together as a kid and hung from his ceiling from strings. He recalled the spring after he'd begun to think a lot about girls. He had removed the planes from their tethers and had taken them onto the porch roof just outside his bedroom window. One by one, he'd doused them with inflammable dope, wound the rubber bands tight, set them afire and let them sail. What a sight! What a whipping!

"May I?" Laney said, pointing to the cockpit. When Barnaby nodded, she pulled herself onto a lower wing by ducking around cross wires and grasping one of the wooden struts linking the upper and lower wings.

"Step lightly there," Barnaby called to her. "If your foot goes through that cotton, you could break a leg."

She checked out the most accessible cockpit—the one closest to the engine. Grasping the leather-covered edge, she peered inside. "Barnaby, how do you fly this thing? There aren't any controls!"

He laughed. "The pilot flies from the rear cockpit. That space is for passengers or any baggage. When the JN-4 was used for airmail, that's where they stowed the mail."

Afraid he might go through the wing covering while stretching for the pilot cockpit, Gray straddled the fuselage above the tail and scooted his way to the back cockpit on his rear.

"That's one way to get in there," Barnaby said with a chuckle.

Gray dropped inside. The small, straight-backed bucket seat was not very comfortable. He latched the webbed seatbelt and flipped the hook down. He looked around. Other than a throttle, the only other controls were a wooden bat-sized stick between his legs and rudder bar on the floor. There were three gauges on the instrument board—one for oil pressure, a tachometer, and a water temperature gauge. He was utterly amazed with the simplicity. Talk about flying from the seat of your pants, he thought.

By this time, Laney had managed to climb inside the front cockpit. When Gray saw Laney's flaming hair through his small curved glass windshield, he wondered what her reaction would be if suddenly Barnaby flipped the propeller and the plane taxied out of the hangar and took off. He decided he didn't want to know and unhooked the belt.

After he and Laney rejoined Barnaby and Elaine, Gray asked, "Have you flown the Jenny since you restored it?"

Barnably glanced at Elaine before answering, "Not yet, but the engine has been started and tested. I taxied it out to the runway and the wheels and other landing gear seem to work okay. I was going to take it up before the latest snow hit. Now I'll have to let the strip dry out and the temperature moderate. That's an open cockpit. You could freeze your ears and nose off.

"Barnaby," Elaine said, "you promised." Her voice quavered.

A pained look crossed his features. He sighed. "Elaine wants Patricia to take it up the first time. Granted, she's an experienced pilot but she's never flown a Jenny."

"And she's not eighty-nine years old either," Elaine said.

23

Laney had made reservations at the General Butler State Park Lodge across the river in Carrollton. The closest bridge was at Markham Dam just upriver from Vevay. Laney drove the Buick while Gray catnapped.

As they rode through Vevay, she reflected about Barnaby's recollection of that night with Victor so long ago. What crime had Victor committed that had put him in possession of something so valuable that he was afraid to cash it in himself? It must have been valuable, indeed, if he'd planned to hold on to it for a generation before passing it on.

The classic Cary Grant film, *To Catch a Thief*, came to mind. Had Victor stolen some jewels or perhaps a piece of art? She remembered reading about a recent theft of a Cezanne landscape from a museum in the UK. Doesn't figure, she thought.

What then? Barnaby said Victor worked for the government in D.C. and later was postmaster in Madison.

Feds would get me for sure.

"Oh my God!" she said aloud and struck the steering wheel. The post office! Could Victor have somehow gotten his hands on some rare stamps?

Laney braked on a dime and made quick right turn without signaling. The guy in the van behind her laid on his horn and in her mirror, she saw him give her the finger. Half a block later, she swung into the

Switzerland County Public Library parking lot and screeched to a stop. Gray snorted and groaned but fell back asleep.

Once inside, she waved at the director who was helping a patron at one of the public access computers as she dashed into the stacks. Ten minutes later, Laney staggered out with every book the library had on stamp collecting. Settling at the nearest table, she began to thumb through the books looking for rare stamps. She knew that if Victor had accessed a rare stamp, it must have been before moving to Madison.

In *Stamp Collectors' Handbook* by Fred Reinfeld, she read that most rare stamps were the result of color errors or a stamp sheet fed improperly to the printer. But by far, the most dramatic mistake was the "invert." An invert could happen if the stamp was printed in two or more colors and fed through the press more than once. If a sheet was accidentally dropped or turned around before going through the press a second time, one of the images could be printed upside down.

She learned that the country's first invert occurred in an 1869 issue of a pictorial series. The fifteen, twenty-four, and thirty-cent values were printed with inverted centers. Later, in 1901, a Pan-American series one-, two-, and four-cent denominations was also printed with the centers upside down. She was scribbling in her notebook when Gray bounded into the library looking for her. He slid into an adjoining seat.

"What's up, Dick Tracy?" he whispered with wrinkled brow.

Ignited with enthusiasm, she shoved the notebook and pen at him. "Figure this," she said. "Barnaby's eighty-nine years old. He was nineteen and Victor was twenty-five when the two of them met. What year was Victor born?"

"Duh."

"Don't make fun of me, just figure it! I'm too excited." She thumped him on the shoulder with her fist.

Gray shook his head in bewilderment but did as he was told in two seconds flat. "Barnaby was born in 1909 and was six years younger than Victor so Victor was born in 1903."

Laney scrunched her face into a frown. "Hmm." Thinking of the Pan American Invert, she realized that in 1901, Victor hadn't even been born yet.

"Hmm, what?"

"Victor worked for the post office, remember?"

"Yeah . . . so?"

"What if he'd come across rare stamps and stole them. That could be the something valuable that Victor was afraid the Feds could get him for."

She scooted the Reinfield book over a little so that he could read about how stamp errors occurred. When he got to the end of page fifty-three, his mouth parted. Laney knew he was dying to tell her she was crazy. Instead he said, "This Pan American stamp was probably the last invert in this century. Postal controls. A print inspector or postal clerk would catch it."

"But what if the postal worker was dishonest?" she said evilly and turned the page.

Gray's eyes rolled then dropped to the book. Promptly, his brows rose sharply. "Holy shit!" he sputtered. He yanked the book away from Laney and stared.

"Laney, an inverted Jenny!"

The two people browsing the Internet jerked to attention and stared. The librarian put a forefinger to her lips and mouthed, "Shh!"

Laney gaped at the stamp of an upside down blue biplane centered on a red frame. Above the plane were the words, U.S. Postage. Below the aircraft was the denomination, 24 cents. "Are you sure it's a Jenny?" Laney breathed in his ear.

"Laney, we saw one with our own eyes. Look at the curved wing stabilizers. The distinctive upper wing cutout roots above the back cockpit! Barnaby said the JN was the only biplane that had that feature."

"Gray, do you know what this means?"

"Slow down, sweetheart. I think we need to read the whole article before jumping to any conclusions."

Laney felt her excitement escalating. "Look! It says right here that a William T. Robey went to the post office in Washington and bought a sheet of the stamps! Victor worked at a post office in DC!"

"Read, Laney."

They began to read the text about the first United States airmail stamp. Evidently, after the sheets of stamps had been run through the press to print the red frame, they were left to dry. A sheet must have been dropped and inadvertently turned around before going through the press a second time to print the blue Jenny. A stamp collector, Mr. Robey, knew instantly that he had a hundred stamps worth far more than the twenty-four dollars he had paid for them. Later, postal inspectors tried to get Robey to return the stamps, but he refused.

It wasn't long before a moan escaped Gray's lips. "Ah Laney, look at the date: 1918. Victor would have been fifteen years old when the invert occurred and anyway, it says only a single sheet of the inverts was printed before the error was discovered."

Laney leaned back in her chair and felt tears of disappointment well in her eyes. Damn it, she wasn't going to give it up that easily. In her gut, she felt there had to be a connection between the Jenny Invert and the something of value Victor had alluded to back in 1928. This time, she was the one who pushed a book at Gray. "Read."

They spent the next two hours devouring everything they could find on the Invert." After enlisting the director's help, they discovered in the 1996 *Smithsonian Magazine* that Robey later sold the sheet of stamps for fifteen thousand dollars, a fortune in 1918.

Finally exhausting all library materials, they turned to the computer. They learned Robey had purchased the stamps at a post office on New York Avenue near 13th Street on May 13, 1918.

"Why are we wasting time reading all this stuff?" Gray asked.

In answer, Laney collected all the copies they had made and nodded toward the exit. "Let's check in at the lodge. I need to make a couple of phone calls," she said. As they crossed over Markland Dam to get to the Kentucky side of the Ohio River, Laney could see a barge carrying coal slowly maneuvering into a lock chamber.

As interesting as the operation was, she couldn't get the stamp information out of her mind, particularly what an encyclopedia had revealed: In 1989, a block of four of the stamps sold at a public auction for one million dollars!

And that was almost ten years ago, Laney thought. My God, no telling what Jenny Inverts were worth today. Would it be so much that someone might commit burglary or even murder to possess them?

24

"Jesse's not too keen about staying at your house tonight. She's jittery as a whore in church, and I'm referring to Jesse, not Blackberry," Shar said into the phone in response to Laney's inquiry about her pet's condition. "Tonight may just be the night that Blackberry pops those babies out."

Laney bit into a triangle of pepperoni, mushroom and banana pepper pizza that they'd picked up on the way to General Butler Lodge. Gray was sprawled out on one of the queen-sized beds in his briefs and T-shirt eating his third slice and washing it down with wine that she had purchased at the Lanthier Winery in Madison. He was flipping TV channels looking for a decent movie to watch.

"Damn," Laney said with her mouth full. "Does Jesse think we need to come home tonight?"

"I'm going over there to look the situation over and I'll get back with you if things look hairy . . . but Laney . . . " Her voice slid into a squeaky Butterfly McQueen. "'I never done birthed any babies before.'"

Laney laughed, but quickly turned serious. "Shar, I have loads to tell you. We've—"

"Me first. This is important," Shar interrupted. "Remember when Scotty first arrived and overheard us talking about her missing mother?"

"Yes . . . "

"I admit it wasn't very sensitive of me, but I asked her why she believed her mother had died like her father."

"Shar, you didn't!"

"Shut up and listen. Scotty said she heard her mother telling the barn cat that *someone made* her father die."

"Get out . . . "

"I swear."

"Shar, as a rule, I don't put much faith in conversations with kitty-cats."

Gray stopped clicking channels and looked over at Laney who was sitting on the other bed, her legs straddling the pizza box.

Shar went on, "When I reminded Scotty that it was a horse accident, she said that her mother didn't know she was listening and to quote the child, 'She told Smoky with eyes full of fright.' "

There was a knock on the door. Gray leaped off the bed and shoved his legs into his khakis.

"Shar, I gotta go," Laney said reluctantly, wanting to get to her second phone call before it got too late. "Someone's at the door."

"Me too," Shar said.

Laney wanted to know more about Scotty's story. "Call me back after you check Blackberry . . . and thanks." She closed the pizza box and scooted off the bed.

"Who is it?" Gray called as he buckled his belt and approached the door.

A small voice on the other side of the door answered, "Elaine Biddle."

He tossed a questioning look at Laney who was retying her silk kimono. "I was planning to call her," she said.

Gray swung the door open and Elaine stood outside. Shadows cupped her eyes like those in old photographs. Her high cheekbones only deepened the hollows. The black parka that she had worn earlier to the airplane hangar was snapped incorrectly and the left hem hung two inches below the right. Road salt was drying on the black toes of her oxfords.

"Elaine, come in," Gray said. He grasped her arm and led her into the room.

"Is Barnaby with you," Laney asked, sticking her head outside and checking both directions.

"I'm alone. I'm supposed to be at my art club meeting in Madison."

Elaine's face reflected the pain of dishonesty.

"But not tonight?" Laney said.

"Not tonight."

Laney took her coat and led her to the nearest bed. Plumping two pillows against the headboard, she got Elaine settled comfortably and handed her half of a tumbler of wine meant for herself. Gray dashed to the bathroom for another glass for Laney.

Laney sat beside Gray on the other bed and asked, "What is it, Elaine?"

"I don't know what to do," she whispered. "I promised Keely . . ."

A jolt of excitement grabbed Laney. She had been hoping that Elaine could throw some light on Keely's death. Laney waited, but Elaine only took a long swallow of wine.

"Elaine, death terminates promises . . . especially if—" Laney began.

"Keely was convinced that someone locked Ray in the stall with that mad horse," Elaine exclaimed, "but I imagine you've heard that preposterous story."

A groan came from Gray.

"Well, as a matter of fact—"

"I told Keely that kind of thinking was insane," Elaine went on, "but she just wouldn't be swayed."

Keely's disclosure to the barn cat suddenly held water, Laney thought.

"At Ray's funeral, Keely confided in me about her suspicions. She was the one who found Ray. When he hadn't come back for breakfast that dreadful morning, she bundled Scotty up and went looking for him. As she approached the foaling stall, she saw blood below the window bars on the outside of the stall. That was her first clue that it may not have been an accident. If the eyebolt had been in the lock hole, the only way for Ray to release it would be by reaching through the bars of the alley window."

Laney swallowed hard. "What did the police think?"

"That the blood might be explained by Ray's confusion after being struck in the head by the horse's hooves. In his panic, he might have reached through the bars. No blood was found on the eyebolt. I'm afraid I had to agree with them."

"But it didn't satisfy Keely?" Laney asked.

"She said Ray knew his horses . . . their oddities and personalities. Talia—that was the name of the mare—blew up after every foaling but he took every precaution with her. Keely thought he never would have allowed himself to get trapped in her stall."

"But what would be the killer's motive?" Gray asked.

"A week before her flight, Keely told me she thought she knew," Elaine replied.

Laney gulped and held her breath "What was it?"

Elaine shook her head vigorously. "I begged her tell me but all she would say was that the fewer people who knew, the better."

" . . . or safer," Gray said, growing anxiety clouding his eyes. He sipped his wine then spoke again after running it all through his mind, step by sinister step. "Keely and Ray are dead. Accidental or intentional? Mabel's apartment ransacked."

His words chilled them all.

"Don't forget that Scotty's stuffed airplane was slashed open," Elaine reflected out loud.

"Barnaby told you?" Laney asked.

"Yes," she said quickly, "this time he did, but he tends to protect me."

"Did he tell you about Victor's secret?" escaped Laney's lips.

A frown drew Elaine's brows together.

"An enigma from the past, Elaine. Victor once divulged to Barnaby that he had taken something of value that he was afraid to profit on," Laney said.

Elaine's hand flew to her mouth. She mumbled, "That could explain the motive, couldn't it?"

"We believe he could have given it to Mabel or Ray. Maybe even Keely or Scotty. It could explain all the violence around the Moore family," Gray said.

Laney leaned forward. "Elaine, did Victor tell *you*."

"That he committed a crime?"

"A federal crime," Laney said.

She dismissed the possibility with a shake of her head. "For heaven's sake. He'd never."

Laney gently led her on. "Did Victor ever talk about his years in Washington before he moved to Madison?"

"Oh, many times. He had loved living in the capital."

"Why did he leave?" Gray asked.

"Opportunities for advancement in the post office were few and far-between. When he heard of a job opening as assistant postmaster at

Madison, he put in for it. At the time, he and Mabel had a child on the way."

"Yes!" Laney said. "So, Victor *did* work for the post office in D.C. What if Victor had come across some rare stamps that could make him rich?" She could still see the red and blue Jenny Invert in her mind.

Elaine inhaled loudly. "*Stamps?* This is about *stamps?*"

Remembering a piece of information she had circled in the *Smithsonian* article, Laney pulled the library copies from her purse where she had jammed them along with her notebook. She leafed through the pages she had stapled together.

"A philatelist named William Robey purchased a sheet of rare stamps at a post office on New York Avenue in Washington," Laney said. "Victor didn't happen to mention which post office he worked at, did he?"

"No," Elaine said.

"Gray thinks I'm nuts believing that Victor got hold of some stamps that were printed in error." Laney shot him a derisive look followed by an air kiss.

Elaine looked at her quizzically as Laney rushed on, slowly pumping her. "Do you know what Victor's duties were at the post office in D.C.?"

"Through the years he had various jobs. Mail carrier most of the time, I believe. Maybe later, postal clerk. I really don't recall."

"One of the best known printing errors occurred when the first airmail stamp was printed. A blue Jenny was printed upside down," Laney said.

"I've heard about those printing mistakes. They're called inverts," Elaine exclaimed.

"The JN-4 was used as the first official airmail plane," Laney said, taking the information from the *Smithsonian Magazine* article. "This Mr. Robey purchased the only known sheet of the Jenny Invert." She showed her a photo of the infamous stamp.

"When was this?"

"That's the kicker," Gray said with a sidelong glance at Laney. "Unfortunately, Victor would have been only fifteen years old, much too young to be working for the post office. The airmail stamps were offered for sale in May of 1918, only two days before the first official airmail flights. The rush to get them printed in time probably added to the chance of a printing error."

A chuckle emanated from Elaine. "Young man, Victor helped his father clean post offices and other government buildings when he was even younger than fifteen."

"What?" Laney cried out.

"One night not long before Victor died, Barnaby and Victor had a long debate over the lack of child labor laws early in this century. Did you know the Fair Labor Standards Act wasn't enacted until the late thirties?" Elaine smiled as she recalled the argument. "Barnaby and Victor were on different sides of the fence on that one. Barnaby had been an activist during his college years in New York and had seen sweatshops first hand. But Victor swore his family couldn't have survived without his meager contribution. He also felt that his childhood connections with the post office helped him get a job there later on."

"Gray, did you hear that? It's possible, after all!" Laney couldn't restrain herself and gave him a brutal kiss on the lips.

"The theft would account for Victor's incessant interest in the Jenny, wouldn't it?" Elaine looked worried.

"You know, even if Victor had had the opportunity to steal the Inverts, we're still assuming that more than one sheet was printed," Gray had to add.

"How will you ever know if that's true?" asked Elaine.

"Unless the stamps are found, we won't," Laney said, "and unless they're found, the attacks against the Moores may continue," she added chillingly.

Laney poked Gray in the gut. "Before we leave tomorrow, we're going to visit Frank Rice. Keely may have confided in him."

"I know it's late, but I promised I'd call you before I left your house. I didn't interrupt anything, did I?" Shar said with a lascivious snicker into the mouthpiece.

"No Shar," Laney said with a casualness that didn't ring true.

"Sorry about that," Shar said. "I'm reporting from the canine maternity ward that nothing seems imminent. Blackberry seems calm and as we speak, is nesting in the kneehole of the desk in the library. I spread newspapers like Gray said and gave her a rawhide bone that she's chewed as slick as snot on a doorknob. Jesse went to bed and has set her alarm to go off every hour to check on her."

"Good, I don't think I could stand any more excitement tonight," Laney said with a brightness that told Shar that Laney was too revved up to sleep.

"What's up?"

"I think we've got a motive for all the violence in the Moore family, and now I'm including Ray's death in that category. Evidently, Keely told her friend, Elaine Biddle, that she believed someone killed her husband."

"Woman, are you saying that poor Keely's remarks to that kitty may have been true?"

"On the mark, according to Elaine."

"Did she get a name?"

"I think that went to the grave with Keely, if indeed, she had figured out who the killer was."

"So, Keely told this Biddle woman she suspected foul play?"

"Yes, and don't forget . . . she indirectly told one other person."

"Who!" Shar said with alarm.

"Scotty."

"Woman, are you suggesting that the child may have inadvertently told Ray's murderer about her mother's suspicions?"

"It's not likely, but she told you, didn't she?"

"What in the hell would be the motive?"

"Stamps."

"Stamps? The yummy gummy stickers you put on letters?"

"The very same, although this particular issue is worth millions and you'd never stick them anywhere but in a bank vault." Laney spent the next ten minutes explaining the Jenny Invert and Victor's possible opportunity to get hold of some of the stamps.

"Amazing, Laney! Wouldn't you have loved to have been a fly on the post office wall that day in 1918? And you say this Biddle guy owns Victor's Jenny? Robert Redford flew one of those planes in *Those Magnificent Men in their Flying Machines*. He tried to save Susan Serandon who was frozen to the wing struts. I'd just as soon eat grubs than go up in one of those crates."

Instead of laughing, Laney's voice became sinister. "Shar, we're assuming that more Jenny Inverts exist and somebody wants them badly enough to kill for them. Tell Malcolm and keep your eyes open."

With the warning, Laney hung up.

Shar dropped the receiver onto the cradle on the desk. Below, Blackberry's expressive eyes stared up at her and she whined.

"Don't even think about it, bitch, and I'm using the accepted meaning of the word for the first time in my life. Chew on your slobbery bone. It'll take your mind off the fact that before long you'll have a passel of little mouths hanging off your tits like ornaments on a Christmas tree."

Shar went down on one knee and kissed Blackberry on the nose. Grunting to her feet, she was about to leave the library, when she noticed that the message light was blinking on the answering machine. When did *that* call come in? She hadn't heard the phone while she was there. Maybe Jesse had missed it earlier. She considered not playing the message back but what if it was someone who wanted to make reservations at the bed and breakfast? Her purple fingernail pushed the button.

25

At six a.m., Laney and Gray tossed their overnight bags in the trunk of the car and set off for Riverview Farm on Route 36 toward Louisville. During a quick stop for coffee and sausage biscuits at a filling station, they obtained directions to the farm that was well known in the area. Nestled in a valley bordered on the north by the Ohio River, the land resembled the farms of St. Clair County where Laney's bed and breakfast was located. Horses and cattle probed the melting snow for grass behind black plank fencing.

The main entrance to Riverview Farm was flanked with pilasters made of an exquisite white Indiana stone that were inset with bronze plaques announcing the name of the farm. Like black crows, eight rural mailboxes were lined up in front of the entrance and the side of the end box had the name, "Rice," printed above the numeral, 1400. Gray followed arrows to the farm office that was built of the same white stone.

They entered a lobby paneled in wormy chestnut where the voice of a woman talking on the telephone drifted from a passthrough. Gray took a seat on one of twin leather sofas while Laney approached the opening. A young woman met her there after finishing her call.

"May I help you?" she asked.

"I understand Frank Rice is the new vet tech at Riverview. Would you tell me where I can find him? We are acquaintances of Keely Moore, his fiancée who was killed recently in an accident."

The woman's eyes darkened. "We were sorry to hear of Ms. Moore's death, however, I had never met her. You should find Frank at barn two behind the office or follow the lane back the way you came to the house closest to the entrance." She pointed out a window.

At barn two, an older man identified himself as the farm veterinarian. He reported that he hadn't seen Frank Rice yet that morning. Gray turned the Buick around and followed the lane back toward the front of the farm where Laney remembered passing a small two-story frame house with a green roof and shutters.

Gray parked the car in the driveway that disappeared behind the house and they followed stepping stones to the front door.

As Laney lifted the brass horse-head knocker, a hideous cry came from inside the house. The sound was so unsettling, they both stepped back from the entrance. They looked at each other in alarm.

"My God, Gray, what do we do!" exploded from Laney. Gray compressed the latch and gave the door a shove. It swung open. "Stay put," he ordered while he roughly thrust the door back at her. It bounced painfully off her knee.

"Not on your life!" Laney retorted, her voice strident. She trailed him into the house.

They found themselves inside a tiny foyer with openings to the living and dining rooms on either side. A dark hallway led toward the rear of the house. Again, they heard groans that appeared to be coming from above them and a moment later, a door slammed at the back of the house.

Gray started down the hall, then saw a narrow staircase rising steeply on his right.

Gray led the way up the steps hugging the wall, one protecting arm against Laney's body. At a tiny landing, Laney glanced out of an octagonal window and caught the tail end of a dark green car that fishtailed around Gray's Buick in the driveway. Beyond her vision, she heard it screech off as it turned onto the farm lane.

Reaching the top of the stairs, Gray put a finger to his lips while they hastened down a hallway with empty bedrooms on either side. A final room, evidently the master bedroom, faced them at the end of the hall. Reaching the open door, Gray's fingers gripped her arm painfully as they peered in.

In a rumpled, king-sized bed, a man lay under the bedclothes.

"What in hell," Gray croaked as he ran to the bed with Laney behind him. Laney looked down at a man with dark brown hair and deep-set eyes above a mouth that lay slackly open. Frank Rice lay on his side, his head resting on a blood soaked pillow. Clots pulsed from a wound in the man's temple. Like a fleshy branch, one arm stretched from under him in an extended position. The other lay lifelessly on the bedcovers. Gray lay two fingers below his jaw. "Laney, he's alive! Barely! Call 911!"

Laney lifted the phone from the nightstand on the left side of the bed. With fingers shaking in panic, she recalled Frank's heartbreaking call to her the day of Keely's funeral and how he had cried when he'd heard about Keely's death.

In the distance, she heard the chilling whine of emergency vehicles and as she dialed, they got louder and louder. Before she could report the location to the dispatcher, shrill sirens and red and blue lights throbbed outside the house.

"Forget it! Someone's already reported it," Gray called to Laney from the window.

Then Laney saw it—a flash of silver beside the telephone. An earring! Not just any earring, but a Scottish thistle pendant that someone must have removed to make a telephone call. A prickly sensation crawled up Laney's spine while the replay of the dark green car careening down the Frank Rice's drive reeled through her mind. The sickening wave of realization and fear that followed almost brought her to her knees.

Gray raised the window and yelled down to the paramedics bounding from an ambulance below. Laney had only moments before they would rush into the room. Her eyes riveted on the thistle earring and she quickly weighed the consequences of the choice she was about to make. As the medics, carrying a stretcher, burst through the doorway, her fingers folded around the earring.

26

F rank Rice was rushed to the nearest hospital in Louisville. Gray had conferred with the paramedics and had reported to Laney that Rice was in a deep coma and the prognosis looked grim. While the police cordoned off the scene, the two of them were ushered into the living room off the foyer and a detective named Grossman from the Carroll County Sheriff's Department began questioning them while criminalists gathered evidence in the master bedroom upstairs. Grossman searched through Frank's wallet for information about his next of kin. When he found a photo of Keely, Laney told the detective that she had died in a hit and run in Atlanta just days before. She also explained that Frank and Keely had been in a close relationship and when Keely hadn't arrived at her new job, Frank had phoned the Lamont home and she was the one who had taken the call.

Grossman raised an eyebrow and inquired why she and Gray were at Rice's house. With a quickness that frightened her, Laney unfolded a tale that Frank had been so devastated when informed of Keely's death, they had decided to pay him a call while in the area visiting other friends. Laney figured the statement wasn't completely false now that they had met Elaine and Barnaby. She did ignore the opportunity to express her suspicions about the motivation for the violence that seemed to pursue the Moore family or reveal the earring she had found and pocketed.

When one of the officers asked for Grossman's assistance upstairs,

Laney and Gray were left sitting alone on a tapestry sofa. Laney fidgeted until she thought she couldn't remain seated a moment longer. Worrying about the earring in her pocket, she had just about decided to bolt, with or without Gray, when Grossman returned to the living room. After checking out their identification, the detective asked several more questions and finally gave Laney and Gray permission to return to Hickory, but warned that if Rice died of his wound, they might be questioned further.

It was mid-morning when, with sighs of relief, they climbed into the Buick and drove out the farm gate. Laney tried to take in a nap but she kept fingering the thistle earring in her suede jacket pocket. *What am I going to do?* she mulled.

"What are you going to do?" Gray asked.

For a second Laney thought she had ruminated out loud. She uttered a feeble, "Huh?"

"Laney, I saw that slight of hand back at Frank Rice's house. You know that's tampering with evidence, don't you?"

Laney's heart plunged to her gut. For a moment she considered inventing some story, but she realized she needed his help on this one. Reluctantly, she pulled out the earring and dangled it in his line of vision as he drove.

"Laney!" he shouted, the car swerving. He braked and pulled off onto the shoulder of the narrow road. "My God, only one person I know wears thistles in her ears." He took the pendant and studied it.

Laney's voice shook as she said, "Shar usually removes an earring before using the telephone. She must have been the one to call in the emergency. When I first saw it, I was hoping that it was someone else's earring until I remembered seeing the dark green Oldsmobile."

"What Olds?"

"The one I saw race out of the driveway when I looked out of the window on the stair landing."

"Malcolm's car?"

"I think so now, although I only saw the rear-end. It was shortly after we heard the door slam in the back of the house."

"Damn! If it was Shar, she must have slipped down the stairs, that dark hallway and out the back door. The Olds must have been parked behind the house."

"I've been wondering what she thought when she saw your pink Buick in the drive. It's so distinctive, she must have known it was your car. And I wonder how she made it up to Carrollton so fast. I just talked to her over the phone last evening."

Gray handed the earring back to Laney and pulled back onto Route 421. "Laney, my biggest wonder is why she was at Frank Rice's house in the first place."

27

"No one's home," Laney said, slamming the phone into the cradle. "I'm going over there and camp on her door step." Sulking, she stepped away from the desk and stood with her arms folded across her chest.

"What good will that do?" Gray asked her. He lay stretched out end to end on the leather sofa in the library where he had been ever since they had arrived home. "Come over here," he said suggestively.

Laney knew that look and what it could lead to, and for the first time in a long time, sex was the last thing on her mind. All she could think of was the thistle earring she had found next to Frank Rice's telephone. Blackberry entered the room and slunk into the desk kneehole. She scratched a spot, circled and lay down.

With great effort, Gray pulled himself up from the sofa and stooped to check Blackberry. "She'll whelp tonight," he announced, straightening. He pulled Laney into his arms and kissed her. "We'll get to the root of this in due time, Laney. Meanwhile, if you're not going to let me jump your bones, I'd better get in touch with these clients that called while I was gone." He picked up a list of four messages that Jesse had left him on the desk behind Laney. "I'll call them at the clinic and get back before she delivers." He started for the door and called over his shoulder, "There's a message on the answering machine. Must be yours."

She sighed and pressed replay.

Ms. McVey, Frank Rice here, returning your call. I'm going away in the morning for several days so there's no need to stop by. I'll be in touch.

"Gray!" Laney cried, but he had already spun on his heels.

"I heard," he said. "What time was the call?"

"Eight p.m."

"So Rice was okay last night," Gray said. "We'd better give that information to the police. It will help them pinpoint the time of the shooting."

"No!"

"Laney, what in earth?" He took hold of her shoulders and his eyes bored into hers. "You're afraid aren't you? Afraid for Shar. It's the reason you took the earring. The reason you didn't tell the police about the green Oldsmobile, isn't it?"

She sat down hard on the red ottoman as the significance of Gray's questions staggered her. An icy frost crept over her heart. "Gray," she beseeched, "Shar . . . she couldn't have . . . you know . . . shot the guy?"

Before Gray could answer, there was a furious rapping at the front door as well as a couple of rings of the doorbell.

"Who in hell?" Gray said, annoyed.

Laney ran out into the hall and looked through the sidelights of the front door.

"Shar!" Laney yanked the door open and Shar rushed by her like a sudden violent squall. "We're in the library," Laney called to her.

Shar pivoted and stormed into the room behind Laney. She carried a small cardboard carton. Afraid, Blackberry shrank farther under the desk.

Shar dropped the box on the red velvet chair and stood swaying from side to side wringing her hands. Her plaid mackinaw looked as though slept in, but her red and puffy eyes said she hadn't slept at all.

"Shar, calm . . . here, take a seat." Laney tried to soothe by offering the ottoman.

Shar shook her head in a fleet movement. "Frank Rice was shot," Shar blurted in a high and hysterical voice.

"We were there," Laney said.

"And so were you," Gray retorted, his eyes leveled at Shar.

Laney winced at his bluntness.

Shar's face collapsed and she sat down hard on the sofa. "How did you know?" she murmured.

"Malcolm's car," Laney said. "I saw you leaving," she paused, "and this." She pulled the earring from her pocket.

Shar's hand shot to her ear, then to the one that was missing the earring. "Where? Oh God, never mind; I remember!"

"Shar, why were you there?" Laney asked, pulling the ottoman over to the sofa after handing Shar the earring. She sat facing her.

Shar put on the earring and dropped her face into her hands.

"Shar, we mean only to help you," Gray said. He sat next to her and put his arm awkwardly around her shoulders.

Shar wiggled from his embrace and stood. She stepped around Laney and walked to the desk and pushed the play button on the answering machine. Frank Rice's voice once more filled the library.

Shar spun and faced them. "Simon."

Laney's and Gray's mouths dropped simultaneously.

"I recognized his voice when I played the message last night."

"Shar, we've been through this—" Laney started.

"Woman, you're not listening to me! I was married to the guy, remember? I drove to Carrollton last night and saw him with my own two eyes!"

Silence, like forked lightning, ripped through the room.

Gray was the first to break the deathly hush. "Frank's telephone message said he was going away for a few days. This morning, the secretary at Riverview Farm didn't tell us he was taking a trip. In fact, she told us where we could find him."

"And I didn't see any packed bags at the house," Laney said, with a growing sense of dread. "It's almost as though he was trying to avoid meeting us."

"Why is this so hard for you to grasp?" Shar retorted. "Simon—Frank if you insist—didn't *want* you to see him, so he told you a big one so you wouldn't come."

"Why?" Laney asked stupidly, though knowing the answer.

"Think about it, Laney. Frank Rice, Keely's significant other, must have known Keely's brother was engaged to me. *Me*, his widow who had been lugging his ashes around for five years. He couldn't take the chance of me accompanying you to Carrollton and recognizing him."

"Wait a minute, Shar. Simon's a blond. Frank has dark brown hair," Laney said with not much conviction.

"Out-of-a-bottle. Got it with me."

Gray scowled in thought. "You're sure, Shar? . . . absolutely positive he's Simon?"

"I checked him out . . . down to his fetching little butt."

"My God, Shar, what in hell do you mean by that?" Gray asked with eyebrows high.

"Later, Gray, this isn't the time," Laney said. She looked at Shar. "I have to ask . . . even with the risk of losing a friend . . ."

"Did I shoot Simon?" Shar asked for her.

"Uh . . ."

"Laney, when I heard Simon's voice on your answering machine, I went crazy. All I could think of was finding that son of a bitch. On my way to Carrollton, torture worse than death went through my mind, but I swear to God, I didn't shoot him." Her eyes were hard gray pebbles.

"After hearing your phone message, I called Mal and told him that Blackberry was acting like she might have those pups any minute. Just in case, I was going to stay the night with Jesse. The sweetheart told me he'd put Scotty to bed and sleep in her room like I've been doing." Shar's eyes softened. But in an instant, her eyes blazed murderously again as she continued her narration.

"Just as I was leaving, Jesse came downstairs to check on Blackberry and begged me to stay with her. When she finally fell asleep on the sofa about three o'clock, I slipped out, jumped into the Olds and took off for Carrollton. Because the phone message said he was going out of town, I wanted to get there before dawn, just in case. I had only the name of the farm. Lost, I wandered through the countryside until I found a service station near Milton. The attendant told me how to get to the farm and once there, I saw Rice's name and address on his mailbox. My eyes were crossing by the time I pulled into his driveway."

Laney and Gray sat mesmerized while she told how she parked behind the house so no one would see her car and knocked on the back door. When no one answered, she tried the front door and found it open, just as Gray and Laney had.

"I heard horrible moans. I found Simon lying motionless in bed, his pillow bloody. He was barely conscious, but I knew in an instant that he recognized me when he begged, 'Help me, Shar,' " Shar's body hunched and shook with sobs. Blackberry, disturbed by all the activity in the room got to her feet, circled and lay down again.

"I admit it crossed my mind to just walk away," she blubbered, "just let him suffer alone like he had left me to suffer alone five years ago."

"But you couldn't do it. You called 911, didn't you?" Laney said.

Shar nodded sadly, stood and moved to the carton on the chair.

"It's all here," she said, opening the flaps and removing several documents.

A birth certificate and social security card were issued to Frank Rice. Only the final document, a death certificate from Puerto Rico, had a different name—Simon Anderson.

Her mouth twisted. "I got word Simon had died in a plane accident in the winter of ninety-three." Anguish contorted her features, and it was a moment before she could go on.

"A U.S. Embassy representative called me from Puerto Rico and broke the news. At least he led me to believe he was from the U.S. Embassy. He gave me a number to call for arrangements. I later agreed to have Simon cremated and his ashes sent to me. It was what Simon had expressed he wanted done if anything ever happened to him. Evidently, it was all a part of Simon's plan to fake his death." She handed the death certificate to Gray.

"Looks authentic to me," Gray said.

"*All* the paperwork from Puerto Rico looked authentic," Shar said bitterly. She began to cry again. "How could I have been duped like that? I even had a memorial service for him at our church in Pittsburgh."

"No one questioned anything? His parents?" Laney queried.

"Simon had no living relatives."

"Don't be so hard on yourself," Gray said. "You were vulnerable . . . the shock of learning of Simon's death . . . the grief you must have felt."

"If he wanted to be rid of me, why didn't he just divorce me?" Shar said.

"He must have wanted to disappear completely . . . start a new life . . . leave no trace," Laney thought out loud.

"But evidently, he found a new life as Frank Rice in Florida and four years later, wooed Keely Moore," Gray said wryly.

Shar whipped the certificate from Gray's hand and stuffed it into the box in anger. At the bottom of the box she retrieved a bottle of brown hair dye. "Simon's box of deception that changed his identity . . . and my life," she said bitterly.

"Did Simon ever express an interest in stamp collecting?" Gray asked.

"Not that I know of," Shar said.

"What did Simon do for a living while he was married to you," Laney asked.

"He worked for a company that searched for free-zone factories around the world. They are factories that import raw materials, especially textiles, and turn them into finished goods that would then be re-exported to the U. S. and Europe. That's why he took that trip to the Dominican Republic and Puerto Rico in 1993. He had a pilot's license and flew the company jet all over the place. He spent a great deal of time away from me."

"But as Frank Rice, he worked with horses," Laney said.

"That's not hard to explain. Horses were an inherent love of Simon's. Even though he was in export, he used to exercise horses at Meadowland Racetrack near Pittsburgh on the weekends. And before I knew him there, he told me he worked part time at a horse farm in California."

"I guess it makes sense if he was in the export business while married to you, he would switch occupations after changing his identity, Laney said. "If he had stayed in export, he might have run across someone who knew him as Simon Anderson."

"You know what I think?" Gray said. "Simon may have learned about the stamps and changed his identity to marry Keely to get possession of them, either through Keely or Scotty."

"Are you also saying that Simon got rid of Keely's husband, Ray?" Laney asked.

Gray shrugged. "Maybe even Keely, herself, if Simon thought she suspected him."

Shar's eyes flashed. "As rotten as Simon was by faking his own death, I can't believe him guilty of murder."

Gray snorted his contempt for the man that had hurt his friend so thoroughly. "Your compassion for Simon is touching, Shar. If I were on death row, I would want you to be governor."

"I have to agree with Shar," Laney interjected "We're all losing sight of, that at this very moment, Simon is in the hospital fighting for his life because someone tried to murder *him*."

Blackberry had been unusually quiet for fifteen minutes. Laney's eyes dropped to the kneehole.

"Good grief! Gray, look!"

Blackberry lay on her side panting. Gray sat on the floor in front of the opening and felt her side. "She's contracting. Laney I need more light. There's a reflector lamp in the carriage house. I'll get my equipment from the Jeep."

"What can I do?" Shar asked.

Gray looked at her with softness and smiled. "Call Malcolm and tell him to bring Scotty to see this."

"You won't . . ."

Laney answered for him "No, we won't tell him about Simon. You must be the one, Shar." She ran to get the lamp.

Shar scrambled for the phone.

"Malcolm said they'll take the farm truck and be here in fifteen minutes," she said a few minutes later.

Gray clamped the light to the rod of a floor lamp and it shined nicely into the kneehole. Blackberry didn't seem to mind the illumination and actually appeared to want them near. Gray arranged an assembly of instruments on a clean towel on the floor.

Blackberry alternated from digging into the thick pile of newspapers to staring at her rear end. She shivered lightly. By the time Malcolm and Scotty arrived, the shivering had increased and the contractions had gotten harder. Blackberry grunted.

"When do the wee dogs come?" Scotty asked, her eyes peeled on Blackberry. She lay on her belly, her chin propped by her hands. Her slim bottom, covered in blue denim, wiggled and scooted to get closer to the action.

"Won't be long now," Gray said. "See how she pushes. There now, that's her water breaking."

Standing behind Gray, Laney craned her neck to see. Shar sat on the floor next to Scotty, and Malcolm, on the sofa, tried to read a *Cattleman's Magazine.*

Blackberry strained and a bubble protruded from her vulva.

"Dinna look like a dog," Scotty squealed.

"That's the placenta bubble," Gray said as the bubble burst and a tiny nose and pink toe appeared.

"A wee neb!" came from Scotty, pressing Shar's nose with her forefinger. Her eyes were large with excitement.

The rest of the pup slid out and Blackberry licked and licked at the puppy still partially encased in its shiny sac until it was free.

Gray grabbed his bulb syringe and compressed the air out before clearing the pup's mouth and nose. He squeezed the blood at the end of the placenta back down the cord into the puppy. "That extra blood can make a weak pup strong," he said. After crimping the cord with a hemostat about a half-inch from the pup's belly, he waited about a minute before taking his pair of dull scissors and cutting the cord between the hemostat and the placenta.

"What's Blackberry doing?" Shar cried. "Gray, stop her. That's repulsive! Disgusting!"

Scotty scrunched up her face.

"Bitches eat some of the placentas, Shar. It gives nourishment to the mother and helps the uterus shrink back to normal. Also aids in milk production," Gray said as he enclosed the puppy in a small towel and rubbed it until almost dry.

"Could I have it?" Scotty asked, scrambling to her knees and holding out her arms.

Gray smiled as he placed the puppy at one of Blackberry's teats. "Scotty, these are Blackberry's babies for awhile. She must get used to them and not be afraid someone will take them away. By tomorrow, I'm sure she will let you hold them as long as you stay near."

Scotty seemed to accept his explanation and settled back onto her tummy to watch more.

She didn't have long to wait. Three more puppies were born in the next hour. Then there was a lull. Laney took the time to make hot chocolate and brought in a large tray of steaming mugs and a plate of oatmeal raisin cookies that her mother had made the day before. Malcolm was the only one who ate.

Although Blackberry was still straining and grunting, Laney was surprised to see that no puppies had been born while she was gone.

Gray looked worried as he listened for additional heartbeats with his stethoscope. "There's at least one more in there," he said. Gray pushed back the vulva and a sac suddenly appeared and dangled, exposing two little feet.

"Damn! It's coming breech . . . hind feet first. With the sac separated, the pup isn't getting any air."

Blackberry strained heavily and the puppy slid out to its waist and stopped.

"Stuck," Gray said and Scotty began to cry.

"It's all right, Scotty. Gray will do his best to save it," Shar said. Scotty climbed onto Shar's lap and buried her face into her shoulder.

Gray scooped up a dollop of Vaseline and greased as much as he could feel of the puppy by running his finger up the vulva. "Large puppy. I can feel the top of a shoulder." Gray contorted his face and with Blackberry's next contraction, he pulled firmly with his finger. The puppy slid out.

"There's the little bugger," Gray said, reaching for his bulb syringe. Gray removed some mucus but the pup was okay. After he cut the umbilical cord, he wrapped a clean towel around the puppy and allowed Scotty to rub it dry and place it on a teat. Its little mouth began to suck.

Gray listened for more heartbeats. "Looks like that's it," he said.

"Like five ain't enough," said Shar. Scotty was relaxed in her arms, almost asleep.

"Not a very large litter for a Border collie," Gray said.

"Doc Mike gets pick of the litter for using his stud," Laney said, "and I already have two others promised."

"Sharlene, we need to get Scotty to bed," Malcolm said, "and ourselves too. We have busy days ahead." He took Scotty from her and helped put on her coat and hat. With one arm around the sleeping child and the other around Shar's shoulders, they looked like the perfect family. But when Laney recalled all of the obstacles the little family had to overcome, her heart ached. Things were about to change and maybe they would never get right again.

28

Before dawn, with guilt caroming off the walls like drunken shadows, Shar finally left her rumpled bed and crept into Malcolm's room. She gently wakened him and whispered in the darkness that she must speak with him. Perhaps it was the seriousness of her tone that made Malcolm not turn on the bedside lamp. With only the glow of a small nightlight near the bath, she watched his form rise from the covers and heard the rustle as he put on his robe. He sat on the edge of his bed and Shar sat on the carpet before him, her legs folded and nightshirt pulled taught over her knees. Her fingers picked nervously at a snag in the fabric, most likely caused sometime by a playful Kudzu.

She began. Not only did she come clean about her trip to Northern Kentucky, but also about the photo and mysterious phone calls she had received in the past month. She spared him nothing: the suspicions about Keely's and Ray's accidents, the slashing of Scotty's toy plane, the likelihood that Victor's theft of rare stamps was behind all the violence. Especially agonizing to relate was Laney's withholding of the evidence that could link Shar to Simon's shooting.

With his hands covering his face, Malcolm's spectacles hung from between the fingers of one hand. A single ray of the rising sun streamed over the windowsill and dappled his rumpled curls with copper. His tartan robe gapped open and his bare chest heaved with a groan of despair as Shar finished the painful account of what had transpired the night before.

And when she was done, the deathlike stillness that permeated Malcolm's bedroom was not unlike the solemn hush while a coffin is lowered into the earth.

Shortly, he rose stiffly from the bedside and barefoot, he edged away from her and left the room.

In a moment, Shar followed and found him in Scotty's room. From the doorway she saw him on his knees by Scotty's bedside, his face close to her sleeping face, his arm tight around her tiny form. His shaking shoulders told Shar that he believed, as she did, that Simon Anderson's reappearance would prevent the child from ever coming to them. There would be no marriage before the custody hearing because Shar was still legally married to Simon.

The ring of the phone on Laney's bedside table shocked her awake. She glanced at the clock. Eight o'clock. She grabbed the receiver before it could waken Gray. He groaned but slept on.

"Ms. Laney McVey, please," a male voice said.

"This is she," she said sleepily after covering her head and the phone with her pillow.

"This is Detective Grossman from the Carroll County Sheriff's Department," the man said just as Laney recognized his voice. "I promised that I would inform you of any change in Frank Rice's condition." He cleared his voice. "Frank Rice died at three o'clock this morning. The crime has officially been upgraded to a homicide and the body has been transported to the medical examiner's department for autopsy."

Laney's heart stopped. He continued. "This definitely puts a new slant on this case. We were hoping that Mr. Rice would gain consciousness long enough to tell us who shot him, if indeed, he saw the person."

"Detective, we'll help in any way we can," she said, and concluded the call with a sigh of relief. Laney flung off the pillow and climbed out of bed. Grabbing her robe, she tiptoed out of their room behind the back stairs and put on a pot of coffee. As she waited eagerly for her first cup, a penetrating coldness chilled her caused by learning about the death of Frank—no, Simon.

Shar! She had to call and tell her.

She took her coffee to the library. Blackberry met her at the door, her teats swollen, her puppies' weak squeals calling from the kneehole.

"Even mothers need to take a leak," she said, addressing the squirming litter. She let mama out and through the sidelights she watched her squat in the yard and hurry back up the steps. She scratched and barked.

"Good mommy," she said, letting her back inside. Blackberry plopped down amid the puppies while Laney rescued one that had managed to wobble out onto the carpet. "Tomorrow you guys go into the pantry." All clinging to Blackberry, their little white tipped tails quivered in a frenzied dance of feeding celebration. She saw that the collie had eaten all of the high-protein puppy chow she had put out and that her water was about gone. She refreshed the bowls before taking her first sip of coffee.

"Gotta get this over with," she said, dialing Shar's number. Malcolm answered but seemed distraught and anxious to get off the phone. Shar's told him, Laney thought uneasily.

When she answered, Laney blurted, "I've news." She heard an intake of breath. "Simon died early this morning." A low sustained expiration came over the phone line.

"Did the hospital . . ."

"Detective Grossman," Laney said. Gray entered the library in his robe and slippers. He sipped on coffee.

"Shar, let me call you back."

"But I need to know . . ."

"I promise . . . in a few minutes."

"What was the phone call this morning?" Gray asked when she hung up.

"Just now?"

"You know when I mean."

"Grossman."

"Frank Rice died, didn't he?"

"Simon Anderson," Laney corrected as she paced the floor. She spun abruptly and held down a button on the answering machine.

Messages deleted, the voice in the little box said.

"What in hell did you do that for?" Gray said. "Police will want to hear that tape to help establish time of the shooting."

"Exactly," Laney said. "Without the message, without the earring, without anyone seeing Malcolm's car, the police can't connect the murder to Shar . . . as long as the identity of the dead man remains Frank Rice." Laney looked down at the carton that Shar had left the night before. "Taking this box linking Frank to Simon was a stroke of genius."

Gray gave her a look of disapproval.

"Gray, we both know Shar didn't shoot Simon so what's the harm in keeping Frank's true identity a secret until Shar and Malcolm marry and the guardianship of Scotty is settled? If all of this comes out before the hearing, Bonnie and Dwayne will get Scotty, for sure."

"Laney you're losing sight of the fact that a man is dead. Murdered. The killer needs to be found."

"Right, and you and I know Simon's murder must have had something to do with Victor Moore and those stamps. Why can't we all keep Simon's identity a secret until after the wedding and custody hearing? Then we can tell the police everything, about Victor's stamps that may be connected to Ray's and Keely's deaths and now to Simon's murder. What do you say?"

Gray gave Laney a long dubious stare while little sucking noises came from below the desk. Gray picked up the phone.

"Who are you calling?" Laney asked with alarm.

"Malcolm and Shar."

So it was agreed that Laney, Gray, Shar and Malcolm would conceal the true identity of Frank Rice and that Shar had visited him on the morning he'd been shot. With forced enthusiasm, Shar hoped for no additional hitches to her abbreviated nuptials that would take place that afternoon. But to be perfectly honest, the subsequent custody hearing was paramount in Shar's thoughts while she and Scotty rehearsed the "Highland Fling," the music they would perform together after the ceremony. It was the celebratory dance after a battle won. Humph, the battle hasn't yet begun, Shar thought. As soon as the four of them told the police that she had heard her "dead" husband on the telephone and she had been to his house, she'd quickly feel the cold grip of steel around her wrists, especially when authorities learned that her marriage to Malcolm and subsequent custody hearing depended upon Simon being positively and absolutely dead, down to the last gasp.

Unhappily, the mental image of Simon lying on his bloodstained pillow crying for her help wouldn't go away. Simon may have committed the ultimate betrayal, but he didn't deserve to die by a bullet exploding in his brain. For among Shar's few good memories of Simon was that he had loved her once and had rescued her from a terrible first marriage wrought with neglect and abuse. It wasn't enough to justify forgiveness, Shar thought wryly, but surely enough to see that Simon's real killer was apprehended. But the truth would have to wait until after the hearing in the wild chance that the court's decision would result in Scotty, Malcolm and her finally becoming a family.

Shar played the chanter only, not wanting to risk the ballooning whine of the bagpipes that might give their surprise away to Malcolm. He was out on the farm but had promised to be back in plenty of time to dress for the ceremony.

Scotty began to dance. Wearing worn bib overalls, red checkered blouse and her black guillies that were beginning to pinch her toes, she delicately moved on the balls of her feet. Shar was still amazed at the tot's agility. In fact, after just two practices, Scotty's dancing skills had become polished way beyond her years. Shar couldn't wait to see her in full Highland dress. How proud Malcolm would be, she thought, as she glimpsed at the kilt, vest and blouse hanging inside the closet.

With Scotty's final bow, Shar glanced at her watch and realized that only an hour remained before Reverend Dunbar and the few friends that she had phoned to witness the wedding would arrive.

At that very minute, Laney and Gray were making the parlor presentable and rearranging the seating for the few guests. Shar and Malcolm hadn't had the time, or to be honest, the enthusiasm to prepare the house and food like they had planned. In fact, with the oppressive recent events, a gloom had settled over the old house and the upcoming nuptials. Not that Malcolm and Shar didn't remain devoted to each other and with a touch or tender word conveyed their closeness. But the urgency of the marriage to obtain Scotty almost became the focus of the event. They were not unlike a childless couple who, under the advice of an infertility specialist, had sex at specific times to try to conceive.

Shar Hamilton, you mustn't dwell on sadness, she told herself. It's your wedding day and dear Malcolm loves you to pieces. But no matter how hard she tried to stop it, the shadow of the custody hearing slithered over her heart and like a snake, wrapped itself around and crushed.

29

"Freddie, I gotta do it," Sheriff Powell said to his deputy. He peered out through the filthy blinds behind his desk to the Vietnam Memorial on the courthouse lawn. The blasted eternal flame had gone out again. He'd have to remember to call the gas company before the vets marched on the courthouse.

"But it's their wedding day, for pity's sake," Freddie said.

Gordon swung to face him. "Like I don't know. Hell, I'm invited."

Freddie cracked his gum, a habit that he picked up when the doctor made him give up junk food. "Couldn't you at least wait until after the ceremony?"

"Grossman said today."

Freddie checked his watch. "Eight hours 'til midnight."

"Okay, okay. Wedding's in an hour. You think you can hold down the fort?"

"No sweat . . . say, Sheriff . . . "

"Yeah?"

"Need me to go with ya?"

"What I need, is a kick in the ass for staying in this job."

30

Scotty squealed her protest.

"Scotty, dear, sometimes you must suffer to be beautiful," Shar said, doing her best to straighten the child's ringlets. She dipped the brush into a bowl and wetted and brushed and wetted some more. When she had the mass of hair grasped in one hand, she slid the thick elastic band around its bulk and shaped it into a bushy ponytail. With additional brushing, goop, and water she twisted the hair into a tight bun on the crown of her head and pinned it in place. After almost asphyxiating the child with hair spray, Shar spun Scotty around to face her.

"There, now let me see," Shar said.

Scotty wrinkled her nose but it couldn't take the moment away from Shar. She was absolutely beautiful.

Shar tugged at the velvet vest and polished each of the embossed buttons with the sleeve of her robe. She straightened the lace trim attached to the neck of Scotty's white blouse and smoothed the tartan kilt that matched her hose.

"I dinna want you to cry, Saugh," Scotty said reaching out and touching the wetness on Shar's cheek.

"Tears of joy . . . good luck on a wedding day."

Scotty's mouth suddenly formed a tiny O and her eyes lit up as the sounds of pipes drifted up the stairs and into the room.

"The music!" Shar said whipping off her robe and tossing it onto Scotty's bed. One of the few preparations Shar had accomplished, was to tape bagpipe music that would be played over the stereo system before the ceremony. As she touched up her makeup in the vanity mirror, she tried to think of how many numbers she had recorded before she would descend the stairs with the playing of "Highland Cathedral."

"Scotty, quick, get my satin shoes in the closet in my room! And don't let Uncle Mal see you!"

Scotty dashed out of the room and down the hallway. In her slip, Shar ran to Scotty's closet where she had hidden her dress after it had arrived from the dressmaker.

Slipping the gown off the padded hanger, Shar dropped it over her head. The ivory tea-length velveteen flowed soft and light over her slim hips like a billowy June cloud. The only adornments were tiny pink satin thistles that flowered around the wrists of the narrow, long sleeves.

"Flower of Scotland" faded away as Scotty burst into the room. She squatted and shoved the cream-colored slippers under Shar's dress and Shar wiggled her toes into them while brushing blush over her cheeks and running a quick comb through her pixie cut. She reached behind her neck to fasten the single button on her dress.

"I do it," Scotty said, climbing upon the vanity chair and working her little fingers over the satin covered button. When she finished, she stared over Shar's shoulder at their reflections. "Bonny Saugh," she said.

Shar reached for a box on the vanity and removed the Hamilton silver thistle brooch her father had given her before he died. An only child, Shar's father had inherited the brooch from his mother to pass on to a daughter should he have one. Shar pinned it to the shoulder of her dress. Perhaps one day it would belong to Scotty, she thought, as the final strains of "Ye Banks and Braes" filtered into the room. She suddenly missed her mother who had planned to be at the other wedding in December but couldn't make it to this one on such short notice.

She lifted Scotty down from the chair and she scampered to her twin bed where she dropped to her knees.

"Scotty, you shall be covered in dust bunnies," Shar said as the child scooted a box from under the bed.

"What's this?" Shar asked, taking it and placing it upon the bed. She lifted the lid and folded back the tissue to reveal a nosegay of white heather trimmed with ivory satin ribbons that cascaded like a waterfall when she raised the bouquet to her face. The card was signed, *Malcolm*. Speechless, she could only weep into the flowers.

The sounds of "Highland Cathedral" filled the house and with a trembling sob, she wiped her eyes with the back of her hand.

"This is it, kiddo," she said and took Scotty's hand. Together, they walked toward the music.

.

31

"It's time," Laney whispered to Gray, giving him a little nudge in the direction of the stereo on the bookcase. Next to her, Malcolm said, "Laney, everything is perfect."

Malcolm wore a short, black Barathea jacket over his shirt, tie and vest. Over his jacket, a Lamont tartan sash swept down across his chest like hills sweeping to the sea. Above his black ghillie brogues, garter flashes were tucked into the cuffs of his knee hose. The matching kilt just brushed the top of his knees. He thought he looked particularly smashing.

As "Flower of Scotland," the unofficial national anthem of Scotland, began to play over the speakers, it was a moment before he realized that the piper had to be Sharlene. She had said she would make a recording, but with the recent unhappy events, he was painfully aware of what an ordeal it must have been to fulfill that promise.

He stood in the archway to the parlor and gazed in amazement at all that Laney, Gray and Jesse had accomplished in a few short hours while Sharlene had been hidden away upstairs with Scotty and he had been out on the farm. Flowers were everywhere: on the console in the front hall, on the table in the dining room, and centered on the mantle between the shiny brass candlesticks in the parlor. And what perfect arrangements they were. Most were sprigs of evergreens softened with clusters of heather and tiny pink and blue silk bows here and there. He could see why Laney had given him strict orders to use the back entrance and stairway when he came in to dress.

"Ye Banks and Braes," his very favorite Scottish song, lilted through the house. He smiled at the few friends that had gathered: Reverend Dunbar, who would perform the ceremony, Laney and Gray, Jesse Mills, Attorney Marshall Knight, Laney's mother, Maddy, with Sheriff Gordon Powell at her side and two very special guests invited belatedly—Barnaby and Elaine Biddle.

It had been years since Malcolm had seen the pair. Sharlene, of course, had never met them and little Scotty, although acquainted with them by phone, had been too small to remember when the Biddles had attended her father's funeral in Scotland.

When Laney called them with the invitation, she had learned that Elaine had finally told Barnaby about Keely's suspicions concerning Ray's death in the horse stall. When Laney had added the new information that Keely's fiancé, Frank Rice, was really Simon Anderson, and that he had been murdered, the Biddles were understandably shocked, but seemed to take Laney's word that Sharlene had nothing to do with the crime. They were so ecstatic about getting the chance to see Scotty after all this time, they agreed to not breathe a word about Sharlene being at Frank's house shortly before the shooting.

"Blast it, Gordon," Malcolm said, elbowing the sheriff standing beside him, "quit looking so glum. This is a wedding, not a funeral."

Gordon smiled thinly.

Everyone began to mingle quietly near the staircase where Laney had told them Sharlene would descend with the playing of the third number. Again, Malcolm was struck by the detail of decoration Laney and Jesse had managed to put together. A simple pine garland draped gracefully from the banister, attached with generous, ivory satin bows.

A brief moment of stillness ensued before "Highland Cathedral" began. All eyes were riveted on the staircase but several stanzas played before Sharlene and Scotty appeared at the top of the stairs.

"My God in heaven," Malcolm gasped and involuntarily took a step forward. The bagpipes swelled and filled the house as they began to descend. His eyes were drawn first to Sharlene and then to the child. Sharlene looked ethereal, though Malcolm never would have ever chosen that word to describe the light of his life before that moment. But at that second in time, Sharlene, in her lustrous ivory gown, was not of this world. At the landing, she stopped to peer down at the child holding her hand and beamed a smile so intense and loving, Malcolm caught his breath.

Scotty wore his family tartan! Where! When! Ah yes. Keely, his dear, tormented sister must have sent it with the child's things. With Scotty's hair swept high and the kilt swinging neatly with her even steps, she looked older to him somehow. Suddenly, Scotty spotted him at the foot of the stairs and broke her tight clasp on Sharlene's hand. With a giant bound, she leaped at him and he caught her to his chest. Sharlene climbed down the remaining three steps and slipped her hand into his. Their friends parted, forming a loving gauntlet of pats and arm squeezes and words of best wishes as the three of them passed.

The group fell in behind them and entered the parlor where mysteriously, Reverend Dunbar had managed to find his place at the mantel to receive the threesome. Malcolm lowered the child to the hearth where she stood between them, each of them holding a hand. The guests seated themselves in the twin settees, wing back chairs and an ancient carved oaken bench with hammered iron supports and rivets. All of the seating had been arranged to face the blazing fireplace. Gray lowered the stereo volume and the pipes faded away. He sat down beside Laney in the Hamilton settee.

Kudzu meandered through the parlor, rubbed against Scotty's legs and then curled into a ball on the hearthrug in front of Reverend Dunbar. Scotty giggled, covering her mouth with her hand.

Reverend Dunbar began to read, "We are gathered here today to witness the marriage of Malcolm and Sharlene. They call upon their loved ones to share in this great and happy moment in their lives."

Begun months before, Malcolm and Sharlene had written the ceremony and had made many changes before they were satisfied with the content.

"Marriage is a beautiful and sacred relationship," Dunbar continued. "There is no other union that can result in the satisfaction and fulfillment of sharing, giving and closeness. Though love stands as the foundation of a happy and enduring home, it will grow and deepen if enhanced by each other's consideration, respect, responsibility, and the understanding that each is a unique individual."

Then Sharlene and Malcolm repeated in unison. "We are as two trees standing side by side. We may be as different as an oak and elm."

Malcolm's stared into Sharlene's smoky eyes and he continued alone, "Even though we share the sun and rain, and bend together with the wind, we come from separate seeds and grow and change with the seasons in our own way."

Then Sharlene replied, "Autumn comes, and though the oak turns scarlet and the elm is touched with gold, our branches touch."

The emotion that Malcolm felt transcended understanding and he suddenly had the strongest desire to kiss Sharlene's mouth. So he did.

"Uh . . . not now, Malcolm," Dunbar said and laughter trickled through the room.

An uncommon blush colored Sharlene's face, warming her gray eyes. Malcolm was tempted to repeat his kiss, but in a bashful diversion, Sharlene quickly handed her bouquet to Scotty and the moment passed.

Reverend Dunbar handed Malcolm and Sharlene the matching Celtic bands that Malcolm had ordered from Glasgow months before.

Their vows were brief, with no mention of obey.

When the rings were exchanged, Dunbar nodded at him and after a pause, Malcolm remembered what he'd almost forgotten. Wanting to appear gallant, but in fact, rather ineptly, he removed his sash and placed it around Sharlene and straightened it at her shoulder and snapped it at her waist. He bent to one knee.

"Sharlene," he said, his voice quivering with emotion, "I can think of no greater gift of my love than to share the tartan of my clan."

Obviously, he had taken her by surprise. Sharlene blinked away the tears. Her hands suddenly fingered the thistle brooch on her gown and without hesitation, she removed it from her shoulder and pinned it to the lapel of his jacket. She smiled. Perhaps the two of them would give it to Scotty on her wedding day, Malcolm thought.

Neither of them spoke. There was no need.

The ceremony about over, Malcolm nodded to the Reverend to remove a crown of dried heather and yellow roses streaming with ribbons from the mantle. Together, Malcolm and Sharlene placed it upon Scotty's head and kissed her flushed cheeks.

With everyone sniffling and smiling, Dunbar announced, "Sharlene and Malcolm are now husband and wife. You may kiss her again, Malcolm."

Malcolm did while everyone laughed.

"Malcolm and Sharlene invite you to their Ceilidh," Dunbar said, pronouncing the Gaelic word for celebration, "kay-lee."

This was Gray's cue to change the music to a CD of Celtic lilts and jigs. While everyone congratulated the couple, Malcolm introduced his new bride and Scotty to Barnaby and Elaine.

Laney and Jesse served the refreshments. Most had been prepared by a Scottish lady in Lexington who, when Laney had contacted her, seemed honored to have been asked, even on such short notice. She had delivered the food herself that afternoon.

A platter of hot Scotch pies—four-inch pastries filled with minced beef and onion—was placed beside another of thinly sliced smoked salmon. Varieties of crackers, scones, and cheeses that included several Cheddars from Galloway and a Crowdie—a simple white cheese made by the same Scottish lady, herself—were placed around the table in the dining room. Scotch bread, Malcolm's favorite, was the first food to catch his eye as he and Sharlene led their guests into the dining room.

"Woman, how did you ever pull this off in only three days?" Sharlene demanded grabbing Laney's arm on one of her trips back to the kitchen.

"It wasn't easy, my friend, but worth every tense moment. However, Jesse did most of the planning while Gray and I were in Indiana and Northern Kentucky."

Malcolm saw the shadow flicker across Sharlene's face. His arm tightened around her waist.

At one end of the table, the wedding cake called a Black Bun, bursting with raisins, currants, chopped almonds, finely chopped peel, and brown sugar waited for the bridal couple. As Malcolm held his hand over Sharlene's and they sliced it, releasing the aroma of ginger and cinnamon, Scotty tugged at Sharlene's skirt. When Sharlene bent to her, Scotty whispered into her ear. Sharlene nodded.

Malcolm served cake and champagne to all the guests and they were toasted again and again. But when next he looked, Sharlene and Scotty were gone.

A few moments later, the Celtic music abruptly stopped and Sharlene stood in the archway of the dining room, her bagpipes resting in her arms.

Everyone ceased talking. "Everyone . . . Malcolm, come," Sharlene said. She led him by the hand to the archway and guided the others to form a semi-circle around and behind him in the area where the staircase began.

She crossed to the other side of the entrance hall and raised the chanter to her mouth.

Wonderful! Malcolm thought, delighted that Sharlene was going to play in the presence of their friends for the first time.

He gave a start of surprise as Scotty walked out of the parlor and stopped in the center of the room. Her fists were perched on her hips while Sharlene played the beginning bars of the "Highland Fling." On the eighth count, Scotty bowed while Malcolm puzzled over Scotty's sequence of movements. Oh Lord, he thought with dismay, surely she wasn't going to try to dance the "Highland Fling!"

But that's exactly what she began to do. While Malcolm's mouth hung unattractively open, his niece performed the unique elements of the oldest traditional dance of Scotland. Arched arms. Grouped fingers. Flying feet in tempo. Beautiful form—graceful yet strong, expressive yet forceful.

But it was the intense rapture that lit up Scotty's face that captivated Malcolm as well as the others that watched. A quick glance to his left revealed Laney's eyes voluminous with wonder, and Gray shaking his head as though he needed to clear his mind to comprehend. Barnaby had tears streaming down his cheeks.

How had this come about? Malcolm wondered. But he pondered only an instant, because he knew instinctively that Scotty's performance wasn't the result of some fluke. His sister had accomplished this miracle by recognizing Scotty's talent early and finding the best instruction she could afford.

With Scotty's final bows, everyone applauded and rushed toward her. But Malcolm reached her first. With his bony knees crunching the hardwood floor, he swept Scotty close and didn't release her until Sharlene wiggled her way through the crush of admirers to share their embrace.

32

"Allow me to help you," Malcolm said, lifting the laundry basket filled with serving platters and bowls and following behind Jesse to her car that was idling at the gate.

"Thank you again," Shar called at the door and waved. She stood on the stoop while Malcolm loaded the basket into the trunk. The night was cold and clear and above her, the Milky Way spilled across the sky.

"Well, woman," she told herself, "you've gone and done it one more time." But unlike following her other weddings when she'd felt as though she had taken a luckless plunge into deep water without looking, she felt in her bones that marrying Malcolm was one of the right things she had done in her life. Who'd have thought it? Proper, decent, and dignified Malcolm pairing with raunchy, rough and mouthy Sharlene. I'll have to watch that mouth around Scotty, she thought.

Scotty. Seems as though she wasn't ever far from her thoughts. Earlier, she'd looked so adorable leaving with Laney and Gray. Exhausted, Scotty allowed Laney to dress her in the new nightgown, robe and slippers that Laney had bought for her. Gray carried her out, asleep on his shoulder, her coat flung over her against the cold. They had promised to keep her for the night so Scotty could help them make Blackberry and her family a new home in the pantry the following morning. But Shar knew they really just wanted to give Malcolm and her time alone tonight. Elaine and Barnaby followed

Laney and Gray to the bed and breakfast to also spend the night before driving back to Vevay in the morning.

Malcolm hurried back to Shar and had just closed the door when they heard a knock. Shar swung open the door. Jesse stood there shivering. "Shar, I forgot to tell you . . . Gordon is waiting to speak to you in the parlor."

While Jesse's fingers fluttered a goodbye, the sensation of the floor suddenly dropping from beneath her made Shar grasp Malcolm's arm.

"Mal, what could he want?" Shar said closing the door.

"I have no idea, but let's get this over with." Together, they walked into the parlor.

Gordon stood near the hearth stirring dying coals with a poker. He turned when they entered. "Forgive me," he said.

"For what?" Shar said sharply.

"For intruding on your wedding night." The smile lines on either side of Gordon's mouth cut deeply into his solemn face.

"Then it must be important for you to do so," Malcolm said, his face as humorless as the sheriff's.

"It is, but I must speak to Shar alone."

Malcolm opened his mouth to protest but Shar laid a restraining hand on his arm. "Mal, please go on up. I'll join you as soon as I hear what Gordon has to say." The Lamont sash slipped down from her shoulder.

Malcolm hesitated, his expression irresolute. He straightened her sash.

"Mal, please," Shar reiterated.

Malcolm kissed her on the mouth, quickly turned on his heel and left the room.

"Would you like a drink, Sheriff?" Shar walked to the wet bar. "Or are you on duty?" she asked acerbically.

"No, to both questions. I'd just rather not. You go ahead."

She poured two fingers of vodka over ice and filled the rest with Bloody Mary mix. She took a long swallow and replenished the glass with vodka. She swung to face Gordon. "Let's get on with it, Sheriff." She swept to the Hamilton settee and sat. "Do sit down." She gestured to the other settee.

"Shar, I'm just doing my job," he said defensively, obviously referring to how she addressed him. He pulled a notebook from his coat pocket and a pen from the spiral.

"Then do it, Sheriff."

He sat down and ran his fingers through his blond crewcut. "Detective Grossman from the Carroll County Sheriff's Department called me this morning." He looked up briefly.

"Yes?"

His eyes dropped back to his notes. "Two nights ago, a man named Frank Rice was shot near Carrollton. He died early this morning. A gas station attendant near Milton reported that a woman fitting your description had asked for directions to Rice's house just an hour before he was found."

"There must be a lot of people that look like me, Sheriff."

"You are a striking woman, Shar. He looked at her and smiled nervously. "The attendant said the woman had a strawberry blond pixie cut and was about six feet tall. Unusual height for a woman, wouldn't you say?"

"Ask the U.S Women's Olympic Basketball Team," she snapped and gulped nervously at her drink. It sloshed over the brim of her glass and soaked like blood onto her wedding gown. She wanted to cry.

"Normally I wouldn't have associated the woman's description with you but it just so happens that Laney and Gray were the ones who found Frank Rice. They were visiting him because he was a close acquaintance of your husband's late sister, Keely Moore."

"What does that have to do with me?"

"In the recent past, it seems wherever we find Laney McVey, you aren't too far away."

Shar leaped to her feet in anger. "That's the most shameless deduction I've ever heard! Sheriff, I think it's time for you to leave."

Gordon stood and pocketed his notebook. "Shar, I'm sorry. Please . . . go to Malcolm."

She turned to leave. "Let yourself out." She took two steps.

"Shar."

Hearing her name, she spun to face him.

"I must call Detective Grossman . . . please, just one question."

"Yes," she said icily while feeling sweat forming under her arms.

"Did you know a man named Frank Rice?"

"No," she answered honestly.

Shar undressed in the room where she had slept ever since Scotty's arrival the Saturday before. She laid the dress and sash next to Scotty's kilt on her twin bed where Laney had left them. The red spill on her gown had dried to a brown stain. Scotty's guillies and hose were tossed haphazardly on the floor.

She showered and as the stream flowed over her body, her hands found her narrow waist, jutting hips and small, firm breasts. Don't think about the hearing tomorrow, she thought. Malcolm is waiting. Tonight is for us.

She dressed in the sheer peignoir she had bought just for this night. As it fell over her head, she spotted her image in the mirror and it reflected an oppressive spirit that felt no passion, no eager anticipation.

Heavy-footed, she walked the hallway to his room but faltered at the door. She thought of returning to her room but finally turned the knob softly and entered.

The nightlight glowed like a shining planet on the wall next to Malcolm's bed. He was still as though asleep, but she knew he was wide-awake and waiting.

She slipped between the sheets and his arms gathered her to him and tucked the down comforter around her shoulders. He whispered her name and folded her into the cocoon created by the curve of his lean form.

"Just sleep," he murmured, his hand caressing the nape of her neck. "We have a lifetime to love."

33

"Gray, we've got to help them!" Laney whispered loudly, pounding the steering wheel of the Whooptie so hard that she hurt her hand. She quickly checked the sleeping Scotty in the rearview mirror. They were on their way back to Taylor Ridge after keeping the child overnight. After moving Blackberry and her pups to the pantry, Scotty had showed Barnaby and Elaine her stuffed airplane and had allowed Barnaby to read from *The Wee Scotch Piper* that she had stowed in her little red backpack Laney had bought her along with her nightclothes. After one of Laney's hearty breakfasts, the couple left for Vevay.

"What can we do?" Gray whispered. "The hearing is at one. You heard what Marshall told Shar and Malcolm. Without a will specifying that Malcolm would be Keely's preference for guardian should anything happen to her, the court would most likely award the child to Bonnie and Dwayne."

"As soon as we get to Taylor Ridge, I'm marching back out into the barn and search through more boxes."

"Laney, I can't imagine Keely putting a will into a cardboard box, even if she did write one."

"Well it sure doesn't look like she put one into a lock box somewhere."

"What about her boyfriend, Frank Rice? Maybe Keely gave him a will for safe keeping."

"Then we've just run out of luck . . . unless . . ."

"Forget it, Laney! The cops are probably crawling all over Frank's place. And after hearing from Shar about Gordon's questioning last night, it sounds as though they already have her under suspicion. It wouldn't do for you to be snooping around."

"It's just not fair. Scotty belongs with them. If she goes to Bonnie and Dwayne, Malcolm and Shar will just lose it," Laney said, swinging into the driveway where the mailman was just pulling away from the Taylor Ridge mailbox.

Scotty's head popped up. "I get it," she said, unfastening her seatbelt. Laney stopped the car and Scotty hopped out of the back seat and scurried to the box. On tiptoes, she could just manage to pull down the lid and retrieve the bundle of mail held together with a rubber band.

"That's a big girl," Gray said, as she climbed back into the Whooptie.

The newlyweds met them at the door and hugged Scotty like it was the last time they would see her. The strain on Malcolm's and Shar's faces foreshadowed the ordeal ahead of them. With a final hug, they ran out to the Oldsmobile as though they were afraid they would break down in front of her.

Gray glumly fixed himself a bourbon and water and retired to Malcolm's den to cancel his calls for the afternoon. When Natine reminded him that he had only worked two half days in the past week, he snapped at her.

Laney heated up a leftover Scotch pie and sliced up an apple for Scotty, but for some reason, she had lost her appetite. While Gray flipped TV channels in the den, Laney and Scotty climbed the stairs to straighten Scotty's room. Laney laid Shar's wedding dress over the banister to be dropped off at the cleaners on the way back to the house. She hung up Scotty's kilt and vest and dropped the blouse and hose into the bathroom hamper. Scotty curled up on her bed with her thumb in her mouth and the plane clutched in her fingers. Kudzu purred beside her.

"Do you feel all right, Scotty?" Laney asked and felt Scotty's forehead. She didn't seem to have a fever.

Scotty unplugged her thumb. "I dinna want to go away," she said, her husky voice faint and sad, her eyes dull.

Oh God, Laney thought, maybe she heard us talking in the car while we thought she was sleeping.

"You will never go away," Laney said with more conviction than she felt. She smoothed Scotty's brow and as though Laney's statement alone had soothed her, her eyes closed in sleep.

34

Shar, Malcolm and Marshall Knight waited in the circuit court on the second floor of the St. Clair County Courthouse. They sat in uncomfortable, vintage oak chairs behind a long desk to the left of the bench. Across the room and behind the empty jury box, elongated windows bathed the room in a cold white light of a northern exposure.

Shar shivered and tensed as three people passed by their table. She recognized Bonnie Day by the woman's excessive gesturing that had set her apart from the other mourners at Keely's funeral and luncheon and the repulsive fox scarf still lolling at the lapels of a purple pantsuit. She was speaking with two men, one an older gentleman carrying a worn briefcase and a second man with raven-black hair and mustache who Shar assumed must be Bonnie's husband, Dwayne.

An attractive man with a dramatic persona, Dwayne, expressed the apparent oppressive tediousness of his wife's remarks by rolling his eyes upward from time to time as they walked slowly across the arena. For someone who had spent less than a minute in Dwayne's presence, Shar was strangely in tune with his assessment of his wife.

The threesome seated themselves in a second arrangement of desk and chairs to the right of the bench. Bonnie's attention suddenly focused on Malcolm. Shar could have knocked her husband in the chops for nodding at the woman. But what else would conventional and agreeable Mal do? Shar thought. Mostly incapable of malice in any form, if introduced to the devil, himself, Malcolm would probably smile and hold out his hand.

A uniformed court officer entered the room from a door to the left of the bench. "All rise," he said.

Shakily, Shar stood, clutching Malcolm's hand for support as Judge Homer Peters entered the courtroom. Oh God, here goes, Shar thought, thinking of Scotty at home with Laney and Gray.

"This is a highly unusual case," Judge Peters began. "Bonnie Moore Day, aunt, and Malcolm Lamont, uncle, have separately petitioned the court for the guardianship of Scotty Moore, age five."

He addressed the attorneys. "Mr. Wells and Mr. Knight, I understand that since both of Scotty Moore's parents are deceased and the petitioners are the only living relatives of Scotty Moore, Mrs. Day and Mr. Lamont have signed a waiver of the twenty-day notice of this hearing."

Both attorneys signified their assent and the court room clerk showed the signed waver to the judge.

"I see that all other documents have been signed and the filing fees paid." Judge Peters shuffled a small stack of papers that the clerk had handed him. "Have the attorneys informed their clients that this hearing is for assigning the temporary guardianship of the child only?" the judge asked.

Again the lawyers assented.

"Normally, the child is present, but in the interest of privacy and the possible emotional harm to the child in question, I have closed the courtroom to the public and have asked that the child not appear. Mr. Wells, I understand you are counselor for Bonnie Day. Am I correct?"

Attorney David Wells got to his feet, "I am, Your Honor."

"Make your opening statement brief," the judge said. He folded his hands over his belly and shut his eyes behind his reading glasses. To Shar, he appeared to be dozing, but she discovered quickly that he was quite alert to what was occurring in his courtroom by his comment after ten minutes of Wells expounding the advantages of living in the home of Bonnie and Dwayne Day.

"I said, 'brief,'" the judge reminded Wells, and the attorney slipped in a couple more accolades for the Days before sitting down.

"Mr. Knight, attorney for Malcolm Lamont," Judge Peters said, "see that you do a better job of restraining your glowing praise for the petitioner."

"Yes, Your Honor," Marshall said, standing. He took a couple steps toward the bench.

"I wasn't aware that it was raining," the judge said, trying to hold back a chuckle when he saw Marshall's flapping galoshes.

"No, Your Honor, but there is a chance of precipitation by nightfall." He combed his fingers through his straggly gray hair and straightened his bow tie.

"Proceed, Mr. Knight." Peters closed his eyes.

Marshall cleared his throat. "I have but one comment for the court. Seldom have I seen a child entrench herself into a household of four hearts so quickly and consummately."

Judge Peters' eyes clicked open. "Uh, four hearts, Mr. Knight?"

"Malcolm, Sharlene and the family pets, Your Honor—a cat named Kudzu and a West Highland Terrier called Nessie." Marshall shuffled back to the table and sat down.

At the other table, Bonnie tittered behind her hand.

"The court thanks you, Mr. Knight." Judge Peters turned to Bonnie. "Mrs. Day, you were the first to petition the court. I would like to ask a few questions. Would you take the stand, please?"

Bonnie moved to the enclosed area next to the bench.

"I understand the child has been living with her uncle, Malcolm Lamont, since just before her mother's death."

"That's correct, Your Honor, but Dwayne and I would have taken the child immediately but Dwayne thought we should do it legally through the courts." She smiled condescendingly at the judge.

"Mrs. Day, how could you provide proper care and guidance for Scotty if you were appointed guardian?"

"Your Honor, Dwayne and I have been married for seven years and are good church-going people. We're not wealthy, but we could provide a stable environment . . . and God knows she hasn't had much stability up to now."

Marshall Knight started to his feet but the judge gave him a peremptory gesture.

"Your Honor," Bonnie continued, "we would do everything in our power to give her the best upbringing we possibly could and certainly the best schooling we could afford." She sniffled. "You see, Dwayne and I have never been blessed with children. I'm sure that Scotty's father, who was my dear brother, and dear Keely—God rest their souls—would want us to be the new parents of little Scotty. We would love her as our very own child."

Shar saw the glisten of real tears in Bonnie's eyes. Damn, Mal really has his job cut out for him, Shar thought as the judge excused Bonnie and Malcolm took the stand.

"The same question, Mr. Lamont. How could you provide proper care and guidance for Scotty if you were appointed guardian?"

Malcolm looked uncomfortable behind his spectacles. He cleared his throat. "Uh . . . Your Honor, financially I am able to provide for the child. But more importantly, we already have a bond that would last, a bond of love and heritage."

"How is that?" the judge probed.

"Your Honor, Scotty and I have strong Scottish roots. She was born in Scotland and only arrived in the U.S. last year. I was also born there. If you could have seen the child at the wedding yesterday." His eyes ignited like sparklers. "Sharlene played the bagpipes and Scotty danced the "Highland Fling" with a jubilant heart."

Shar watched a subtle smile on Attorney David Well's face slowly grow into an ear-to-ear grin.

Oh Mal, don't mention the wedding! Shar screamed inside, but knew instantly it was too late.

"Wedding?" Judge Peter's queried. He peered at a document in front of him. It's stated here that you were only engaged to be married . . . 'a Christmas wedding planned,' it says."

"I was, Your Honor . . . at the time I signed the petition, but Sharlene Hamilton and I were married yesterday."

The judge raised his brows but didn't comment.

"Your Honor," Bonnie's lawyer interjected. "May I address the court?"

"Only if it is relevant to this testimony."

"It is, Your Honor. It's evident that Mr. Lamont rushed his nuptials in order to appear to have a stable home situation in time for this hearing, however, the court should be aware that this is Sharlene Hamilton's fourth marriage."

Shar's head fell into her hands and she lamented quietly, "Down the tubes."

Laney unzipped Scotty's red backpack and hung her nightgown and robe on a hook in the bathroom. She dropped the Mickey Mouse slippers below and placed her toothbrush into the holder on the vanity wall. When she checked another compartment, she discovered the stack of mail secured with a rubber band that Scotty had retrieved from the mailbox and smiled that she had placed it inside her pack.

Scotty was still sleeping soundly so she went downstairs to join Gray in the den.

"Where's Scotty?" Gray asked as she entered.

"Sleeping. Gray, I think she heard us talking in the car."

"Oh, no."

"She told me she didn't want to go away."

"Shit. She doesn't need this."

"No . . . nor does Malcolm and Shar." She tossed the stack of mail on the desk. "I wonder how the hearing is going." She took a swig of Gray's bourbon and water that was leaving a ring of condensation on Malcolm's blotter. Her eyes rested for a moment on the stack of mail.

Gray flipped to "The Young and the Restless."

"Gray!"

"Hmm."

"Look at this!" Laney ripped the rubber band off the pile of mail.

"Laney, for God's sake, don't be tampering with Malcolm's mail." He snapped back the lever of the recliner.

"Gray, this envelope . . . the return address! It's from Frank Rice!" Laney waved the fat white envelope in front of him.

"A letter from a dead man?"

"It's postmarked two days ago, the day he was shot."

She lifted the silver letter opener off the blotter.

"Laney, you can't!"

"Wanna bet?" She slid the point under the flap and ripped.

"Dammit, you have no right! It's addressed to Malcolm." He reached for it but she twisted away and dashed across the room away from him.

Her back to Gray, she peered inside. It contained a large envelope and a single sheet of paper. She reached for the envelope.

There was no mistaking the words that shot out at her like a slingshot. "Gray, it's Keely's will!" She danced around the den with Gray trying to keep up with her.

"Laney, come down to earth and open the damn thing."

"Oh thou who woust not allow fair maiden to open sweet missive?" she mocked. "Oh God, pray let there something about guardianship," she said, tearing it open.

They speed read, skipping words and phrases, even sentences.

Laney found it first and she drank in the words that soothed like warm, sweet honey on a raw throat.

Tears of joy spurted from their eyes. They hugged and jumped and danced, until Gray suddenly stopped dead and looked at his watch.

"Get Scotty, while I call the courthouse," Gray said. "Let's just hope to hell we're not too late."

35

Gray called Malcolm repeatedly, but got no answer. Figuring that Malcolm had turned off his cell phone while in the hearing, Gray dialed the Circuit Court Clerk's office in the St. Clair County Courthouse. When he got a busy signal, Gray assumed it was because of the heavy docket just before Thanksgiving recess. While Laney drove toward Hickory and Scotty sucked obliviously on her thumb in the back seat, Gray dialed the two numbers alternately. Finally, he managed to get through to the clerk's office just as they turned into Court Row, a narrow street on the south side of the courthouse.

After explaining to Madeline Grayson, the Circuit Court Clerk, that he had a document that could affect the outcome of the hearing, Madeline told him she would try to get a message to Judge Peters, but made no promises. Familiar with the guardianship case and very sympathetic with Gray's position, she added that unless it was because of an act of God, the judge frowned on any interruptions while court was in session.

Laney double-parked outside the courthouse and for once, Gray didn't say a word even though the Whooptie had one of the sheriff department's patrol cars blocked in. Scrambling out of the front seat, Laney held the back door open for Scotty.

Gray lifted Scotty onto his shoulders while Laney took the stairs two at a time. Just as they approached the clerk's office, Madeline rushed out the door.

"I was just on my way to my execution," she said, waving a note for the judge at Laney.

Laney slapped the will into her hand. "Maybe he'll only wound you if you give him this."

Madeline looked down at the writing on the envelope and then up at Scotty who was holding onto Gray's hair for dear life. She smiled at them. "I only wish I could admit you, but the hearing is closed to the public. No harm in waiting just outside the courtroom though. She crossed her fingers, took a deep breath and disappeared up the long flight of stairs to the second floor.

Judge Peters' response to Attorney Wells' reference to Shar's many marriages was brief and firm. "Mr. Wells, I will not turn this courtroom into a battlefield for warring parties." A spasm of irritation crossed the judge's face. "The child's best interest is the court's primary concern in this guardianship case and the character of each of the petitioners will come out in due time."

Shar sneaked a glance at Bonnie and Dwayne.

Bonnie's mouth had tightened into a stubborn line but Dwayne's had curled with indignation as though the judge had reprimanded him personally. He combed his mustache nervously with his fingertips, turned to their lawyer and whispered behind his hand.

Madeline Grayson entered the courtroom and crooked her finger at the bailiff. They met at the bar where there was an exchange of whispers. The officer looked at the envelope in her hand and shook his head slowly but took it and gave it to Judge Peters.

"Ms. Grayson, has there been a nuclear meltdown or other such catastrophe? If so, I shall clear the courtroom," Judge Peters said to Madeline caustically. He peered over his half glasses with eyes that could paralyze.

"Your Honor," she mumbled, "I thought it of the greatest importance . . . I'm sorry," Madeline slunk out of the courtroom.

"What if it's a warrant for my arrest?" Shar whispered to Malcolm and he clutched her cold hands in his.

The judge took the plump envelope from the clerk. He studied it for but a second. "The court will take a five minute recess."

"All rise," the bailiff just managed to say before Judge Homer Peters—his robe flapping about his pant legs like the wings of a blackbird— swept from the courtroom

"Do we have time to call Scotty?" Shar asked Malcolm as she glanced at the wall clock over the Judge's bench. They stood at one of the long windows behind the jury box.

"Maybe." He turned on his cell phone and punched in the number.

As they waited, Shar stared out at Bank Row. A meter maid was writing out a ticket for a white Nissan that was double-parked behind a patrol car.

"The Whooptie!" Shar cried, spinning away from the window as Malcolm turned off his phone. "That's why you can't get hold of Laney. She's here, Mal. Those papers Madeline rushed to the judge . . . The cops must have found out about Simon and she's here to warn me. It's the beginning of the end, Mal! I know it!"

Marshall motioned to them to return to their seats.

"All rise," the bailiff called.

Malcolm put his arm around Shar's waist and held her close to him as the judge reentered the courtroom carrying a document.

After everyone resumed their seats, Judge Peters briefly looked over his glasses and said. "This clause is from the last will and testament of Keely Moore:"

> *If any child of mine is under the age of majority at my death,*
> *I hereby nominate, constitute and appoint my brother, Malcolm*
> *Lamont, currently residing at Taylor Ridge Farm on Squire*
> *Road in St. Clair County in the Commonwealth of Kentucky,*
> *U.S.A., as the guardian of each child of mine.*

Gasps were heard from both tables. Malcolm was on his feet, pulling Shar into his arms. Tears rained down his face, mingling with Shar's.

"No!" Dwayne spat involuntarily, then threw up his hands in disgusted resignation. Beside him, Bonnie sat rigidly, her expression stoic and unreadable.

"This court is still in session!" Judge Peters stated fiercely, his gavel cracking sharply. When the courtroom quieted, the judge continued reading from the will:

> *If this person for any reason, shall fail to qualify or cease to act as such guardian, I hereby nominate, constitute and appoint my sister-in-law, Bonnie Moore Day, currently residing in Switzerland County in the state of Indiana, U.S.A., as successor guardian.*

Dwayne's lips that had been pursed with suppressed fury, slid into a smirk.

Peters laid down the will and spoke to the court. "When a child's parent nominates a person as guardian in her will, the court gives first consideration to the person named, especially when the person named has already petitioned the court requesting the child. However, children aren't property that one can pass on to someone. A parent can only recommend that the court appoint the guardian she prefers.

In this county, we have a social services agency that screens proposed guardians for history of abuse or neglect. If I am satisfied with their report, I will issue permanent guardianship of Scotty Moore to Malcolm Lamont. Until that time, and since the child has been living in the Lamont household since her mother's death, the child will remain with them. This court is adjourned."

Shar swore that when Judge Peters banged his gavel, the sound pealed like church bells through the courtroom.

36

"Woman, thank you for being so indescribably wicked. If you hadn't opened Malcolm's mail, Scotty wouldn't be sleeping between her Spitfires and Messerschmitts upstairs," Shar said, her eyes wet with good will toward her friend.

They sat in the breakfast nook. Laney and Gray had followed them home after the hearing and they had eaten leftovers, including the rest of the Black Bun fruitcake.

"This was like enjoying our wedding dinner all over again," Shar said as she refilled everyone's liqueur glass with Old Bailey's.

"Malcolm, will you join me in one last toast?" Gray asked. The two men held up their glasses. "To the most incorrigible wenches we have ever known," Gray said.

Malcolm, who was a bit tipsy from the Scotch he had drunk before dinner and the wine he had consumed with his meal, added. "May they remain forever naughty." He winked at Shar.

"I think it's time we leave," Laney said. "I'll get our coats." She dashed into the den while Gray helped Shar and Malcolm put the dishes into the dishwasher.

Laney zipped up her green suede jacket and felt for Simon's envelope that contained his letter. She had found it on the den floor where she had dropped it after discovering Keely's will. When they arrived back at Taylor Ridge, she had tucked it into her pocket when Shar wasn't looking. Laney reasoned that she needn't bother the newlyweds with the letter tonight. Let them have some happy moments without the worry of whatever Simon had written before he was murdered. Laney patted her pocket and retrieved Gray's worn leather jacket. She hadn't had time to read it herself, but there would be plenty of time for her and Gray to read Simon's final words, she thought wistfully. Gray's toast came to mind. After all, she had to live up to her reputation, didn't she?

Scotty lay on her side, her favorite things around her—the plush plane, Kudzu, and Nessie. Her rosebud mouth twitched as though pulling at her thumb but the digit was dry.

Shar bent and kissed Scotty's forehead. "Mal," she whispered to him standing beside her in the dim light of the bedroom, "am I foolish to think that we can have her forever?"

Malcolm kissed his two fingers and rested them on Scotty's cheek for a moment. He motioned for Shar to follow him out of the room. Once in the hall, he took her hand and led her to their bedroom, closing the door behind them.

Cupping her face, he ran his thumbs across her cheeks and kissed her mouth. When he finally pulled his lips from hers, his eyes narrowed to tiny points that seemed to pierce her very soul. "Sharlene, I will make you a promise. No matter what the court finally decides, no one will ever take this child from us. I swear it."

The resolution in his eyes both frightened and assuaged her. What would Malcolm do if she was arrested and the court ruled to take Scotty away from them? Would he forsake his high principles, take the child and run? It was a question best left unanswered for now. It was enough that he felt as she did, that God's will had brought Scotty to them and mere destiny could not take her away.

37

"Twice in one day, Laney? Malcolm and I underestimated the extent of your unscrupulousness," Gray said as he climbed into bed.

Laney, propped against several pillows, had just pulled Simon's letter from the envelope.

"Admit it, thou without sin or guilt, you're dying to read Simon's letter." She waved it in front of him. "I just felt that Shar and Malcolm needed a night to themselves."

"We could also use a night to ourselves," he said in a hurtful tone.

"Okay." She folded it and tucked it under her pillow. She turned off the bedside lamp. All was dark. Neither moved. Neither spoke.

Several minutes passed.

"Laney."

"Hm?"

"What do you think Simon said?"

She giggled.

A minute later, they both were devouring the letter. Laney read aloud:

> *Dear Malcolm,*
> *I am sorry for the delay getting Keely's will to you. She left it in my self-keeping last summer with the instructions to get it to you in the event of her death. She told me that it had been pre-*

pared by a solicitor in Edinburgh before she moved to the U.S. At the time she gave it to me, I never thought that anything would take her from us so soon.

Now, I must add something you won't want to hear. In recent months, Keely had been exhibiting very anxious, even fearful, behavior. While we were living in Florida, on several occasions I overheard her making inquiries into certain people's whereabouts on a particular day five years ago. Phone calls to Scotland, Indiana, and Kentucky appeared frequently on our phone statement. I confronted her and she told me that she believed her late husband had been murdered. She did not know for certain why someone would want him dead, but did recall what Ray's mother had once told him, that thanks to Victor, Scotty would be well taken care of someday. Keely fretted over the possibility that Ray might have told someone other than herself of this conversation and the person might believe Ray owned something of value. According to Keely, Ray loved to tell tall tales and he often stretched the truth. Unfortunately, Mabel died before revealing what Victor owned of value, if anything at all. The conversation may just have been the ramblings of an old lady. Mabel did not die a wealthy woman.

Devastated by Keely's death, days passed before I could think clearly enough to follow up on some of the information that Keely had gathered. It's all making alarming sense to me now. Ray's death was not an accident! I'm sure of it. Naturally, I'm thinking that if someone killed Ray, the same person may have decided Keely was getting too close to the truth and killed her too.

Tomorrow I am going to the police.
Frank

"Laney, do you know what this means?"

"It means a lot of things—first, that Simon may also have gotten too close to the truth and was eliminated."

"Hell, it means more than that." Gray frowned. "Think seriously about this, Laney. Ray and Keely's murders were made to look like accidents, but whoever killed Simon just didn't care if it looked deliberate or not. The murderer is getting careless which means he or she is getting scared, maybe desperate."

A quick shiver ran through Laney. She looked down at the letter. "This confirms what we suspected, that Victor may have had something of value."

"Stamps."

"Yes, the motive behind Ray's murder."

"But the way Ray died . . . trapped in that horse stall. How could the murderer acquire the stamps that way?"

"The letter said Ray liked to fabricate stories. He could have told someone he had something valuable hidden somewhere. Hell, for all we know, Mabel may have even told Ray they were stamps. The murderer could have killed Ray and then searched where Ray bragged he had them stashed. The killer didn't find them though. That much we know for sure."

Laney yawned and turned out the lamp. She heard Puccini purring at the foot of the bed. "Gray, don't you wonder what information Keely had gathered?"

"No!" His loud voice stopped Puccini's motor. "It got Keely killed and Simon too. Which brings me to the first order of business in the morning. This letter goes to the police."

"It's Malcolm's letter."

"Could have fooled me."

38

"Malcolm will do the right thing," Laney said to Gray while she maneuvered the Whooptie into a parking slot in front of a grimy building on Main Street. For the first time in a long time, the car didn't stall on her.

"Even if it results in Shar's arrest?"

"It won't happen."

"Tell that to the police. Shar was the last one to see Simon alive."

"There they are," Laney said, really not wanting to hear any more. "I'll give it to Malcolm and be right back with Scotty." She grabbed the letter off the dash.

Shar, Malcolm and Scotty were climbing out of the Oldsmobile that was parked two cars down from the Whooptie. When Scotty spotted Laney, she gave her a sunny smile. Laney only wished that the expressions on Malcolm's and Shar's faces were as welcoming, but she had expected that they would be upset from their reaction when earlier, Laney had read the letter to them over the phone. Shar had sobbed and Malcolm had quickly rung off to comfort his wife.

Laney handed Simon's letter to Malcolm. "I hate this, Malcolm."

"Not as much as we," he said, "but we need to disclose all of it. No one is safe until we do," he whispered into Laney's ear. The protective way he rested his hand on Scotty's head indicated that he worried that the child might become prey for the killer.

"Take good care of her," was his final comment before he and Shar climbed the narrow stairs to the office where Attorney Marshall U. Knight waited for them.

Marshall had cleared two appointments from his calendar after Malcolm, his voice frantic and breaking over the phone, had told him that he and Sharlene needed to see him immediately. Marshall was only on his second cigarette of the day when his secretary showed them into his office. The seriousness of the problem was etched on their faces and they clung to each other's hands as though they would collapse if separated.

As quickly as possible, Malcolm told Marshall that Laney and Gray had discovered Keely's fiancé shot and bleeding on the second floor of his house on Riverview Farm in Northern Kentucky.

"This is about Gray and Laney?" Marshall inquired, stubbing out his cigarette. Smoke fogged the room.

"No," said Malcolm. "This is about Sharlene. Sheriff Gordon Powell questioned Sharlene after the wedding. He wanted to know whether she knew Frank Rice, because someone fitting her description had asked for directions to Rice's house just about the time of the shooting.

Marshall asked, "What did you reply, Sharlene?"

"I told him 'no.'" Shar licked her dry lips and shifted her feet.

"Did you lie to the sheriff, Sharlene?"

"Not exactly."

"I can't help you," Marshall said, getting to his feet. He opened the door to his reception area in dismissal.

"Sharlene," Malcolm said. "We said we would tell Marshall all of it."

"Nothing will leave this room if you don't want it to," Marshall said.

Shar stared at her hands and nodded. Marshall shut the door.

She raised her face to the dingy overhead light, its meager glow somehow gratifying in the drab room.

"I knew Frank Rice. He was my second husband. He died five years ago in a plane crash."

"I beg your pardon," Marshall said.

"His name was Simon Anderson then. He faked his death and took the name, Frank Rice."

"Oh my goodness," was all Marshall could reply to Shar's extraordinary statement.

Shar told Marshall about the phone call from a woman telling her that Simon was alive and then later receiving the photograph. She passed the picture to him.

"This is not conclusive evidence that this man was Simon," Marshall said.

"I wasn't exactly sure of it myself until I recognized his voice on Laney's answering machine. Then, I was positive it was Simon."

"So you—" Marshall led her.

"Decided to see for myself."

"You were angry?"

"I was pissed." She thought a second and her eyes narrowed. "Frothing! Raging!"

"Ahem . . ."

"Look, Marshall, he had put me through hell and he had been living with my fiancé's sister before she was murdered."

"Murdered?"

"Mal, give him the letter," Shar ordered.

Malcolm handed it over a pile of documents teetering on Marshall's desk.

Marshall read while Shar regarded him through anxious eyes.

By the time Marshall had finished, he had paled considerably. "Do you know what this item of value was that Victor possessed?"

"Rare stamps," Malcolm uttered and he told Marshall about Laney's investigation in Vevay that made them believe that Victor may have gotten hold of some Jenny Inverts while he was associated with the post office in Washington, D.C.

"At this point, I'm more interested in what you found when you arrived at Frank's house," Marshall said.

"Simon."

"How did you get into the house?"

"The front door was open."

"Did he recognize you?"

"Yes."

"What did you do?"

"Are you asking me if I shot him?"

"Yes." Marshall's eyes never wavered as he waited for her answer.

"No."

"What *did* you do when you saw him?"

"I called 911."

"Did you touch anything?"

She turned and looked at Malcolm and he nodded.

"I used a tissue to handle the phone and I took a box of items that proves that Simon changed his identity."

"Do you still have them?"

"Yes."

"Why didn't you go to the police?"

Shar didn't answer.

"Simon died the following day," Malcolm answered for Shar. "We were afraid she would be charged with murder." He wrapped Shar's hands in his, pulled them to his mouth and held them there.

Marshall looked troubled. "Shar, I don't want to frighten you but what better reason to kill Simon than pure revenge for what he had done to you?"

Shar stared saucer-eyed at him. "But I didn't!" Her voice was shrill as a siren.

"A second motive is perhaps even more incriminating," Marshall said. "If you had told the police that you were in Simon's house about the time he was shot, the court may have refused to allow Malcolm temporary guardianship of Scotty. It must have also occurred to you that if Simon were alive, you would still be legally married and couldn't marry Malcolm."

"Yes."

"Marshall, when we give this letter to the police, won't it suggest that the person who killed Ray and Keely also murdered Simon Anderson?" Malcolm said.

"Not necessarily." Marshall lifted the letter. "Granted, it would be difficult to connect those two killings to Sharlene. She had never met Ray or Keely. But the motive and opportunity to kill Simon aren't going away unless the real killer surfaces. That reminds me, did the police find the murder weapon?"

"No," Shar said quickly.

A little too quickly, Marshall thought. "Sharlene, did you see the gun?"

"Of course she didn't," Malcolm answered testily.

"Mal . . ." Shar began, but wouldn't look him in the eye. Instead, she chipped away at a fingernail.

It was so quiet in the room, Marshall could hear his pulse throbbing in his temples. Again he asked her, "The gun, Sharlene?'

Shar spun out of her chair and started for the door as though she would exit, but instead she stopped and pivoted. "The gun was on the floor next to Simon's bed."

"Sharlene!" Malcolm was aghast.

Marshall exploded. "You took the gun? Why?"

"Sharlene, it could have been a suicide attempt." Malcolm said.

"It wasn't."

Marshall waited for her to explain.

"The bullet had entered his right temple."

He waited.

"Simon was left-handed. He was lying on his left arm."

Marshall's lips parted at her perceptive insight. "But why take the gun, Sharlene?"

"It looked like the same thirty-eight I had given Simon on his birthday six years ago. That gun was registered in my name."

Marshall sighed and reached for his cigarette pack. If he could get Shar out of this one, it would be a miracle. "Where's the gun now?" he asked.

"In the Ohio River."

39

Instead of going to breakfast with Laney and Scotty, Gray insisted that Laney drop him off at the clinic. "If I don't get back to work, I'm going to lose clients," he explained. "I won't starve. Natine always makes coffee and last time I looked, there were a couple of stale donuts in my desk drawer. He reached into the back seat and playfully bored a forefinger into Scotty's belly before leaving the Whooptie. Her bubbly laughter buoyed up Laney's spirits.

The day was absolutely heavenly. Indian summer, Laney thought. It happened often in Kentucky—a few days of mild weather in late fall. Every bit of the snow had disappeared and the temperature was already in the sixties. She rolled down the window and the sunny clean air made her almost believe it was spring.

Laney drove to the Finish Line. The restaurant was Laney's favorite spot to eat. As they exited the car, they heard the drone of a plane.

"Look Scotty," Laney said pointing overhead. "An ultra-light."

Scotty squealed.

"The pilot sits under the wings and flies just like a bird."

"I want to do it." The blue of Scotty's eyes rivaled the sky.

"Perhaps you will some day." They watched until the plane disappeared, probably returning to the Georgetown Airport in the next county.

"Entering the restaurant, Laney saw that the two tables of regulars known as the "breakfast club" were just breaking up to go to work or to the retiree bench in front of the courthouse. They all chatted briefly and she introduced Scotty around. She automatically searched the dining room for her friend, Jesse, then remembered she usually didn't work until afternoon. Another waitress dressed in yellow jockey silks and cap seated them in front of a window and took their orders.

Scotty made short work of the silver dollar pancakes while Laney, not particularly hungry, nibbled a grilled biscuit and drank three cups of coffee.

Laney was thinking of Shar and Malcolm, who at that very moment were unloading on Marshall Knight. What in heaven would Marshall think when Shar showed him Simon's letter and admitted she had been the person who had found him bleeding, possibly only minutes after he had been shot. This time, Laney wasn't so sure the eccentric little attorney could prevent Shar from being the number one suspect in Simon's murder.

She looked over at Scotty who was licking strawberry preserves off of a thumb that had helped shovel the pancakes onto her fork. Scotty hadn't cared for the traditional maple syrup topping.

What if Shar was charged with Simon's murder and arrested? Laney thought, her meager breakfast beginning to toss. Would the court award Scotty to Bonnie Day? Oh God, no!

If only she could find those blasted stamps! She was sure they would ferret out the killer. What *had* Mabel done with them?

"I want to see the wee pups now," Scotty said, her bright smile red and sticky.

Laney dipped a corner of her napkin into her glass of ice water and wiped Scotty's face. "Let's do it," Laney said. She paid the tab and brooded about the stamps all the way home.

The phone was ringing as she let herself into the house. Blackberry sat by the front door. "Let her out, Scotty," she called, dashing into the library.

The caller was Barnaby. "Laney, I've been trying to get you all morning. The weather is glorious and I am planning to take the Jenny up tomorrow if the weather holds. I thought maybe everyone could come up to see her fly. I will even taxi Scotty around the runway beforehand. Do you think she would like that?"

"She would love it! I'll check with Shar and Malcolm and let you know. What time is the big event?"

"Early afternoon if the winds are low. The forecast calls for another day like today so I'm hopeful."

She rang off as Scotty ran into the room. "Blackberry dinna want to come," she said.

"It's all right, Scotty, she needs time away from her puppies now and then. She'll let us know when it's time for the next feeding. This would be a good time for you to play with the puppies, don't you think?"

Like a top, Scotty's little denim-covered body spun and hurtled out the door. Her short footsteps faded down the hallway. What a joy this child will be to Shar and Malcolm, Laney thought. She stared at the photo of Scotty's mother on the desk and the promise she had made to discover the truth about her death and help Scotty find some happiness in her life. She'd learned much since then, but it was not enough. The stamps still eluded her and someone wanted them so badly, he'd killed three times trying to obtain them.

The multicolored airplane with its ugly row of black sutures lay on the desk where Scotty had left it. Had Bonnie cut the plane open the day of the funeral, thinking that her mother had hidden the stamps inside?

Wait a minute. She had almost forgotten about the mysterious blond woman in a black cloche who had come and gone from the funeral luncheon without anyone seeing her clearly. When she rushed away in that dark car with Switzerland County plates, had she been afraid someone would recognize her? She could have been the one.

But wasn't there another incident concerning Scotty's plane? It wagged at her memory but before she could recall it, she heard scratching at the front door and Blackberry's distinctive bark.

"Feeding time," Laney sighed and let the dog inside, following behind her to the pantry where Scotty sat among the squealing puppies. Scotty scrambled out of the box and the dog gingerly took her place. Scotty plugged the puppies in.

"It's such a pretty day, let's take a walk," Laney suggested. "I'll show you where we canoe in the summer. We'll take a snack for lunch and eat on the dock."

While Scotty washed her hands, Laney found two bananas, a chunk of cheddar and a small, unopened tin of shortbread cookies that Malcolm had given her. She stowed them all, including bottled water and the wounded airplane, in the red backpack that Scotty had brought with her. She left a note on the front door for Shar and

Malcolm telling them where they would be.

Scotty followed Laney through the kitchen garden, dormant except for the twiggy lavender and a sprig or two of parsley that frost hadn't nipped. Laney carried the backpack. She led the way down the stepping stones and past the rock springhouse where she stored the two canoes for her guests to use.

When they reached the floating dock, Scotty jumped in place to make it rock like a boat while Laney struggled to spread a napkin and place their snack on the weathered wood.

"Next summer, we'll take a canoe ride with Blackberry," Laney said. "That's her very favorite thing to do. By then, her puppies will be grown and in their new homes, I hope.

"You know Scotty, the first time your Uncle Malcolm ever heard your Aunt Shar play the bagpipes was right here in this very thicket of sycamore and ash. She marched right through the fog like a ghostly piper. I think your Uncle Malcolm was almost as enchanted that morning as when you danced the "Highland Fling" at his wedding."

Laney smiled at the dreamy expression that came over Scotty's face as she looked out at the wooded valley. Her head swayed right and left as though she could hear Shar's chanter playing some lilting melody.

Scotty reached for her backpack. She unzipped a narrow compartment and pulled out *The Wee Scotch Piper*. "Would you read ma book?"

"You certainly do love this book," Laney exclaimed, taking it.

"Gran gave it to me."

Laney froze. "Mabel? Scotty, when did she do that?" she asked, looking down at the book in her hand with new interest.

"It came the day before we go from Scotland." Scotty's voice rasped the edges of her brogue.

So, another gift from Mabel . . . and just before she died, Laney mused with just a hint of effervescence forming in her gut. She turned the book over. Just an ordinary book, she thought, but an absurd thought crossed her mind: What a hoot if Mabel had somehow hidden Victor's rare stamps in the book.

So, regardless that Scotty sat gawking in puzzlement and that the book had been handled and read numerous times, Laney feathered the pages as though the stamps might just tumble from the pages.

It didn't happen.

"Let's eat lunch first," Laney said, setting the book aside and feeling chagrinned by her wishful and foolish expectation.

Suddenly famished, she gobbled a banana, a piggish wedge of the cheese and several shortbread cookies while Scotty just munched on the cookies.

Gathering Scotty into her lap, she again lifted *The Wee Scotch Piper*. She turned to the dedication page and read aloud:

> *To every child of every land,*
> *Little sister little brother,*
> *As in this book your lives unfold*
> *May you learn to love each other.*

"Your Gran must have loved you very much, to give you such a lovely book," Laney said, giving Scotty a squeeze. She closed the book. "It's getting quite worn. Look how the dust jacket is yellowing."

The cover pictured an older gentleman with a lamb under his arm and a black haired little boy wearing a kilt and carrying bagpipes. The dark green border was beginning to tear away. Laney turned the book over. The back of the heavy, paper dust jacket had torn away along the edges revealing the pale blue hardcover in several places.

"Could you fix it?" Scotty asked.

"We could put a clear plastic cover over the dust jacket like they do with library books."

"Take that oot," Scotty said. She pointed to what appeared to be a piece of waxed paper peeking from a gap in the torn book jacket.

Laney's heart stopped.

"Oh God, Oh God, Oh God!" she babbled. She felt strangely disembodied as her breath quickened and she threatened to hyperventilate.

"Scotty, scoot over for a second!" The child moved quickly, Laney's frantic tone frightening her. "It's okay sweetie, really it is," Laney reassured her with a pat on her thigh and tried to smile through lips that were turning numb.

Scotty grabbed her plane, thrust her thumb in her mouth and sat on the bobbing dock staring at Laney's face.

Opening the book to where the dust jacket folded over the back cover, Laney carefully pulled it away.

"My God, I don't believe it!" Laney gaped pop-eyed. A large glassine wrapper was glued to the back cover. And inside the glazed and murky cloud of the envelope, flew Jenny after Jenny after Jenny!

40

It was a subdued Shar and Malcolm who came to pick up Scotty after their meeting with Marshall. The lawyer had told them that he would turn the letter over to the sheriff's department and would represent Shar at any interrogation that might result from the fresh evidence. He made no bones about the seriousness of the situation that faced her and Laney noticed that Shar's hands shook as Laney offered her a mug of coffee.

Laney, herself, was unusually nervous and reticent as she placed a plate of the Scottish shortbread cookies on the breakfast room table. Malcolm shoved one after another into his mouth while Shar refused to touch a single one even though she hadn't eaten all day.

While rushing up the hillside after the exciting discovery, Scotty had questioned Laney about the mysterious envelope found in her special book. Laney, holding the book tightly to her chest, explained that it was their little secret, rather like the one she and Shar had kept from Malcolm about her Highland dance lessons in Scotland.

As soon as they reached the house, Laney carefully pried the envelope from the back of the book. It was no easy task as the adhesive that had been used to secure the envelope had hardened to a brittle slab. No matter how carefully Laney tore it away, pieces of the envelope remained glued to the book.

The stamps appeared to be a single sheet folded over several times to fit inside the envelope. Laney couldn't really determine the stamps' condition because of the cloudy wrapper. For all she knew, they could be stuck together, but she controlled the urge to unseal the envelope because she was afraid of damaging them further. She dropped the glassine bag into an eight by ten-inch manila envelope. She put it into her oversized shoulder bag hanging over a kitchen chair and zipped it shut.

She led Scotty into her bedroom behind the stairs for a nap and read to her one more chapter from the book. For the life of her, Laney couldn't have told anyone what she read.

"How about some exciting news?" Laney asked the glum pair sitting across from her."

"The only exciting news I want to hear is that those damn stamps have been found," Shar said.

Laney smiled thinly, thinking about how excited they would be if she told them about the stamps in her bag. But a plan was forming in her mind and she didn't want to divulge the discovery quite yet. Shar and Malcolm would have to wait a couple more days.

Instead she said, "Barnaby called and he's taking his Jenny up tomorrow for a test flight. He invited all of us up to Vevay to witness it and even offered to taxi Scotty around the runway beforehand. Want to go?"

"Sharlene," Malcolm said, his face lighting up, "Scotty would love it and we could do with a few hours away from all this worry. What do you think?"

"Whatever, Malcolm." Shar sat slumped in her chair with her chin sunken into her chest.

Shar's pain tugged at Laney's heart, but for any plan to succeed, she had to be the only one who knew the whereabouts of the stamps.

However, that wasn't her only concern. *Whoever* knew where the stamps were hidden could be in jeopardy. With a shiver that crept up her spine and left her weak, she realized at that moment, only she and Scotty had that knowledge.

41

"Hey," Grover Smith called to Laney from atop a stack of hay bales. He threw a bale down to the bed of his truck to join the four others in a haphazard pile. "How about this weather?"

"It's wonderful," Laney said, pacing impatiently while Malcolm's farm manager, Smitty, as he was affectionately known, threw down a couple more.

Smitty hopped his way down the tiers of hay until he was standing in front of her. "Something I can do for you?" he said. He pulled off his John Deere cap, wiped sweat off his brow and ran his hand through his coffee-colored hair.

"I need some information about Scotty."

"Scotty, huh?" His face lit up. "She's a sweetie."

"It's about the welcoming party Malcolm held for Scotty and Keely in Florida over a year ago. You told Shar about Scotty locking herself in the bathroom, remember?"

"Oh that . . . yeah."

"Scotty told me that some little kid wanted to play with one of her toys and she didn't want him to."

"Wasn't quite like that, as I remember."

"How was it, Smitty? You wouldn't think so, but this could be important."

"You mean important like whether or not Malcolm gets permanent guardianship of that little girl?"

"So you've heard about the custody suit?"

He nodded. Removing his cap for the second time, he scratched his head.

"I was helping Malcolm out by playing bartender. The bar was set up in a corner of the living room. Malcolm had invited a horde of people to meet Keely and many had brought along their kids to meet Scotty. Everyone was standing around talking with drinks in their hands. No one was paying the youngsters any mind when this little kid came over to Scotty. She was sitting on the sofa playing with that toy airplane she likes so much. The little boy asked to hold her plane and Scotty smiled and handed it to him. The little kid took off running. Scotty ran after him and grabbed the plane back."

"Was that it?" Laney was disappointed.

"As I recall the incident, no. I saw a woman say something to the little boy. The kid approached Scotty again and told her he was sorry, and Scotty, trusting as she was, let him hold the plane again."

"And . . ."

"The little imp took off with it again, with Scotty right on his heels. The kid ran smack into the same woman who snatched the plane out of his hands. When Scotty reached for it, the woman twisted away from her and began to make her way out of the crowded room. Scotty started to cry and Keely rushed over and asked her what was wrong. Scotty told her and I heard Keely explain to Scotty how she should share her toys. Scotty gave her mother a furious look and ran out of the room. The next thing I heard, someone had tried to use the powder room and found that Scotty had locked herself inside. I figure you know the rest . . . the locksmith and all. When Scotty finally came out of the bathroom, she was carrying the plane, so I figured Scotty had snatched it away from the woman. Lots of spunk in that child."

Laney was so excited about this woman's obvious attempt to get Scotty's toy, she couldn't contain the elation in her voice when she asked, "Did you get the woman's or child's name?"

"No, and the woman beat an exit while Scotty was in the lavatory. Good riddance, if you ask me."

"Did you tell Malcolm about this?"

"It wasn't my place to squeal on one of his guests."

"What did the woman look like?"

"She seemed attractive as I remember. Blond hair. Nice legs. Good figure. Not that I usually notice things like that. She wore a wide brim straw hat that dipped in front, so I couldn't really see her face clearly."

"How old do you think she was?"

"Now that's hard to say. I remember thinking that I first thought she was either the little boy's mother or grandmother, but she left without the kid. The little boy was about the same age as Scotty at the time—four, maybe a little older. Laney, I don't see how this can help Malcolm."

"I'm not so sure how it can either, but if I can find out who that woman was . . ."

"Maybe Malcolm still has the invitation list."

"That's an idea," she said, but recalled that no one had invited the woman who had come to the funeral luncheon, so it was possible the woman who attended the Florida party hadn't been invited either.

"Say, I heard from Malcolm that everyone is going up to Indiana today to see one of those old biplanes fly. Ya lucky dogs. That'll be something."

"That certainly will, and I'd better be going. Thanks, Smitty."

"For what? I'd do anything to keep that youngster with Malcolm and Shar." He slapped his cap on his head and climbed back up the bales like a mountain goat.

Walking back to the house, Laney chewed on a hay stem while wondering about the two mysterious blond women in the face-concealing hats. They had to be the same woman. If so, was she the same person who had killed Ray, Keely, and Simon? The woman would had to have been in Scotland the morning Ray died, in Atlanta the night Keely was struck down, and in Northern Kentucky when Simon was shot.

Was she someone she knew? Laney tried her best to remember more about the woman she had seen at the luncheon. She was also blond with nice legs and figure. But there was something else, Laney brooded, something she just couldn't put her finger on.

And Smitty had first thought the woman was the little boy's mother or grandmother. Could she have been an older woman in disguise?

As Malcolm locked up the house to leave for Vevay, Laney hung back and asked him if Elaine and Barnaby had accompanied him to Scotland for Ray's funeral.

"No," he said, "they were already in Edinburgh when they got word Ray had been killed."

42

Gray griped all the way to Milton, Kentucky. "As much as I want to see that crate of Barnaby's get off the ground, I shouldn't be taking another day off work." He patted Laney's thigh. "That book of yours better have block-buster sales if we're going to have enough money to pay for our honeymoon."

"Can you shut off that racket for a few minutes?" Shar shouted from the backseat of the Buick.

Laney lowered the volume on the aria from *Don Pasquale* and turned in her seat. Shar looked dreadful. Her already thin face had turned skeletal, her depressed eye sockets, dark. Hastily applied blush and lipstick only exaggerated her gauntness.

Shar and Malcolm's reprieve from worry had been short—only one night to savor the decision of the court. Then the bomb dropped. Marshall's disclosure to the police about Shar would once more raise the question of who should have permanent custody of Scotty.

If only she could tell Shar about finding the stamps, Laney thought. It would give her hope that this nightmare was coming to an end. But she was still afraid for anyone to know.

But the time to put her plan in action was getting closer now that Malcolm had told her that the Biddles had been in Scotland when Ray was killed. Furthermore, she recalled that on the day she had met the Biddles, Barnaby had told her that Elaine was away on an art club trip to Florida the weekend that Keely was hit by that blue car. Could

Elaine have stopped off in Atlanta? Was it unreasonable to believe that a seventy-year-old woman could have committed murder?

The blue car! That's the key, she thought. If she could find the car with tinted windows, it could be the definitive proof. She searched her memory. The Biddles had driven Barnaby's van to the wedding and she hadn't seen another vehicle in the parking lot the day she and Gray had first visited the airstrip. Laney promised herself she would do some snooping around once they got to the airstrip.

Scotty, sitting between Malcolm and Shar, squirmed under the restraint of her seatbelt. She seemed to be the only lighthearted spirit in the car. When told she would get to taxi in the biplane that had once belonged to her grandfather, she whooped and galloped around Laney's kitchen like a warrior readying for battle.

"Saugh, could I go up in the plane?" she asked. Malcolm chuckled.

"What's so funny, Mal?" Shar asked.

"The name Scotty has given you."

"She can't help that she can't pronounce my name—though it's pretty close, wouldn't you say?"

"Sharlene, in Gaelic, a sough is a willow," Malcolm crowed.

Great gales of laughter rippled through the car.

Shar snickered and replied to Scotty's question. "Listen up, Scotty girl. This willow doesn't want to become a weeping willow so I won't permit you to take part in the test flight of an eighty-year-old biplane."

Scotty seemed to take Shar's ruling in stride since it didn't seem to douse her spirits a bit. Obviously, the ride in her grandfather's plane would be enough.

Gray turned into the small airport about noon. They hadn't gone fifty feet when ahead they could see a biplane parked at the end of the grassy strip. Laney noted that it wasn't just any biplane, but the Jenny that Barnaby had so painstakingly put back together over the years.

Scotty shrieked. She unhooked her seatbelt and bounced in her seat until Laney was afraid she would hit her head on the roof of the car.

"Easy there, Lindbergh, you'll get to do your stuff in due time," Shar said.

As they passed the plane, they could see that a large crowd of people had come out to see the flight. Scotty was now on her knees looking at the Jenny through the rear window. They parked where they had before, on the side of the largest hangar that was the home of the Jenny. But today, over a dozen other cars and trucks had squeezed into the lot and overflowed onto the grass. Laney recognized Elliot Cook's grimy pick-up and Dwayne Day's yellow beetle. She only hoped that Bonnie hadn't accompanied her husband.

Barnaby and Elaine rushed out the door of the gothic cottage as all of them alighted from the Buick. Barnaby was dressed in gray twill work pants and shirt and as he got closer, Laney saw that he had clipped on a black, leather bow tie for the occasion.

Elaine, a red sweater flung over her shoulders, swooped down on Scotty and gave her a hearty squeeze. "I've prepared lunch before the big event," she said. She herded them like sheep toward the house. Through clinched teeth, Laney imagined the woman putting Simon's gun to his head and pulling the trigger. Her gut did a roll.

Elaine led them through the small living room to the left of the entrance and into an even smaller dining room. They sat, elbow to elbow. Elaine ladled thick potato soup and passed the bowls. A basket of sliced crusty bread followed.

"Barnaby, is everything ready for the flight?" Gray asked while holding the bowl of tossed salad for Laney. She forked out a small portion onto her plate.

"She's tiptop. Patricia and Dwayne are seeing to all the pre-flight checks. I still have a few authentic accessories I'm trying to locate, but nothing that will delay the flight today."

"Will I get to ride soon?" Scotty said, her eyes shining like star sapphires.

"After lunch, sweetheart," Barnaby said.

"Could Saugh and me go together?"

"In your dreams, pumpkin," Shar said stone-faced.

"She's only going to taxi," Malcolm reminded her.

Elaine passed a plate of homemade sugar cookies glazed with icing.

Reposed and satiated from the lovely lunch, Laney was beginning to question why she had suspected Elaine of the crimes in the first place. Yawning, she grabbed her shoulder bag from the back of the chair and excused herself. The only bathroom was at the back of the house and to the left of the Biddle's bedroom. Through a window over the cast iron claw-foot tub, she could see the front of the large metal hangar, and she noticed a car parked in the grass on the left side of the building. Strange, she thought, as she washed her hands, I wonder why they didn't park in the lot. It struck her as so odd, she shed her sneakers and climbed inside the tub to see the car more clearly.

She gasped. The vehicle was a dark blue sedan with tinted windows! Hastily, she put her shoes back on, moaning with the discomfort of wet socks caused by a puddle from someone's morning bath. Leaving the bathroom, she tiptoed back down the hallway and out the front door. Shutting it softly behind her, she bounded down the three steps, cut across the lane and around the hangar.

As she approached the rear of the parked car and could read the license plate, she recalled that the first two numbers in Indiana plates indicated the county code. The 78 jumped out at her. Switzerland County! They were the same as those on the dark-colored car she had watched speed away from Taylor Ridge after the funeral luncheon. But then, she was in Switzerland County and would expect most of the visitors would be from there. She quickly wrote down the rest of the numbers in her notebook.

She tried the driver's side door. Locked. She walked around to the passenger door. Although also locked, the window was open about an inch. "Damn!" If only she had a coat hanger. Cupping her eyes with her hand, Laney squinted to see inside but the darkened windows did their job. She thought she could make out a lock button on the windowsill.

She dashed to the front of the hanger and peeked around. She could see that the crowd at the plane had increased and more cars were parked in the grass on the highway side of the runway. Laney ran to the hangar door and slipped inside, recalling her other brief visit here with Gray.

It was a few moments before her eyes adjusted to the gloom and leaving the door cracked for light, she made her way to a workbench against the right wall.

Greasy engine parts rested on a dirty cloth and other parts were scattered over grimy issues of flight magazines. Pegboard lined the wall behind the bench where several spools were hung. Laney found a roll of stiff wire. She unrolled a length and bent the wire back and forth until it broke. After replacing the spool, she ran back to the car. Twisting a small loop into one end, she lowered it inside the window glass and tried to hook the lock button. Two adjustments to the wire and she had it. The button snapped up!

She took a final look around and opened the car door.

A *Backstage Magazine* lay on the passenger seat and a faint odor of White Diamonds perfume teased her nostrils. She tried to remember where she had last smelled it. It hadn't been long ago. She had received a bottle of Elizabeth Taylor's favorite scent on Christmas and found it too heavy for her taste. She punched the glove box button and as it opened, something hairy fell out. Thinking it alive, she jumped back, her heart racing. The scent grew stronger but the object on the floorboard lay lifeless.

"Good God!" A woman's blond wig! Laney lifted it to her nostrils. The source of the scent! And it came to her. The woman at the luncheon had worn the same perfume. Whoever wore this wig must have been the woman who drove away in this very car with Switzerland County plates.

She looked inside the glove compartment and pulled out large crumpled black object. The black cloche!

Hearing distant voices, she stuffed everything back into the glove box and softly shut the car door. She walked quickly to the corner of the building and peered around. She could see Barnaby, Elaine, Malcolm, and Shar walking down the lane toward the plane. Scotty was skipping ahead of them.

She fumbled for her address book and cell phone in her purse. Flattened against the side of the building, she phoned Gordon Powell at the St. Clair County Sheriff's Department. She was told he was out of the office.

"Damn!" she said. She asked for Deputy Freddie Rudd. When he answered, she explained to him that it was an emergency and imperative that she obtain certain information immediately. A long explanation followed and when Freddie still balked, she reminded him that Gordon had once given her similar data. She paced a path in the grass as she waited for him to return, but it was Gordon who eventually spoke into the phone.

"Laney, you are messing around in police business again," he reprimanded her. "Is Shar up there with you?"

"Yes."

"Detective Grossman from Carroll County is coming to Hickory in the morning to question her." Gordon exhaled loudly through his nostrils.

"If I'm right about this, he might not have to. Please Gordon, you won't regret this, I promise."

"What's your cell phone number? Give me Gray's too."

She rattled them off.

"I'll call you right back."

"Oh there you are," said Gray when Laney almost smacked into him as she stepped around the corner of the hangar. "We didn't want you to miss the flight." He held out her green suede jacket and she put it on.

"I felt a little queasy and needed some air, so I took a walk."

Gray's eyes abruptly darkened with concern. "Laney, what is it?" He laid his hand on her arm. "You're trembling." He drew her into his arms.

She couldn't help it; the tears flowed.

"Sweetheart, tell me," he murmured.

"Gray, I've found them!" she blurted.

He regarded her quizzically. "Found what?"

"The stamps! Victor's Jenny Inverts." Laney's lips trembled the words. She knew she shouldn't be telling him.

Gray, his hand on his heart, stepped backward in shock. "Whoa! Where?"

Standing in front of the hangar, Laney explained as quickly as she could how she'd discovered them in Scotty's storybook, a gift from her grandmother.

"Let me see them," he said excitedly.

"For Pete's sake, I can't right here!"

"But that's incredible! Scotty had them all the time?" he said loudly.

"Shush! If the killer hears that I have them . . . "

"Killer?" Gray looked around with an incredulous grin.

"Elaine Biddle. It has to be her. Everything fits."

"Laney, my God, no!"

"She was in Atlanta when Mabel's apartment was ransacked. She was in Scotland when Ray died."

"Laney, I'm not going to argue—"

"Then quit, for God's sake! I have other evidence." She dragged him to the corner of the hangar and pointed to the blue Ford she had just broken into. "That's the same blue car that was at the funeral luncheon. And, in case you've forgotten, Keely was struck by a blue car with tinted windows?"

"I didn't forget."

"Elaine was on an art trip the day Keely was killed," Laney interrupted.

"Where?"

"Ta-da! Florida! Guess what? I-75 goes right through Atlanta."

"Dammit, Laney, as much as I hate to admit it, you may be on to something."

"Something else. I found a blond wig and a black cloche in the glove box of that car." She thumbed over her shoulder as they began to walk down the lane. "Elaine was disguised that day at the luncheon. No one saw her face. According to Smitty, a woman disguised in a similar way tried to get Scotty's plane away from her at Malcolm's welcoming party for Keely."

"But what about the night Simon was shot? Elaine was with us at General Butler State Park."

"For an hour. If Shar made it to Simon's before we got there the following morning, Elaine could have too, even if she had to swim the backstroke across the river."

Laney went on, her voice suddenly cracking, "God, Gray, I was the one who set up Frank, I mean Simon. I told Elaine that night we were going to see him the following morning to ask him if Keely had told him anything."

"Don't start blaming yourself."

She whispered in Gray's ear. "I have a plan to get Elaine to admit it."

Gray stopped in his tracks. "Laney, you can't. It could be dangerous."

To emphasize her determination to see this through, Laney stopped and looked him in the eye. "As soon as the flight is completed and the crowd thins, Elaine is going to learn that the stamps are right under her nose. She won't be able to resist getting her hands on them."

Gray's expression tightened and he paled.

"I'll detail more of my plan after the flight," Laney said, not liking the frigid stare he was giving her. "Gray, trust me. I know what I'm doing." She patted the purse on her hip and walked into the crowd.

Gray watched her until she was out of sight. In frustration, he cracked his knuckles, a habit he had quit in his teens.

43

Barnaby's color was high with excitement as he mingled with his friends and aviation enthusiasts in the crowd. He stopped to answer questions from a reporter from the *Vevay Reveille=Enterprise*, the same newspaper that Laney had read about Victor's crash of the Jenny back in 1928. Barnaby held up a photocopy of the article for the cameraman while Barnaby's daughter, Patricia, and Dwayne Day made last minute adjustments on the aircraft.

Dwayne inspected the plane's shock absorption—bungee cords wrapped around the axle—while Patricia crawled under the tail and looked for any cracks in the skid.

"Scotty, Victor Moore's granddaughter, will get the first ride in the Jenny, although it will be on the runway," Laney heard Barnaby say.

"Will you be the pilot?" the reporter asked.

"I'm afraid not," Barnaby said. "My wife laid down the law. But my daughter, Patricia, will take her up. That's almost as sweet."

While Dwayne oiled the rocker arms on the engine, Patricia made her way over to her father who was standing by the wings. He introduced her to Laney and Gray.

Patricia was a pretty girl with her mother's brown eyes, but without the yellow lights. She had dressed in barnstorming gear—tan jodhpurs, a bomber jacket and knee-high leather boots. Aviator goggles rested on her leather cap and the straps were unfastened.

She had Elaine's high cheekbones and trim figure, but unlike Elaine who was outgoing and confident, Patricia spoke softly and guardedly. Laney remembered well how she had shrunk from conversing when Gray and she had first met her in the hangar several days before. Laney could bet on it that the Amelia Earhart getup was Barnaby's idea, not hers.

"Scotty, let me show you where you'll sit," Elaine said, holding out her hand. Scotty hesitated, searching Shar's and Malcolm's faces for reassurance now that the moment had come. Smiling, they nodded and Shar buttoned Scotty's toggle coat and pulled her denim hat down over her unruly curls. With a final kiss, Shar sent her off with Elaine.

It took every bit of Laney's willpower not to yank the child away from Elaine, but she quickly realized that normalcy was paramount if later, she were to get Elaine to act upon the stamp discovery. She rationalized that with the crowd around them, any danger to Scotty was unlikely.

Patricia pulled herself up on the lower wing and Elaine lifted Scotty up to her. With Patricia holding her about the waist, Scotty peered inside the cockpit. As she grasped the leather-covered edge, Laney could hear her laughing and jabbering.

"This will be the thrill of her little lifetime," Malcolm said as they watched Scotty's face.

"We're all going to get a thrill before the day is over," Gray said. Laney bumped him hard with her hip while smiling innocently.

While Patricia waited at the plane, Elaine returned to the group. "Laney, you've been chosen to hold Scotty," she said. "Patricia said that the child is too short to see out if she sits in the cockpit alone."

"What about you, Shar?" Laney said.

"No way. Anyway, with my long legs, Barnaby would have to cut a hole in the fuselage."

"Malcolm?" Elaine urged.

"I think not. I'll keep my new bride company."

"Gray?" Laney asked.

"No thanks. I'll hold your purse for you."

Laney caught his smirk. "Like hell you will," she whispered in his ear. "I'm not letting it out of my sight." She put the strap over her head and arm, bandoleer style.

"We're getting a bit of a headwind. Let's get on with this," Barnaby said, rushing over to them. He held up two pairs of aviator glasses.

"What are these for," Laney asked.

"You'll see soon enough," Barnaby said, winking at his wife.

Gray walked with Laney to the plane and helped her climb onto the wing. With a grunt, she struggled into the cockpit. Gray handed Scotty up to Patricia and she maneuvered her into Laney's lap. Momentarily removing Scotty's hat, Laney hooked the child-sized glasses onto her head and did the same with hers. Laney was reminded of a couple of barn owls she had seen staring at her from a limb of a maple tree one summer evening.

As though she were mounting a horse, with a great swing of her leg, Patricia climbed into the rear cockpit.

Patricia gestured to Dwayne and he pulled hard on the propeller. Nothing. Again he flipped the prop and the engine roared to life with a teeth-rattling noise. It seemed that Patricia checked the few instruments forever before giving Dwayne a "thumbs up." He removed the wheel chocks. Patricia gave the engine a small burst of throttle and the plane began to taxi slowly down the grassy strip.

With the first movement forward, Laney felt Scotty's body stiffen. Then she squealed and giggled while the crowd cheered and waved. Patricia opened the throttle a bit more, enough to give Scotty the sensation of flying but not enough to allow the plane to levitate. The finest spray of oil and grease speckled the windshield and their faces. When the plane clattered and bounced over the uneven turf, Scotty laughed and shouted with glee.

Patricia cut the throttle as the plane approached the end of the runway and the plane eased into a one-eighty turn on the wide strip. Then back they came, the Jenny rattling and rumbling, while inside the cockpit, Laney and Scotty bobbed and jostled together like apples in a tub. When they came to a slow stop near the crowd, Dwayne lifted the tailskid and helpers held the wing tips as they turned the plane around. Patricia held back the throttle to keep the plane from taking off.

Barnaby and Gray appeared behind the left wing and Gray lifted Scotty out of Laney's lap and handed her down to Barnaby. Just as Laney placed her foot on her seat to scramble out of the cockpit and Gray reached for her hand to steady her, a mighty roar erupted from the engine. The plane jerked forward and Gray, with a sharp cry, tumbled off the wing. Laney was thrown face-forward onto the seat. With flailing hands, she grappled for the back edge of the cockpit to regain her balance while the cracking rumble of the engine pierced her ears.

Through Patricia's cloudy windshield, Laney could make out her expression of willful purpose as she opened the throttle. With strangling fear, Laney heard the scream of acceleration as the plane thundered down the grass runway.

"Patricia, stop!" Laney shouted, but her words were ripped from her mouth. Laney could see Gray struggle to his feet and begin to run after the plane, his hand outstretched, as though if he could only reach the wing, he could stop the plane's roaring takeoff. Behind him, Shar and Malcolm, their arms locked around their child, and Barnaby, his lips forming a growing cavern, stood in a frozen tableau before a backdrop of stunned onlookers.

"Patricia!" Laney screamed again, but intent on tasks at hand, Patricia seemed unaware that she was there. As the plane accelerated, Laney felt the strong push against the seat and her arms weakened until she collapsed against it, her face pressing against the leather-covered edge. With all her might, she twisted her body around until she was facing forward. She took hold of two of the four wooden struts that ran from the upper wing into the fuselage near the corners of the cockpit.

The wheels riding the bumps became a clatter, then a drum tattoo. The trees at the end of the runway rushed toward them. Closer and closer they came. Faster and faster the plane accelerated. Suddenly, the clacking quit as the ground dropped away and they skimmed skeletal limbs.

They gained altitude and like a giant bird, they banked toward the river and made a gentle turn until Laney could make out the approaching airstrip—the hangars, the gothic cottage, the single runway, the crowd. Gray! she thought. He would be terrified for her. *She* was terrified for her. She could have been killed when the crazy woman took off like that and Gray too, when he fell from the wing. Thank God he wasn't hurt, she thought with relief, recalling his desperate run for the plane. What in hell was Patricia thinking?

Laney released one of her hands that was frozen to the front struts and gave Patricia an interrogative gesture while glancing back at her and mouthing, "What the hell?"

Patricia answered with three tight, fast barrel rolls.

After his fall off the wing and futile run after the Jenny, Gray was as confused and rudderless as the stock market before an election. He couldn't take his eyes off the Jenny as she cleared the trees.

"Laney! Laney!" he screamed into the sky.

"Gray, are you all right?" Barnaby said, rushing to his side.

"I think so," he said shakily.

"I don't know what got into my daughter, but if I would trust Patricia with my Jenny, you can be sure that Laney is in the best of hands. You have to know how much I regard her flying abilities." He said the words with conviction while his eyes blinked rapidly.

Gray rubbed his elbow and felt the throb from the growing lump on the back of his head. How in the hell could Barnaby trust someone who had just jettisoned him off the wing like excess baggage. He thought for a moment. Could Patricia not have known he was still on the wing?

He was still pondering this possibility when his cell phone rang. He reached inside his windbreaker pocket. "Yeah?" he said with annoyance that he had to interrupt his concentration on the biplane.

"Gray? This is Gordon. Where's Laney? I tried to get her on her cell."

"Ha, it's not likely she'd hear it. As we speak, she's about a thousand feet up."

"Huh?"

"Forget it."

"Well, she wanted to know the registration on that tag."

"Tag?"

"License plate. Look Gray, you need to talk to her. She's fooling in police business again. I only looked this up as a favor to her and she's way off track. That car isn't registered to Elaine Biddle."

It was a moment before Gray recalled his earlier conversation with Laney about Elaine and murder and stamps. Right now, he wasn't interested in the intrigue over Jenny Inverts. The Jenny he was interested in had just banked and was coming in fast toward the strip.

"Hey Gray, you there?"

"Yeah."

"When Laney comes down to earth, tell her some gal named Patricia Biddle owns the blue Ford." Gordon hung up.

"Patricia Biddle!" Gray cried out as the plane zoomed closer. Gray's mind spun out of control. Patricia! *Patricia* owns the car with the tinted windows, wig and cloche? For a second he lost his focus on the plane and chewed on a lip. His palms grew clammy as like it or not, his interest in the Jenny Inverts abruptly re-engaged.

Overhead, the Jenny's motor noise changed pitch and his head snapped up. Gray watched with numbed horror while the Jenny carrying Laney and a woman who may have killed three people, corkscrewed across the winter sky.

44

They were the most terrifying moments in Laney's life. One second she could see the crowd with cupped hands over their eyes, staring into the sun. In the next, the earth was spinning away on its axis in a revolving vertigo. The horizon was above her, beside her and below in a whirling dizziness while her body slammed the cockpit. Her fingers, white with her grip, clutched the wooden struts. She thought her hands would be ripped from the struts when three times upside down, she dropped away from her seat.

Then, as quickly as it began, Patricia's maneuver ended and they banked once more. Laney, afraid to invoke a similar response from Patricia by looking back at her, instead closed her eyes and quivered in her seat.

She had to admit that Patricia was good. Those rolls had obviously been done before, but never in the Jenny, she reminded herself. Hadn't Barnaby mentioned something about a flying club that Patricia had belonged to? All at once she remembered the aviation magazines in the hangar. Aerobatics club, she could bet. But what was Patricia trying to prove by taking her up in this antique biplane and scaring the bejesus out of her?

"Laney?" a puff of a voice shouted through the crackling drone of the plane.

Afraid, Laney didn't turn.

Again Patricia called her name, louder, accompanied by a quick tip of the wings that got Laney's attention. Her gut did a three-sixty. She released her grip on a single strut and turned.

Patricia's outstretched hand was resting on the top of her curved windshield, so close to Laney that she could see the calluses on her palm and the grease beneath her fingernails.

Patricia screamed two words that were barely audible through the noise of the engine. Through her goggles, Patricia's eyes locked with Laney's like a heat-seeking missile.

"What did you say?" Laney yelled at Patricia, giving her a questioning look.

"The stamps! Give them to me!"

This time, there was no mistaking what Patricia said. Laney was instantaneously thrown into confusion. How had Patricia learned that she had the Inverts? She'd told only one person about finding them— Gray, and he certainly wouldn't have told anyone. Damn! Realization struck her like a punch to the solar plexus. Scotty! She had seen them, had known she'd put them into her purse. Maybe she had unintentionally mentioned them to Patricia when Elaine had taken her to the plane. She had seen Scotty talking to her. But what possible concern were the stamps to Patricia anyway? It was Elaine who owned the car, the wig, and the cloche. It was Elaine who wanted the Inverts. It was Elaine who had had opportunity to vandalize, slash and kill, wasn't it? Her breath quickened and she gulped air furiously.

Why hadn't Gordon returned her call with the registration information? Or maybe he *had* phoned, but with all the engine noise, she hadn't heard the ring or couldn't receive on her cell phone this high up. She unzipped her bag and removed her phone, again closing up her purse. With the wind whipping her hair wildly about her face, she cautiously slid the phone to her ear.

Could she get through to Gordon from this altitude? Through a crackling in-and-out reception, she thought she heard Freddie's voice before, in a blaze of terror, all hell broke loose.

"What in hell is Patricia doing?" Gray yelled at Barnaby after partly recovering from the shock of seeing the Jenny spiraling across the sky.

"Barrel rolls," Barnaby said. "It's a positive maneuver . . . quite safe."

"Safe, my eye! For all we know, Laney doesn't even have her seatbelt on!

"Surely Patricia . . ."

"Listen, Barnaby, I have reason to believe . . ." Gray stopped, suddenly unsure whether or not to reveal his suspicions about Barnaby's daughter. Damn it, for all he knew, Barnaby and his wife, Elaine, could also have been involved in the murders. At the edge of the crowd, he saw Elaine speaking to Dwayne. He was nodding and he suddenly turned and vanished into the crowd.

Gray sidled up to Malcolm who was holding Scotty. Next to them, Shar's eyes were transfixed with horror, as were Malcolm's. Only Scotty had a look of delight on her face, her neck craned at the plane that once belonged to her grandfather.

Gray addressed Malcolm, "Don't you think you should take Scotty? . . ." Gray cocked his head toward the parking lot.

"Yes, yes . . . of course," Malcolm said, turning toward the lane.

"Shar!" Gray called.

Shar pivoted and rushed to him. She was shaking uncontrollably. Malcolm, with Scotty, continued toward the car.

Gray placed his arm around Shar's shoulders conspiratorially and walked quickly beyond the hearing range of Barnaby. "I think you should know about this," he told her, "Laney found the Jenny Inverts."

"Get out!" She punched him hard in the arm while her pale face suddenly flushed and her eyes pooled tears. "Where were they?" she asked in a quivering voice.

"In Scotty's bagpiper book she got from her grandmother." His eyes scanned the heavens for the plane. He spotted it making another slow turn.

"You don't mean it!" Shar said. "The little bugger!"

Then Gray told her the rest of it—Laney's suspicions about Elaine, the blue car with its unexpected contents, and Laney's plan to entice Elaine with the stamps after the flight.

"Why that conniving, murderous biddy! And Elaine had my little Scotty in hand! I'll pull every goddamn white hair out of her little head!"

"Hold it, Shar, there's more." When he gave her the details of Gordon's call, Shar stood thunderstruck.

"Do you mean to tell me that Laney may be with "Patricia the Whacker" in that bunch of parts flying in formation?"

"Yes . . . I mean, I *think* Patricia is the one. . . . Christ, Shar, there's nothing we can do! I feel so helpless."

"Do you think Laney has figured it out?"

Before Gray could answer, they watched as the Jenny approached the field again. They stared with fascinated horror as the biplane did a quarter loop and began a vertical climb.

"Jesus! She's got to know it! Look!" Gray screamed.

But with one look, Shar covered her eyes as the plane climbed and climbed, higher and higher. With the engine sputtering, the plane decelerated, its airspeed slowing close to zero until it hung in silent suspension as though in a stall. The crowd gasped in unison as the plane pivoted in a turnaround until the nose was pointing straight down.

The Jenny dropped like a stone toward the ground. As though they were experiencing the plunge themselves, people shrieked.

"God no!" Gray screamed, as the earth rose up to converge with the plane.

Not unlike a steep climb in a roller coaster, Laney was thrown backward in her seat until she was lying on her spine staring upward through the windshield at the brilliant blue sky. Pressed against the seat, her hands couldn't reach the front struts. The phone fell from her hand and was swept away behind the slipstream. With one hand, she clutched the leather-covered edge of the cockpit and her other hand gripped a strut at her shoulder. But she felt her body slipping from the seat.

The belt! Laney thought desperately. She had to get the belt fastened. Still grasping the strut with one hand, she felt for the mesh straps that she had seen when she first climbed into the plane. If only she had fastened it then. She recalled Patricia's words when she had lifted one end, "No need for a belt. We will only taxi."

Her hand groped beneath her legs, and she grasped one strap, then alternating hands, found the other just as the plane's vertical climb lost momentum. The engine crackled and popped and then was silent. "God help me," she screamed, fumbling the clasp together and flipping down the hook. Her cry pierced the sky in the silent seconds of the turnabout.

The rough clickity-click of the eight-cylinder, OX-5 engine cut in as the nose pointed downward and they began a hellish descent. Faster and faster they dropped, and Laney's body pulled against her belt and she braced her hands on the wooden cross member in front of her. Oil from the rocker arms misted her goggles and she was glad she couldn't see the earth that she knew was racing toward them.

This is it, she thought, I'm going to die! But all at once, she felt the nose lift and they finished the maneuver with another quarter loop. When Laney opened her eyes and wiped her goggles with her fingers, they were once more flying horizontally away from the airstrip and her hammering heart was threatening to burst out of her chest.

"Laney?" Patricia called.

Laney knew what was in store for her if she didn't give her the stamps. Without hesitation, she unzipped her bag, removed the envelope and turned to hand it back to Patricia.

Instantaneously, Laney had a thought. Wait a damn minute! Patricia didn't want to die any more than she did. Her only purpose was to get hold of the Inverts. She wanted the stamps. Period! The aerobatics may have been frightening, but Patricia had made sure that they'd been performed while the stamps were safely in her bag. What if . . .

Impulsively, Laney dangled the envelope over the edge of the cockpit.

"No, stop!" Patricia shrieked, but the plane remained horizontal.

Laney managed an inward smile, although outwardly, her face was unable to pull one into place. Affirming her determination, she waggled the envelope. She won't risk it, she thought almost smugly. Laney turned so she was facing Patricia. "You land this goddamn plane or I swear, I'll drop them!" she shouted.

Patricia's eyes narrowed but she held the plane level and banked toward the river.

"Where are you going?" Laney yelled, as Patricia flew west. Laney knew the airstrip was in the opposite direction.

"To land the Jenny," Patricia retorted.

It was only minutes before the plane was joggled by a gust of wind. Laney tried to tighten her belt but found that it wasn't adjustable.

45

With the final quarter loop, the plane peeled off toward the river. When it didn't reappear, Gray didn't waste anymore time. "Barnaby, get over here," he said. Shar stood beside him in shocked silence until Barnaby approached.

Barnaby, who had seen the second maneuver, was pale and shaken. "Gray, she never should have done a hammerhead. If Laney didn't have her seatbelt on, she could have pitched out of the plane."

Elaine rushed over to her husband. "Why is Patricia doing this Barnaby? I thought the plan was to just take the plane up for a short test. Did you give her permission to take a passenger with her and perform aerobatics?"

"Certainly not! Why would I subject Laney to danger and risk my eighty-year-old Jenny?"

"Barnaby, the press is having a field day with this," Elaine said with trembling lips. "They got both of those procedures on tape."

As far as Gray could see, the elderly couple was truly disconcerted by what their daughter had done.

Elaine searched the horizon. "Barnaby, a storm is getting up in the west. If Patricia plans to land here, she'd better do it soon."

Gray flinched reflexively because it was obvious to him that Patricia wouldn't fly back to this strip after that exhibition. He was particularly worried that Patricia had somehow found out about the Inverts that Laney had in her purse. But how? He looked toward his pink Buick in the parking lot. Malcolm had just fastened Scotty in the rear seat and was climbing into the front passenger seat.

"How long can the Jenny go without refueling?" Gray asked. His fingers combed frantically through his hair.

"The Jenny has a forty-gallon tank, enough fuel for two and a half hours if you were to push it, but you wouldn't want to cut it that close."

"Barnaby, there's a front coming in. Where would *you* land?" Gray asked anxiously.

"Right back here. That was the plan."

"But Patricia isn't following the original plan. We know that now," Elaine said with a catch in her voice. "Another thing, she told me just before takeoff to tell Dwayne to look for her to land in Madison. I thought it was odd at the time, but I assumed it was only an alternate course of action if the weather worsened. If she plans to land in Madison, she's flying right into the storm!" she stated with panic in her voice.

Gray thought back. That must have been the gist of Elaine's conversation with Dwayne after the Jenny did the barrel rolls. He looked toward the parking lot. The yellow VW was gone.

The biplane not reappearing, the crowd began to thin. The media, their equipment safely stowed in the van, pulled away.

Grabbing Shar's hand, Gray headed for the Buick. On the way up the lane, the wind shifted and they felt a lowering in the temperature. Gray punched the number of the St. Clair County Sheriff's Department into his cell phone and continued walking while he waited for Freddie to locate Gordon.

"What are you going to do?" Shar asked with fear for her friend shaking her words. There were tears in her eyes.

"After I talk with Gordon, I'm going to question Scotty about her conversation with Patricia before her ride in the Jenny."

Shar's long strides barely kept up with Gray's. "Gray, I forbid you to scare her in any way."

"Gotcha. Gordon?" he said into the phone.

"What's happening up there?" Gordon asked.

"Marshall filled you guys in on this Jenny Invert scheme, didn't he?"

"Yeah, and I must admit it's the wildest incitement to murder I've ever heard of. Detective Grossman and I have men on it."

"Well, it gets wilder, so listen up. I'll try to give you the short version." A few minutes later, Gordon was screaming in his ear, "Laney's up the air with Patricia Biddle?"

"Afraid so."

"Does Patricia know that Laney found the stamps and has them on her?"

"I could almost bet on it. I'm thinking little Scotty let the cat out of the bag. Laney was an unwilling passenger in this flight. I think the stunts were performed to intimidate Laney enough to get her to hand over the Inverts."

"What time are they due to land."

"The plane holds enough gas for about two and a half hours of flight. They took off over an hour ago but I have reason to believe Patricia plans to come down in Madison." Gray fell sick as he continued, "But they could be forced down before then. There's a squall line approaching fast. Look, I'm going to drop Scotty and Shar off at a motel in Madison and try to get to the airport before the plane lands."

"Forget that, Gray. If this woman has killed—"

"Just try and stop me." Gray hung up. As the wind lashed at his pant legs like a whip and Shar's pixie whirled a tornado around her head, all Gray could think of was Laney in that rickety biplane flying into the storm.

Laney was prepared to continue tormenting Patricia or even drop the envelope if the situation warranted it. She just wasn't sure how far she could push her. One thing seemed pretty certain, that as long as she was in the plane with Patricia, she was a lot safer with the stamps, than without them. At this point, she didn't care where they landed. She just wanted to get her feet on terra firma again.

They followed the Ohio River, a blue-green, satin sash between black bands of leafless trees lining the banks. Behind the trees, checkered fields of brown and green studded with barns and houses rolled into wooded ridges.

Laney didn't like the looks of a great dark cloud that was moving in fast toward them. It was only minutes before the plane was joggled again by a burst of wind.

Ahead, Laney saw an area along the river studded with houses and buildings. Madison, she deduced. Maybe Patricia will land the Jenny at Madison Municipal Airport west of the city. Please oh please land there, she implored silently.

The wind picked up and when an extended rush of cold air buffeted the plane, Laney slipped the stamps back into her purse.

They were over the city when the black sky enveloped them and it began to rain great sheets of water accompanied by flashing lightning. The plane was jolted by turbulence that slammed them downward one second and upward the next. Drenched to the skin, Laney began to shiver with cold and fright.

"Thank God!" Laney said aloud when she spotted a long asphalt strip in the distance and the miniscule Quonset hut, white terminal building and hangars of the Madison Airport.

Suddenly, she heard the engine falter. It coughed and sputtered and a couple of cylinders cut out, then two more stopped firing. The rain on those exposed rocker arms! Laney thought in a panic, but really didn't know much about the OX-5 engine other than what Barnaby had told them in the hangar that day.

The engine spat and with a final explosive pop, quit for good. She turned to look for reassurance from Patricia but didn't get it. Her expression was as dismal as the storm front they were confronting.

This is it! Laney thought in terror.

Quickly, the Jenny slowed and with her heart flip-flopping, Laney waited for it to drop out of the sky. But as fast as the squall had begun, the wind and rain suddenly abated. And for a dazzling moment, the setting sun escaped from the ominous cloud and gilded the simple cotton wings. As the Jenny descended in a soft and gentle glide, it passed through a magical window of stillness and calm. All around her, the vintage wooden fuselage creaked its proud and somber past while the rigging wires sang like an angel choir.

This must be what Victor loved so about flying his Jenny, Laney thought and incredibly, all at once, she was at peace and unafraid while silently, they drifted closer and closer to earth.

46

Ducking into the Buick, Gray lost no time in questioning Scotty. Twice, Shar, who had slipped in the back seat beside her, glared at him when the questioning got too intense. Scotty, her eyes wide with innocence, related to the three of them, how when Patricia held her on the wing of the Jenny, she had babbled to Patricia how her grandfather's biplane looked just like the stamps in Laney's purse.

"The stamps have been found?" Malcolm cried. His eyes were enormous behind his glasses.

"They were in ma wee piper book," Scotty said.

Radiance transformed Malcolm's face as he digested the significance of the find, but abruptly faded when he realized something was not right if Patricia had consequentially taken Laney aloft against her will. Gray decided to wait until Scotty and Shar were safely at a motel, before telling him what Laney had discovered in the car registered to Patricia.

Silent and tense, Gray sped down Highway 56 as fast as he dared. But soon a driving rain joined the blustery winds and he was forced to slow. Lightning rent the somber sky.

When they reached Madison, as much as he wanted to rush directly to the airport, he turned north onto Route 62, his eyes searching for a motel. Finally he spotted a Best Western and pulled quickly in front and waited while Malcolm checked for a vacancy.

"Maybe I could go instead of Mal," Shar said. Scotty was asleep under her arm.

"Not this time, Shar. Your place is with the child. I promise we will call you as soon as I know anything."

Malcolm rushed out and gathered up Scotty. "Got the last room," he said.

"Shar, call Aaron, our farm manager and tell him we may not get home tonight. Call Smitty, too," Gray said.

Packing Scotty on his shoulder, Malcolm and Shar rushed inside the lobby. Five minutes later, while the squall line passed through overhead, Gray and Malcolm were again on their way.

"Step on it!" Malcolm cried after hearing that the blue Ford with tinted windows hidden behind the hangar belonged to Barnaby's daughter, Patricia, and was likely the vehicle that had run his sister down in Atlanta.

Laney was shaken from her brief quiescence when the howling of the cross wires intensified as the Jenny lost altitude. Patricia banked and lined up for the approach. Laney saw that she was aligning the plane with the grassy strip between asphalt runway and the taxiing strip.

Even without engine power, the Jenny closed the distance with alarming speed. Bucking and shaking from blasts of crosswind, Laney thought they might overshoot it. Closer and closer they came, but even with the upper wing flaps down, they were coming in too fast. With a dead engine, there was no way Patricia could go around and have another shot at it.

"Patricia, there's less than half the runway left!" Laney yelled just as the wheels touched down and bounced the Jenny back into the air. Again they hit hard. There were no brakes to slow them, no way of throttling back. Two more rebounds on the drenched grass slowed the plane slightly and brought them to the end of the strip.

Then disaster! They hit a rut in the thick turf and the plane went up on its nose and made a single revolution on its prop and landed upright on its landing gear.

Time stood still. Laney couldn't believe they were on the ground and that she was in one piece. Suddenly, through the blur of shock and paralyzing fear, Laney was aware of hands pulling at her clothes, rip-ping and pulling at her purse. She remembered the stamps and pried Patricia's groping fingers from her bag.

"Patricia," a male voice inquired, "what the shit?"

"She has the stamps on her!" Patricia yelled at him. "In the purse!"

"Stamps? The Inverts?"

Dwayne! Laney thought. He's in on it with Patricia. From the corner of her eye, she spotted the yellow VW near the airplane wing.

"Goddamn it, help me!" Patricia yelled, and Dwayne hesitated for only a second more before climbing the wing and trying to yank the purse straps over Laney's head.

"No!" Laney screamed and Patricia beat at her face with hard, quick blows. She felt the sting of tears and pain as her nose began to bleed.

In the distance, Laney saw a single vehicle racing to the scene. Where was everyone? she thought in a panic, then realized that they had landed silently on the most remote area of the strip and that the small airport had no tower. Still strapped in her seat, Laney struggled feebly with Patricia and Dwayne to keep possession of her purse, but they soon overpowered her and Patricia tore the bag away just as Laney recognized the approaching vehicle. There was no mistaking the streaking pink blur. She heard the wail of emergency vehicles in the distance.

"Dwayne, let's go!" Patricia yelled, while she unzipped the bag and removed the manila envelope and tucked it inside her leather jacket and zipped.

The Buick cut behind the Volkswagen and squealed to a stop. Patricia hurled the purse at Laney and she and Dwayne leaped off the wing and ran for the VW.

Laney unlatched her belt and climbed on the seat and jumped to the wing. She realized her mistake too late as her foot slit the wing covering like a sledgehammer breaking through ice. Her shoe, caught between a spar and cross-rib, caused her to sprawl between the rigging wires that had sung to her only minutes before.

Trapped for the moment, Laney shouted at the figures alighting from opposite sides of the Buick, "Gray, they've got the stamps!"

The sirens got louder and Laney could see three police cars race onto the tarmac. She figured Gray must have called them.

Patricia had only made it into the passenger seat when Malcolm yanked her out by her arm and twisted it behind her back. His other arm choked her neck in a hammerlock.

Dwayne climbed in behind the wheel but Gray caught the swinging door. While grappling with Gray, Dwayne somehow managed to start the engine. Laney, struggling to release her foot from the wing, glared at him through his windshield.

There was no way Dwayne could move forward because of the Jenny directly in front of the VW, so he shoved the gear into reverse. Gray dove to his right as the VW shot backward—into the Buick.

It was like hitting a Sherman tank. With a crunch, the rear end of the Volkswagen folded up like tissue paper and because the engine was in the rear, the radiator began to hiss and spew steam.

Gray leaped upon Dwayne like a madman and ripped him from the car. He held Dwayne at arm's length and swung. Dwayne crumpled.

By this time, the police cars had arrived on the scene. Laney, her foot finally freed from the wing, limped to where Malcolm was holding Patricia. With a speedy unzip of Patricia's jacket, Laney snatched the envelope.

"I think these belong to a little girl named Scotty," she snarled, and as Malcolm reeled with astonishment, she kneed Patricia in the gut.

47

They piled up like puppies in the motel room's only bed—Shar and Malcolm on one side, Laney and Gray on the other, with Scotty dividing the couples. Laney's wet and blood-stained jacket hung over the shower rod in the bathroom and her various other garments, all soaked through from the rain, hung here and there over the furniture.

When Malcolm, Laney and Gray had arrived at the motel after a long interrogation at the Jefferson County Sheriff's office, there was a great celebration with soft drinks, beer and sandwiches picked up on the way. First, Laney ducked quickly into the bathroom so Scotty wouldn't see her bloody clothes. As Laney climbed into the tub, she noticed the oily residue in the bottom where Shar had scrubbed Scotty clean of oil and grease. Laney took a long, hot shower and wrapped herself in the blanket that Shar handed to her through the door.

Clearing a circle in the steamy mirror, Laney saw a bulbous nose and a small bruise forming under her right eye above her blanket "cloak."

"Queen of Stupidity" she said to her royal reflection, but gave herself a tiny bit of credit that she had managed to make it out of the day's happenings at all.

As they devoured everything in sight, nothing but Scotty's wonderful plane ride was discussed until, exhausted from excitement, she nodded off.

Instantly, everyone talked at once, except for Gray who was quiet, his arm tight around Laney's shoulders as they leaned against the bed pillows.

"Woman, don't keep me in suspense any longer," came from Shar. "That quickie phone call from the police station won't hack it. I want details, the more explicit, the better."

"I really can't tell you very much. The police here in Madison wouldn't divulge anything other than Patricia had been arrested for abduction and assault. Dwayne is being held for accessory after the fact. I certainly didn't hesitate to press charges."

"I believe in the days ahead, more serious charges will be added," Malcolm said.

"Well, pooh!" Shar said, screwing up her mouth. "At least let me see them."

"The stamps?" Laney teased.

"Woman, what do you think?"

"I can do that. Hand me my purse."

With great ceremony, Laney opened the manila envelope. In awe, they stared through the glassine covering and commented about the 1918 blue and red issue until in total exhaustion, one by one they fell asleep.

48

Christmas Eve at Stoney Creek Farm

A new layer of snow had been cleared for Laney and Gray's overnight guests as Malcolm, Shar and Scotty, carrying overnight luggage and shopping bags full of gifts, walked the curving brick path glowing with luminaries. Christmas wreaths flashed tiny lights from every window and red bows adorned the twin porch lights.

"Blackberry," Scotty cried and broke rank as the Border collie flew around the corner of the house. Scotty's shiny red boots planted oval tracks off the path. Running circles around the child, the dog left a wake of fluffy snow like a sparkling spindrift from the sea.

"There you are," called Laney from the open door. Behind her, Gray, Maddy and Gordon grinned and waved them all inside with hugs and good cheer. Only two days before, Maddy had returned from a week's cruise to the Bahamas with friends.

Coats were tossed on top of each other on the sofa in the library, and Puccini did his kneading thing on Scotty's toggle coat before finally settling in for a short winter's nap.

Scotty reached the parlor first and stopped in her tracks. Her hands flew to her mouth smothering a whoop. "A bonny, muckle Christmas tree!" she exclaimed with a brilliant smile that rivaled the tree lights.

"Muckle big it is," Malcolm said of the glorious tree that brushed the ceiling in the far corner of the parlor.

Instead of using the tiny white lights that Laney had brought from her Pittsburgh apartment two years before, she had found strings of traditional red, blue and green ones that her sister had stored away in the attic. The tree was transformed into a breathtaking jewel box of rubies, sapphires, and emeralds. From every branch, hung a unique antique or homemade ornament. Wide streamers of gold and silver ribbon trailed the full length of the tree from an oversized bow on the top. Beneath, presents wrapped in vivid, shiny papers and bows covered every inch of the tree skirt.

But it was the child staring at the tree that left everyone's eyes teary with the joy of the season. Scotty, drawing in her breath in delight, her eyes shining, her spiraling curls gilding in the firelight and remarkably, her sunny, unsinkable spirit still in tact after her recent losses.

Malcolm, his eyes glistening with happy tears behind his glasses, broke the moment of reverie with a clearing of his throat. "Scotty, let's put our gifts with the others."

She ran to him and with her tiny hands, reached inside the shopping bags again and again. Each time she stooped, her calf-length scarlet jumper brushed the floor. Each time she straightened, they glimpsed her favorite faded sneakers below her white tights.

"Could I open one wee gift now?" she asked.

"Just one," Shar said and Scotty selected the glossy red box from Barnaby and Elaine.

While Scotty pulled on the bow, Gray fixed toddies.

"The turkey is begging to be eaten so we only have time for a single drink," Maddy said, accepting a glass of cabernet from Gray.

While everyone got cozy in front of the fireplace, Scotty tore at the paper on her present. Finally, she lifted the cardboard lid and amid the tissue, found it.

"Saugh, Uncle Mal, ma goggles!" she cried.

Elaine and Barnaby, even though suffering excruciating pain over the upcoming murder trial of their daughter, had sent the aviation glasses Scotty had worn on her "ground flight."

Everyone chuckled when Malcolm fitted them over Scotty's eyes and she scampered down to the pantry to play with the puppies.

"Now, how long are we going to have to wait before we get some of our questions answered?" Shar asked Gordon.

"Shar, you know we can't discuss much about the upcoming trial."

"Nothing? . . . nada?"

"Most of the police investigation was in the newspaper anyway," Gordon said. "*The Hickory Times* was particularly thorough in their reporting of Patricia's arrest and subsequent confession. I can talk about that."

Maddy busied herself by passing around a tray of Stilton, Harvarti and cheddar cheeses with assorted crackers. "Well, I for one, was out of town when that article was printed," she said.

"I'll be glad to fill you in," Malcolm said.

"Mom, you already knew I got the murderer wrong," Laney said.

"I could see how that happened," Malcolm said. "You didn't know that Patricia also was in Scotland with Barnaby and Elaine the week Ray was killed." He looked at Maddy and explained, "Barnaby was guest speaker for the Scottish Aero Club in Perth. You know, if Keely had told me her fears about Ray's death, maybe I could have made a connection," Malcolm said. "Seems funny, now."

"What?" Laney asked.

"That Barnaby's talk to the Aero Club was entitled, 'How to restore a Curtiss Jenny.'"

Malcolm went on. "While in Scotland, Patricia took the train to Edinburgh for the dinner with Keely, Ray and the new baby. When Ray drove her back to her hotel, they had drinks in the hotel lounge. That's when Ray bragged about the stamps and that they were hidden in a fireproof box in the tack room of the barn."

"You mean to tell me Mabel had given Ray the stamps?" Maddy asked.

"No, but we think Mabel had told Ray that the stamps would be Scotty's some day. Evidently, Ray liked to fabricate stories. I guess it made him feel noteworthy or a cut above other people.

"Anyway, two days after Ray told Patricia he had the stamps, she parked a rental car on the farm road and sneaked into the foaling barn through the rear door. She wasn't aware of Talia's foaling the night before and certainly didn't expect to see Ray in the barn that early in the morning. Patricia ducked into an empty stall when she heard him come into the barn. She watched as he pulled the pin on Talia's door and entered the stall, leaving the door cracked. Hoping that it might prevent Ray from catching her in the act of searching the firebox in the tack room, Patricia slipped out of her hiding place and quietly slid the mare's door shut and shoved in the pin.

"And of course, when she looked inside the box, she didn't find the stamps. To be fair, Patricia didn't know the horse had a violent streak and when she heard the mare going crazy in the stall, she panicked. Rushing to the stall, she realized she was too late. Ray was lying still and bloody in the straw. Patricia unhooked the pin and cracked the stall door so it would appear as an unfortunate accident."

Malcolm excused himself to check on Scotty.

Maddy took the opportunity to ask how Patricia managed to kill Keely.

"Patricia accompanied her mother on an art club trip to Florida the week Keely and Scotty were to fly to Lexington," Gray said. "During the trip, Elaine confided to Patricia that Keely thought Ray's death wasn't an accident and that she thought she knew who killed him. While checking into the Jackson Hotel in Atlanta, who do you think Patricia saw alighting from the airport shuttle?"

"Keely?" Maddy said.

"Yes, and while Keely ate a late lunch in the hotel restaurant, Patricia got her mother settled in her room. With the excuse of doing a little shopping, Patricia rushed back to the lobby and saw Keely get into a cab. Following in her own car that was still at the check-in entrance, Keely led her to Peachtree Courtyard where Patricia waited outside."

"Evidently, Keely got suspicious of the dark blue car that was parked near the care facility, so when she got into another cab, she had the driver let her off at a park near the hotel," Gray said. "Rather than check into the Jackson, Keely spent a cold night in the park like that homeless person reported to the police. Early in the morning, she was on her way to hail a cab to the airport when Patricia, waiting in her car, saw her emerging from the park."

"The rest is history, as they say," Shar said sadly.

"Didn't Elaine wonder where her daughter was all this time?" Maddy asked.

Gray answered. "Patricia called her mother and said she had run into a friend while shopping and she had invited her to spend the night. She promised to pick her mother up the following morning for the return trip to Indiana."

"Two down and one to go . . . Frank Rice," Malcolm said bitterly in the doorway of the room.

"Simon," Shar corrected him.

"Ah, Malcolm . . . I didn't realize you'd heard," Gray said apologetically.

"It's all right," Malcolm said. "Hopefully, this will be the last time we discuss these miserable crimes."

Laney continued for Gray, "Elaine visited Gray and me at General Butler State Park in Carrollton. I told her we were going to question Frank Rice in the morning. When she got home, she must have told her daughter."

"Elaine just couldn't seem to keep anything from Patricia, could she?" Shar said.

"I first thought they were very close," Laney said. "But now I'm inclined to believe it was more of a one-sided relationship. Patricia used her mother to gain information."

"When Patricia heard from Elaine that Gray and I were going to question Simon, Patricia drove to his house, found the door open, and just in case Keely had told him of her suspicions, used his own gun on him to keep him from talking to Gray and me. She hoped that it would appear to be a suicide but evidently didn't realize Simon was left-handed."

"Now, I can see how you first suspected Elaine. You couldn't have known that Patricia was with her mother on two of those trips or privy to the same information," Maddy said.

"But the mistake could have cost Laney her life," Gray said.

"I'd like to have a nickel for every time you've said that in the past month," Laney said.

Laney then addressed Gordon, "Maybe you could answer this for all of us. Dwayne certainly knew about the stamps when he helped Patricia rip my purse off after my Jenny flight. How long had he known about them?"

"For some time, it seems. Dwayne admitted vandalizing Mabel's apartment looking for them."

"Did Bonnie also know about them?" asked Shar.

"Probably," Gordon said, "and Bonnie may have suspected that Dwayne had something to do with Mabel's burglary. Dwayne had been arrested for a burglary once before."

"No!" several of them said in unison.

"That would explain why Bonnie appeared so nervous when I told her that Keely had gone to the care facility seeking answers about Mabel's fall and the subsequent vandalism," Laney said. "Bonnie and

Dwayne had both rushed to Atlanta when they heard about Mabel's fall."

"The arrest happened six years ago in Madison, but he got off on a tech," Gordon said.

"Enough police talk," Maddy piped in. "Let's eat before Tom dries up and blows away."

Over a wonderful dinner—the giblet gravy disguising the dryness of the turkey—they chattered and laughed and toasted until Malcolm and Shar spotted Scotty who was still wearing her goggles, falling asleep over her custard pie. They excused themselves and carried Scotty upstairs to one of two guestrooms connected by a joint bath.

When they returned to the dining room, Malcolm told them, "Getting her ready for bed, was like undressing a rag doll."

Shar added. "She protested when I removed her glasses. I predict that they will become as precious to Scotty as the stuffed airplane and the piper book. She's sleeping with all three of them tonight."

"I bet she is already dreaming of sugarplums and airplanes," Laney said, beginning to clear the table.

"Santa has provided ample aviation gifts under the tree," Malcolm laughed.

"Could I change the subject?" Gordon said suddenly, his expression serious. "Shar, I have some information that is personal. It's about Simon Anderson. We can talk privately, if you like." He stood to move to another room.

"Gordon, sit down, will you?" Shar said. She glanced at Laney and Gray, but her gaze settled on her husband. "Mal, Gray and Laney have been involved with this case from the beginning. I want them to hear anything you have to say about Simon, personal or not."

Gordon finished his wine with a loud swallow. He wiped his lips with his napkin. "After examining the documents that you discovered under Simon's bed and the driver's license in his wallet, the police found them to be forged instruments, possibly all procured from an Internet site. Only Simon's Puerto Rican death certificate was not fake. We did our own little investigation and enlisted the help of the FBI.

"On one of Simon's export trips to Puerto Rico and the Dominican Republic, he accidentally uncovered drugs being smuggled out of one of the free-zone factories he had set up for one of his clients. He reported the information to our government and volunteered to infiltrate the ring to get names and smuggling routes. This was a big operation, and I mean *really* big. He and a second operative leaked a lot of information to the FBI until they were suddenly exposed. Simon managed to escape but his partner was found dead in a ditch. He had been tortured in inexplicable ways. Shar, this was while he was married to you."

Shar took a deep breath while waiting for Gordon to continue.

"Witness Security, more popularly known as the Witness Protection Program, offered to give Simon witness protection if he agreed to testify once the criminals were apprehended. Simon refused the offer for one basic reason," Gordon spoke directly to Shar. "You."

"Me?"

"He told the U.S. Marshall he didn't want to uproot you and have you always worrying that his identity would be found out. Instead, he somehow managed to obtain a bona fide death certificate and got the rest of the documents himself."

"But the plane crash?" Shar protested.

"Now that's when things get interesting," Gordon said. "Patricia—"

"Patricia! What in hell does she have to do with the plane crash?" Shar cried.

"Sharlene, let Gordon get on with it," Malcolm said. He had scooted his chair as close to her as he could and was stroking her shoulder.

"To fake his death, a plane needed to crash and burn," Gordon said. "At the time, Patricia Biddle was a pilot for the Marshals Service. That's the service that transports federal defendants to and from court in vans or transports prisoners in the service's mini airline. She met Simon in Puerto Rico while she was on an assignment and he was trying to arrange his faked death. It was Patricia that salvaged a derelict two-seater airplane at some remote airstrip and outfitted it good enough so that it would take off—but never land. Simon set the plane on autopilot and parachuted. The plane crashed into a mountain and burned fifteen minutes later."

"I wonder if their association might explain the photo of Simon that I got in the mail," Shar said.

"It does," Gordon said. "Patricia secretly snapped it while they were working on the derelict plane together. It seems she had a thing for Simon and later tried hard to hook up with him while he was in Florida, but it was so soon after leaving you, he wasn't interested.

"Then Patricia met Dwayne in Vevay and learned from him that the

Inverts had never been in Ray's possession, but were supposed to go to Scotty when Mabel died.

"So while Mabel was in the hospital, Dwayne vandalized her apartment looking for them. Shortly after that, Patricia, disguised as a blond, bribed some little kid at Keely's welcoming party to try to snatch her little plane."

Foiled again, Laney thought.

"Here's where it gets complicated. A couple months ago, Patricia heard from Dwayne that her old friend, Keely Moore, was planing to marry a Frank Rice who Patricia knew was really Simon Anderson whom she had helped fake his death.

"At the same time, she learned that Malcolm Lamont was going to marry Shar Hamilton, the woman Simon had been married to. It really ticked her off, so she decided to have a little fun."

"Why that bitch! So, for kicks, she made those phone calls to me and sent photos to Keely and me!" Shar spat.

"Right, although I'm sure Keely was glad to receive hers because, for a reason known only to Frank and Patricia, he wouldn't allow any photos of himself to be taken," Gordon said.

"But in my case, Patricia was hoping that if I knew that Simon was still alive, I couldn't marry Malcolm. What fun for her, the dirty . . . " Shar's eyes blazed.

"It was shortly after sending the photos that Patricia heard from her mother that Keely suspected Ray had been murdered. Sooo . . . Patricia killed Keely and disguised again, slashed Scotty's plane at the funeral luncheon, looking for those damn stamps," Gordon explained.

"Gordon, I'm anxious to know this. The State Forensic Anthropologist has had my urn for three weeks. Whose remains have I been carrying around for five years?" Shar asked.

"I got the report yesterday from Karen. She couldn't tell whether they were human or animal ashes. If she had found remnants of teeth, she could have determined whether or not they were human. She thinks they are probably dog or cat remains from some crematorium.

"Shar, I hope all this has helped vindicate me a little for our untimely conversation the night of your wedding. You have no idea how painful that was for me."

"I shall show mercy," Shar said with a wink. "Joking aside, Gordon, thanks to you, Laney, Gray and Mal, I am here tonight instead of rotting in some jail cell this Christmas Eve."

Malcolm added, "And rather than Scotty abiding with Shar and me, she'd be residing in the unaffectionate household of Bonnie Day. I'm sure that you've heard that permanent guardianship has officially been awarded to me. We will start adoption proceedings after the first of the year."

"I understand the stamps were professionally evaluated," Maddy said.

"Ah, the stamps . . . the object of the long and damnable quest," Malcolm said sadly. "I hope to never see them again."

Shar patted his hand. "The stamps were found to be in terrible shape," she said. "Through the years, they had been exposed to heat, cold, and light so most were either faded or stuck together. Mind you, the philatelist thought ten of them could be salvaged from the sheet in good condition."

"However," Malcolm added, "if they are put on the market, the increased number of Jenny Inverts would devalue them somewhat. So for now, as trustee of Scotty's estate as well as her guardian, I will put them in trust for her."

"Now," Gordon said with a long sigh, "if you will excuse us, we will call it a night." He rose and with Maddy, went upstairs to their room. Laney, Gray, Shar and Malcolm also stood. Without speaking, the four of them stacked dishes and carried them into the kitchen where Laney loaded the dishwasher. Plates clattered. Silverware clinked. They fed Puccini and Blackberry, and the fat, wiggly puppies that were just about weaned.

"I think we will also retire," Malcolm said. "I remember my mum telling me that for parents, morning approaches quickly on Christmas Day. But when I was a child—"

"Let's never forget how that was," Laney interrupted and extinguished all the lights except those on the tree and the flickering embers of the fire. The four of them stood in the center hallway while the lights cast rainbows of color on their faces.

Laney felt the loving arms of Gray, Shar and Malcolm around her and remembered the warmth of Christmases past. The grandfather clock in the hall struck midnight and it was Christmas Day.